MAX
The Best of
Braithwaite

MAX
The Best of
Braithwaite

by Max Braithwaite

McClelland and Stewart

The Canadian Publishers
McClelland and Stewart Limited
25 Hollinger Road, Toronto   M4B 3G2

Printed and bound in Canada
by John Deyell Company

Canadian Cataloguing in Publication Data
Braithwaite, Max, 1911-
Max: the best of Braithwaite

ISBN 0-7710-1634-4

I. Title.

PS8503.R34A6 1983   C818'.5408   C83-098718-5
PR9199.3.B735A6 1983

Grateful acknowledgement is made to the Ontario Arts Council
for their assistance in the publication of this book.

*This book is dedicated
to the most important
women in my life:*

*Elizabeth Copeland,
whom I never met;
Mary Copeland Braithwaite,
who always thought I would amount to something;
Amy Treleaven,
a great mother-in-law;
and most of all,
Aileen, with whom
I have worked and played
and loved over the years.*

The following works have been previously published:

Monster in the Cellar: *Maclean's*

The Night They Danced Till Dawn:
McClelland and Stewart Limited

We Mean Business: McClelland and Stewart Limited

Why Shoot the Teacher: McClelland and Stewart Limited

The Rise and Fall of the Dumbells: *Maclean's*

Irish Immigration: *Maclean's*

Never Sleep Three in a Bed: McClelland and Stewart Limited

Max Braithwaite's Ontario: J. J. Douglas Limited

I Want to Be Alone: *Canadian Home Journal*

New Baby – A Cure for Middle Age: *Chatelaine*

Lusty Winter: McClelland and Stewart Limited

A Privilege and a Pleasure: J. J. Douglas Ltd. and Paperjacks

The Western Plains: McClelland and Stewart Limited

The Year of the Killer Flu: *Maclean's*

"What Are You Doing Now, Darling?":
Canadian Home Journal

The Night We Stole the Mountie's Car:
McClelland and Stewart Limited

McGruber's Folly: McClelland and Stewart Limited

The Commodore's Barge Is Alongside:
McClelland and Stewart Limited

Contents

Introduction

When I met Jim Harris, the editor of *Liberty* magazine, in Toronto in 1945, it was the first time I'd come face to face with a real live editor. And when he asked me what I'd done in civilian life, I said, with a straight face, "I was a writer."

Not entirely a lie. While teaching school in Saskatchewan, I had written, along with Mac Mooney, an article called "School Drought," which sold to *Maclean's* magazine in 1937. And I'd sold a short story and a radio play and had written and acted in a radio series for the Saskatchewan Dairy Pool.

During the ten years of the Dirty Thirties, I had been wondering how I was ever going to get out of Saskatchewan and into the world of writers. Then, by a stroke of luck, the navy transferred me from HMCS *Unicorn* (an old garage on First Avenue in Saskatoon) to HMCS *York* (the Automotive Building in the CNE grounds in Toronto). I had made it.

And almost the first person I met on "the ship" was an honest-to-gawd free-lance writer. His name was Jack Mosher, a sea-cadet officer. He was – and is – a lively, funny, altogether fascinating person. Best of all, he'd sold stories and articles to the *Star Weekly, Collier's,* and other publications, including *Liberty* – something I'd been trying to do without success. He introduced me to Jim Harris.

So, here I was finally in the right place at the right time. I had actually met a real live editor, and I was somewhat surprised to find that he was a person like myself. Because of all the rejection slips I'd received, I had some vague notion that an editor was a monster who hated all writers and who spent the bulk of his time writing them nasty notes. But Jim, a tall, handsome man who looks like comedian Steve Allen, just tilted his head slightly, as he does when interested, and said, "Why don't you write something for us?" And I said, "O.K." My writing career began right there.

I wrote an article for Jim titled "Servicemen, Where Do You Go From Here?" and he bought it. Then I wrote another and he bought that. Then I sat down and did a half-hour adaptation of James Thurber's wonderful story, "The Catbird Seat," and Hugh Horler bought that for Buckingham Theatre.

At the same time I was doing some veteran's rehabilitation stuff for the CBC, which was produced by Don Fairbairn. And when the corporation said they wanted a serial about a returning serviceman and his family, Don and I worked out the idea for a series to be titled *Your Family*, which ran for twenty-six weeks. Some of the episodes were good and some not so good, but it had some of Canada's finest radio actors in the cast, including Bob and Margo Christie, Doug Masters, Ruth Springford, and my eight-year-old daughter Beryl.

In my spare time I wrote an adaptation of Stephen Leacock's *Sunshine Sketches* (the first Leacock ever adapted for another medium), and it was produced by Andrew Allan on his *Stage* series. I was also writing the air-force segments of a big recruiting show, and some public relations material for The Tea Bureau.

As can be guessed, I was extremely busy, but I was learning that if I was to succeed as a free-lance writer and support my family doing it (three children at that time), I had to work harder than most people ever work and stay healthy. I managed both, never missing a day's work through illness until 1969, when I got gout.

Versatility was also important, and a bald-faced audacity that made it impossible for me ever to admit that I couldn't write anything as well as anyone else could write it. An example of this is a job I did for Ford Theatre. Alan Savage, the producer, who had already repeated my "Sunshine Sketches" for the theatre and a couple of other adaptations, phoned me at my home just outside Streetsville and said, "Max, Ford Theatre is doing well, but most of our originals are by U.S. writers. We need an original three-act play by a Canadian."

"O.K.," I said.

"Good. There's a bit of a rush on this. We have a space in a month's time and we'd like it by then."

"O.K.," I said.

"And we'd like it to be a comedy."

"O.K."

"Oh, there's one more thing. You know how scarce housing is now; well, we'd like it to be a comedy about that."

"O.K."

The fact that I had never yet written a three-act original radio play didn't even give me pause. Before he'd finished talking, I was thinking of a situation where a guy wins a prefabricated house in a contest and then, because of many building restrictions, can't find a place to put it. Prefab houses were something very new in 1947, and I remembered a *New Yorker* cartoon in which a big truck is stopping in front of a lot and a woman says, "Look, dear, our house has come."

So I wrote a three-act comedy titled *Home Free*, and Ford Theatre staged it with Don Harron in the lead role. It was reasonably successful.

This points up another fact that I have learned about writing; you learn by doing it. There are, scattered over this broad land, a number of places where for a fat fee a person may supposedly learn how to write. These courses are presided over by professional or non-professional writers who should know better. I have had a number of offers to teach in such places but, except for one short stint in Lorne Greene's School of Radio Arts, I have always refused, believing it to be a waste of my time and that of the students. Besides, I hate teaching. I suppose young aspiring writers have a good enough time at these courses, and the instructors have an equally good time name-dropping and yarning, and if anyone wants to spend his or her money and time in this way, who's to say they shouldn't?

Everything about the mechanics of writing can be learned.

If you are smart enough to be a writer, you are smart enough to learn from the models that are all about you – plays, novels, articles, poems. One must study them assiduously of course, rather than just read them for pleasure. Not much that anyone tries to teach you will help.

In my own personal experience I have discovered that the most helpful person to a writer is a good spouse. I don't mean by bringing money to the partnership, although that would certainly be useful, but by being understanding and non-demanding. A spouse's ability to edit, spell, and type have had a great deal to do with many a writer's output. Thomas Hardy's wife Emma copied manuscripts of his novels in longhand. My wife Aileen has made it possible for me to turn in copy that astounds editors with its neatness and correctness.

I met Aileen when we were both teaching in Saskatchewan. Both dirt poor. During my teaching "career" I never earned more than seven hundred dollars a year. As a result of this poverty, we never had great expectations of what our physical environment should be. Running water and flush toilets and electricity are still the ultimate in luxury to us.

Besides, when I was courting my darling, walking the long dusty roads or the grasshopper-infested pastures, I assured her that if she married me I would take her away from all that. We would live in Toronto or New York, I said, and be rich and famous and associate with brilliant, witty folk. She believed me, and I have at least made a stab at it.

Everything we did since our teaching days, when we dwelt in an uninsulated shack with no running water or indoor plumbing and subsisted on sixty dollars a month, has been an improvement. So when we first saw that the Streetsville house had no running water or indoor plumbing, facts that would have turned many couples away, we were undaunted.

This house was heated, I use the term loosely, by a monstrous coal-burning furnace. To understand what I think of coal-burning furnaces read "Monster in the Cellar," which is included in this collection.

For a couple of years I wrote regularly for *Maclean's* magazine under the able direction of editor Ralph Allen and articles editor Scott Young, and had become one of their "regulars." This was, I think, the most difficult and least profitable writing I have ever done. Both these master craftsmen were most exacting in their requirements. Allen particularly filled the margins with caustic comments such as "Who he?" and "Oh, come now!" or "Who says?" and the like. Most articles had to be rewritten before they were accepted, and this was tedious work. (Allen once remarked to an assistant, "This will have to be rewritten before we can reject it.") I mean, by the time you've gone over the life and times of a Jersey cow breeder three times, it can become tedious. And once sold, for two hundred dollars or whatever, the articles had little if any residual sale. People steal from them freely under the name of research, but that brings nothing. One of my *Maclean's* Flashbacks, on the Irish immigration, which was all original material, and another on the Dumbells, for which I was able to interview Captain Plunkett and Al Plunkett and Red Newman and Patty Rafferty for hours, have been used by people ever since who are writing or broadcasting on these subjects.

It's a great life, this writing life, and I wouldn't exchange it for any other. It's the easiest line of work to get into. All you need is a typewriter and some paper. Don't even need an office or a desk. Some of the best writing has been done on a kitchen table. University degrees don't mean a thing. No producer or publisher ever asks for your curriculum vitae; all he wants to see is the script or manuscript. You don't need influence in high places or pull, or family background or any particular colour of skin or a clean criminal record. But you must have a lot of ideas, a fair amount of talent, a lot of drive, good health, an abundance of good luck, and a helpful spouse. But these things are mandatory for success in any business or profession.

I have been lucky. I seemed to have had all my bad luck between 1925 and 1935 and have been making up for it ever since. When I was discharged from the navy in December 1945, the whole communications business – radio, magazines, books, public relations – was entering its most expansive time. These were the halcyon days in Canada. Plenty of work for everyone, reasonable prices, loads of opportunity, so that even a free-lance writer could make a good living, raise a family, and have a lot of fun. The best years that Canada has ever known, perhaps will ever know, and we hit them just right.

What follows is a sampling of the writing I've done since I got out of the navy in 1945 up to 1982. Most of the pieces are in chronological order, so that they depict a writer's progress from magazine writer to radio writer to television and movie writer to novelist. I hope you enjoy it.

MAX
The Best of
Braithwaite

Monster
in the Cellar

How does a humour piece evolve? Well, here's one way.

One day, after I'd become a regular contributor to *Maclean's* magazine, I received a bulky envelope from Scott Young in which there was a carbon copy of an article and a note that read something like this: "We have had this piece in the vault for some time, but it is unpublishable in its present form. We've paid off the original writer. Maybe you can punch it up, and we can salvage something from it."

I began reading the piece. It was about the good old wood- and coal-burning furnace, which at that time dominated just about every basement in Canada. The piece covered the history, kinds, costs, maintenance, and so on, and was just about the dullest thing that I had ever read. It was so awful that it was funny.

I began thinking about it as I walked across the road and down the neighbour's long, long driveway to his outdoor tap where we got our drinking water. The people who lived in this house raised Great Danes and every trip was a fearful adventure. Luckily, this day there was no sign of the dogs, and as I walked towards the tap with my empty pail and back with my full one, I thought of this furnace piece, and the more I thought of it the funnier it became and by the time I got back inside our kitchen I was laughing out loud at a humour piece I'd written in my head. I sat down and typed it out and sent it to Young, and he bought it and ran it as "Monster in the Cellar," with a good illustration.

Scott told me later that he and Allen had had a hard time getting the piece past Arthur Irwin, who couldn't see anything funny in it. Finally he'd said, "Well, if you two think it's funny, I guess we'll run it."

Which points up the difficulty of selling humour articles. People don't agree on what's funny. I've met people who can't see anything funny in Leacock. Or Thurber. As Scott Young once told me, "To sell a humour piece here, you have to make everybody in this place laugh, and some of them haven't laughed in years."

So, if you want to write humour – or must – do it in book form.

This was one of the few pieces for which I had a supplementary sale. Bernie Braden, before he went to England, did a radio series called *Bernie Braden Tells a Story*. He told it on the air and then recorded it. I don't have the record now and I don't think he sold many. Anyway, I never made any money from that.

The other day I received a note from the editor of *Maclean's* which said in effect . . . . "What do you know about furnaces?"

What do I know about furnaces! That's like asking Mackenzie King what he knows about politics, or Casanova what he knows about love, or a physiotherapist what he knows about physics. All my life I have been intimately associated with furnaces . . . inside and out.

However, just to bring myself up to date on any new wrinkles that may have developed in furnaces in the past couple of years (this is going to be pretty scientific, so look out!), I interviewed some of the foremost heating engineers in the country. Funny thing . . . to a man, they begged me not to quote them or even divulge their names. So I won't. After all, I may be a fugitive from justice someday myself.

I have decided to cover this subject under the following headings:

1) Functions of the furnace;
2) Kinds of furnaces;
3) Characteristics of the furnace;
4) !X" . . . X!!?*!!!

If these don't completely cover the subject, go ahead and

think up some of your own. Who's the expert here anyway?

To cover the first heading first, furnaces have many functions, as follows:

The furnace is primarily a machine for manufacturing ashes. The raw materials used in this process are paper, wood, garbage, or coal. Coal is best, both as to the quantity and quality of the ashes produced, but it is also the most expensive. Coal can be obtained from Pennsylvania or Alberta depending on whether or not you want to keep your Canadian dollars in Canada. Old scraps of lumber aren't so good since they sometimes put nails in the ashes.

Ashes have many uses about the home. You can sprinkle them on your walk in winter to keep callers from breaking their necks. Or you can forget to sprinkle them when your mother-in-law is coming over. They may also be used for filling old holes. There is another use which is associated with sackcloth, but none of my experts seemed to know anything about it.

Good ashes are hard to come by. No one has ever figured out a better machine for manufacturing them than the good old furnace. I don't know why anyone would want to, when the average furnace will produce about five tons of ashes for every ton of coal thrown into it. Making ashes out of the coal is not as simple as it sounds, however. There is a great deal more to it than just throwing coal into one end and taking ashes out the other. But this will be covered later under heading No. 4. What's the good of having headings if you don't follow them?

Another important function of the furnace is that it satisfies that primitive urge we all have to build fires. Building them in the furnace is a lot safer and cheaper than building them in the barn, say, or against the back fence. This urge to make fires goes away back to the dawn of history and even today it is usually around dawn that most fires are built.

It's funny about this urge . . . next to a couple of others it is the strongest urge of the human race. I know a fellow who has installed at great expense and sacrifice one of those new oil-burning things (also to be discussed later under "Kinds of Furnaces"). He never has to go near it. There's a little doin's on the wall, and when the room gets too hot or too cold it sends a little message down to the oil burner that starts it up or shuts it off.

Well, what does this fellow do when he comes home from a hard day at the office? Does he mix himself a drink, sink into a soft chair, and say, "Thank heaven for modern science"? Not him. He climbs into a bunch of old clothes, gets hold of an axe, and spends an hour cutting up wood for his fireplace. He gets all worked up getting the fireplace going, almost burns down the house, and just makes the house too hot in the end. Then he sits in front of the fire and watches it.

The Indians used to have a saying: "White man make big fire and sit way back; Indian make small fire and sit up close." That has nothing to do with furnaces but it's a pretty good quotation so I thought I'd throw it in.

The third function of the furnace (you'll be beginning to see that a furnace is a pretty handy thing to have around the house) is to provide exercise for what is sometimes referred to as the male animal . . . or the man of the house . . . or that blasted husband of mine. Carrying ashes up the cellar steps and out through the kitchen provides exercise for just about every muscle in the body . . . including the muscles of the inner ear.

The next function is what might be called the psychological one. It provides a sort of whipping boy around the house (for the benefit of the layman, that means something to curse at besides your wife). When he gets what-for upstairs the husband can always go down to the basement and kick the devil out of the furnace. It nearly always needs a kicking anyway.

Also, shaking up the furnace, cleaning it, and carrying ashes out through the living room gives the man of the house something to do when the little woman is occupied with strictly feminine matters like entertaining her bridge club or the WCTU. One of my experts, whom I shall call Dr. X, has made exhaustive tests to prove that the blood pressure of the wife varies in direct ratio with the amount of ash dust in the air. An important if not revolutionary discovery.

Furnaces also provide furniture for the basement. Try to visualize what *your* basement would look like without a furnace . . . . O.K., that's enough. Can't go on dreaming all day, you know.

It is obvious that the furnace must be the perfect furnishing for a smart basement because practically every basement has one. Try to imagine a game of Ping-Pong with no furnace for the balls to get behind, no pipes to bump your head on, no shaker to bark your shins against. Another heating engineer interviewed – whom I shall call Dr. X(i) so as not to confuse him with Dr. X (who is confused enough as it is) – estimates that if there were no furnaces 98.07 per cent of all houses would not have basements at all. Where would they store their ashes?

There was one other function of the furnace that I was going to mention, but for the moment it eludes me. Oh yes, I remember. Furnaces sometimes provide heat. Many persons will deny this, but I think I can prove that under certain conditions the furnace may help to keep the members of the family warm.

Take the way a man gets heated up when a grate slips out just when he's got a good fire built up. Take the way a wife warms up when the old man brings the ashes through the kitchen. Isn't that heat? It can help the children, too. Take when it begins to get a bit chilly, around about September, say, and the kiddies are sitting on the floor with their little teeth chattering. The father can always say, "You, Harold, go down and cart those ashes out of the cellar. That'll warm you up." And if Harold doesn't go, well, there are other ways of warming him up, too.

"Oh, but that's a very indirect function," I hear you say. I agree. In fact I'm willing to scratch heat making right out of the list of furnace functions if you want. Let's keep this scientific.

So much for the function of the furnace. Now for the kinds. Basically there are two kinds of furnaces – little and big. The little furnaces are found in big houses and the big furnaces in little houses.

Under the main classifications there are several subclasses according to the kind of coal the furnace is supposed to use in the manufacture of ashes. The hot-air furnace is the type for which you can't get lump coal. The hot-water furnace is the type for which you can't get pea coal. And the steam furnace is the type for which you can't get a different kind of coal.

Hot air is the kind I know best – furnace, that is – so let's stick to that. (I've been stuck with one all my life.) Forty-seven per cent of the people of Canada use hot air for heating, a fact which, according to an eminent psychologist, is responsible for 18.07 per cent of all nervous trouble, 22.7 per cent of all crime, and 99.09 per cent of all suicides in the country.

There is a disquieting tendency nowadays to classify as furnaces a number of other contraptions that use oil or gas or electricity. Some of these I'm told are even built right inside the walls of the house instead of being in the basement. Imagine! These things, of course, aren't furnaces at all, since they do not perform the basic function of a furnace: namely, manufacture ashes. They have some other function, but I don't quite know what it is. Got something to do with after-dinner conversation.

Why, some people are even talking about using atomic fission instead of furnaces to heat our houses. I don't know. My experts were just about equally divided on this. Some were in favour of fission, others dead against it. Some sample quotes from them may help to clear this up in your mind. It sure didn't in mine.

Dr. X: Atomic fission? . . . . Yes and no.

Dr. X(i): There is no question in my mind but that the atom is here to stay. But don't quote me on that. I like to live as well as the next guy.

Dr. X(ii): Fission, you say? Heck, son, I ain't been fission in years. Used to catch some great bass in the creek down home, though. Why, I remember one . . . .

No point in giving you the rest of the learned doctor's quote. Tell the truth, I think he got a little off the track.

But to get back to the real, or simon-pure, furnace – and believe me we'll be getting back to it time and time again before the birds are back and lush warm days proclaim that spring is really here at last – the third heading under which I propose to discuss this subject is "Characteristics of the Furnace." (Boy, wait till we get to that last heading!)

To understand the furnace's characteristics we'll have to throw in a little history. The furnace was invented by the Chinese as what wasn't – many, many years before our civilization began. In fact, it is the original Chinese puzzle.

Furnaces are extremely sensitive to heat and cold. They should always be kept warm because that is when they work best. In the fall and spring, for instance, when there is just a bit of chill in the air, it is easy to get a roaring fire in the furnace . . . in fact impossible not to. During the cold winter days, on the other hand, the furnace is sluggish and often refuses to work at all.

Furnaces have three distinct sets of pipes. There is a pipe that runs into the bottom of the furnace through which the cold air enters the furnace; and there are pipes running from the top of the furnace through which the cold air leaves the furnace. There is another pipe running from the furnace to the chimney. This one is too ghastly even to talk about.

Nearly every furnace has two little chains that come up through the floor of the kitchen. I could find nobody who could tell me what they are for. One day last summer I tried tracing the ones in our house just to see where they did run to. Well, you know what it's like trying to trace anything through a basement. I got lost. Finally ended up inside the furnace. I lost interest in the chains then because I found too many interesting things to attract my attention. Like my favourite croquet mallet that I'd blamed the kids for losing and a foot-long mouth organ I'd been saving ever since I was in a mouth-organ band in high school in Saskatoon. Boy, what a band that was.

All furnaces are ugly. With dispositions like theirs how can they help it? I hear a lot of nonsense talked about painting furnaces in pastel shades to brighten them up. Pastel shades, for gosh sakes! Can you imagine going down into the basement and being confronted by a furnace in pastel shades? It's enough to shake a man's reason. How are you going to kick a furnace in pastel shades? Or curse at it? Or even get near it? You'd have to put on a dinner jacket to go into the basement at all.

Now for the final chapter in the nauseating subject. How to Make the Furnace Work. I shall try to keep calm through this, but can't promise anything.

In order to get the most out of any furnace – most ashes, that is – you must know how to work it. There is no rule of thumb here, except to keep your thumb out of the way when you bang the door shut. What I mean is each furnace has its own individuality and there is nothing for it but to adjust yourself to it. For instance, some furnaces smoke when the draught is open, others when the draught is shut, and others when it is open or shut. This is all subject to temperature, humidity, barometer reading, wind velocity, and how much time you've got to get to the office. The only time a furnace doesn't smoke is in the summer, unless of course you happen to be burning garbage.

A good pair of hard-toed shoes is essential when tending a furnace. You can mash your toe pretty badly kicking a furnace with a soft-toed shoe.

Some people are trying to beat the rap by installing a lot of fancy geegaws upstairs. Finger-tip control, they call it. You can tend the furnace without going into the basement at all. No good. The geegaws are even more complicated than the furnace and go on the hummer just about as often. Besides, take away a man's excuse for going into the basement every so often and you don't leave him much.

The furnace should be cleaned out at least once a year. There are people with big vacuum cleaners that go around doing this. But just try to find one. I phoned thirteen last summer and they all promised to come on Tuesday, but they never showed up.

Finally I put a big sign up in front of the house which read, "FURNACE SUPPLIES FOR SALE . . . WHOLESALE." Then I placed a cleverly concealed bear trap just inside the gate. I got a furnace cleaner!

A friend of mine was so desperate for someone to come and clean his furnace that he raised his son up to be a furnaceman. Sent him off to an expensive technical school and all. As graduation day approached he got so excited he could hardly see. Thought at last he was going to get his furnace cleaned. But as soon as the kid graduated, he joined a union and went on strike. So my friend's furnace is still dirty.

Well, as far as I know that is just about all there is to say about furnaces without getting into profanity. Anybody who can't make his furnace work now had better move south.

The Night
They Danced
Till Dawn

The one-room prairie school house is gone. When Fil Fraser
and I were looking for one in which to film *Why Shoot the
Teacher* we travelled for miles over prairie trails without seeing one. Many have been hauled onto farmyards to act as
granaries or chicken houses or pig barns. Others have burned
down or just slowly rotted away. They have been replaced by
large brick schools with gymnasiums and libraries and
teachers' rooms and all the tools of modern education, to
which the children are hauled in buses.

In their day one-room school houses were the centre of
the "district," serving as dance-halls, venues for political
gatherings, meeting places for the IODE or the Women's In-
stitutes, and, oh yes, institutions of learning. They did their
part in mitigating the awful loneliness and isolation of the
early pre-radio, pre-television, pre-hard-top-road days. They
served a need that no longer exists and so they no longer exist.

Many remember them with nostalgic affection, but I am
not one of those. To me they will always be cold, bleak,
meagrely equipped shacks in which no child or teacher
should have been required to spend most of his days. They
may be adequate for housing chickens or pigs or cows, but
never human beings.

The following piece is from *Why Shoot the Teacher*.

Over the course of the years I've attended dances in posh wardrooms, army messes, and ballrooms five times as big as Willowgreen School. I've waltzed, rumba'd and cha-cha'd to small combos and big bands whose members are world-renowned musicians. But the dance that sticks in my mind for all time is the one in Willowgreen School when Orville Jackson played the fiddle and Grandma Wilson chorded on the organ.

I first got wind of it after school on Friday when, instead of slouching down the aisles making desultory passes at dust, Charlie McDougall and his band of helpers began by energetically pushing all the desks to the sides, back, and front of the room.

"What's the idea?" I asked.

"Dance tonight."

"Here?"

"Yep."

"Who's coming?"

"Just about everybody in the district, I guess."

"Nobody said anything to me about it."

He merely shrugged at this and then, as an afterthought, "Oh yeah. Dad said to tell you they'll need your bed for the babies."

With that puzzling announcement he set to cleaning the floor as though he actually cared about getting the dust off it.

The bit about my bed bothered me to the extent that, after eating my supper of roast pork and bread, I got out the broom and swept my own rooms. Then I picked up the half dozen or so brown-stained cigarette butts from the edges of the table and shelves where they'd burned little black grooves. I even washed the dishes and the table-top and put away the pork. Then I pulled the covers straight on my bed, hung my shirt on the back of the door, and kicked dirty socks under the bed. The place looked almost tidy.

The Montgomerys were the first to arrive – and I had my first sight of Harris Montgomery who later was to become my mentor in socialism, advisor on morals, and instructor on the new economics. Seeing him then with the neat, if big, Mrs. Montgomery, I could hardly believe my eyes. He was the untidiest man I've ever seen, a sort of middle-aged beatnik. His eyes got you first, wild, and small beside the great bridge of his nose. Then the nose, sharp and hooked, extending down to his upper lip. His wrinkled face was lean, mouth slightly pointed, cheeks with shiny skin peeling from much exposure to wind.

He treated his wife always as a petty bourgeois and she treated him with that silent, tolerant contempt that wives have for husbands whom they've given up on.

When he saw me Harris Montgomery leaped forward, grabbed my hand, shoved his chapped face within six inches of mine, jabbed my chest with a nicotine-stained finger and demanded, "What do you think of Cole?"

"I don't know," I stammered. "I'm afraid I haven't met him yet."

"No, no, no, no! The Cole in England, I mean. The economist. G.D.H."

"Oh. That Cole?"

"Yes, yes. You've read him, haven't you?"

"Well, uh . . . ."

"Great thinker. None of your mealy-mouthed bull manure about him. We'll have a talk about him. You live downstairs, don't you?"

"Well . . . yes."

"Good. We can go down there. Get away from all this damned falderal. I've been looking for somebody with some goddamned brains in his head to . . . ."

But at this point Mrs. Montgomery captured him. "Hang up the Coleman," she commanded. "It's so dark in here you can't see your hand before your face."

"Women!" Harris Montgomery muttered darkly. It was his most venomous expletive, and it summed up all the nonsense, muddled thinking, and waste effort of the capitalist world.

But he lost this battle long ago. So he took a large gas lamp and hooked it on the end of a strong wire that extended down from the middle of the ceiling, and the whole room changed miraculously. I began to feel like a party.

27

"Now take these things downstairs." Mrs. Montgomery handed him a big wicker basket of provisions, and turned to her younger sister who came through the door carrying something bundled up in blankets. "You can put the baby downstairs on the teacher's bed. Is your fire going?"

"Uh . . . yes . . . yes, it is."

"Good. Harris, get that wash boiler of water out of the sleigh and put it on the stove down there. And don't spill half of it on the way down the steps. Teacher, maybe you could help him."

So, with nothing more than my sweater on, I went out to the sleigh to help Harris with the water. As we did so another sleigh pulled by a team of ice-flecked Clydes came slanting dangerously over the drift at the gate.

"Wahooo!" A youth in a sheepskin mackinaw and no hat leaped out of the back of the sleigh, waving in his hand a mickey of gin. "It's a great night for the race!" he bellowed, crooking his arm over my shoulder and shoving the bottle at me. "Have a drink, pal."

Involuntarily I was reaching for the bottle when I heard Harris Montgomery's warning. "Cut it out, you damned fool, Jake. That's the teacher!"

"Oh!" Jake, who was just about my age, sobered immediately. "Gawdamighty, I'm sorry, sir."

He shoved the bottle into his pocket, hurried off to unhitch the horses, and from the sleigh box came the sound of female giggles – young female giggles.

So, neatly and completely, I'd been categorized as "the teacher." Something from outer space, without feelings, Ichabod Crane, a nothing.

For a second I was swept by frustrated rage. Here was a party in my own place, and I couldn't even be part of it. Of course, if I'd had a jug of liquor hidden down in the furnace room or in the barn as the others did, I could have invited them for a drink. But I had neither the money nor the opportunity to get a jug, and even if I had the news would have spread like a prairie fire that the new teacher at Willowgreen was a drinker. Not that he took a drink or was sociable or a good sport. Just a drinker, and who's going to send their kids to a school run by a drunkard, I'd like to know.

So they came, the old and the young, each with their bundles, many with babies. Some had come from as far as twelve miles, a three-hour journey over a winding snow trail. In the bottoms of their sleigh boxes they'd put stones, heated in the stove and wrapped in newspaper, for foot warmers. Some of the sleigh boxes were half filled with straw so that the children could snuggle down out of the wind like mice in a stack.

Why did they come? It was a break in the dreary drag of the winter months. They were sick to death of playing rummy and cribbage and the sound of each other's voices. They'd had a bellyful of togetherness, babies, grandmothers, old-maid aunts, grown-up sons with no place to go, huddled in a few drafty rooms like foxes in a den, satiated with the sight and sound and smell of each other. This was their chance to break out for a few hours, see different faces, hear some gossip. Find out about that cow of Mark Brownlee's that was due to calf, the vicissitudes of fate, the shortage of feed, the uselessness of the Bennett nickel – a five-cent bonus on every bushel of wheat paid through the good offices of a prime minister who, like everyone else, was rendered confused and inept by the magnitude of the Depression.

Soon the school house was full. My bed was covered with tiny bodies stacked like cordwood across it. Every so often a mother would come down the steps, listen at the closed door and, if she heard anything, tip-toe in and shove a soother into the mouth of the restless one. My kitchen-dining room was plugged with food, boilers for coffee, cups, plates, and outdoor clothing. I had been dispossessed.

Upstairs were all the people in the district over the age of three. The very young squirmed on the laps of the very old. The little girls, with fresh hair ribbons and pressed print dresses, dashed about between their elders, chatted breathlessly, giggled, excited beyond comprehending by they knew not what. The little boys, on the other hand, hands shoved embarrassingly deep into knicker pockets, stood about not knowing quite what to do.

Almost to a man the male adults wore blue serge suits bought, heaven knows how many years before, through the Eaton's mail-order catalogue. When the history of American costumes is finally written, the blue serge suit must surely have a special place as the worst fitting, the shiniest, and most durable of all articles of clothing. Most of these were wedding suits and saw duty only at church, weddings, dances, Christmas concerts, and special political meetings. Some had been handed down from father to son to grandson.

The women, a half dozen of whom were in various stages of pregnancy, all had the same look of tired resignation. But, miraculously, as the evening progressed and the dancing became more animated, I was to notice this expression gradually change, the eyes regain a little of their sparkle, the cheeks a slight splash of colour and, from behind the tired, worried countenance, I got the occasional fleeting glimpse of what that face had been before the years – only a few, really – of drought and cold and worry and child bearing had cast them in the sad mould. The prairies are hard on women.

Of young girls there were only three. Two unbelievably homely and the other as unbelievably beautiful. A dark-haired, round-cheeked, full-lipped, thick-bosomed girl whose shapely legs and thighs, which showed often as she was "swung out," made my mouth go dry.

It was a gay crowd but I wasn't part of it. Mrs. Montgomery had made a few introductions, but they'd fallen flat. They mistook my natural shyness for a stand-offish attitude, and each attempt I made at light conversation came out all wrong. Finally I found myself standing around with my hands in my pockets, trying to keep out of people's way.

But I had my eye on the dark-haired beauty and I knew what I was going to do when the music started. I fancied myself pretty good at the flea hop, and foxtrot, and the waltz, and could do a passable Charleston. I'd show these damned yokels a thing or two. After all, I hadn't been nicknamed "Twinkle Toes" at Nutana Collegiate for nothing.

With a smattering of applause, the fiddler, Orville Jackson, took his place beside the organ in the corner. A short, bandy-legged man of about sixty-five, he wore a khaki peaked cap indoors and out. I soon discovered why. Most of his front teeth were gone and, in order to keep his pipe in his mouth while playing, he hung it from the peak of his cap by a thread. He cradled his fiddle in his left arm with the butt against his chest and began tuning it.

As he did so, Grandma Wilson, who must have weighed close to 300 pounds, came forward and sank down on the organ stool, her ample bottom overlapping on all sides. She threw her beefy hands at the organ keys and came up with a wail like a sick cat. Orville tapped his right foot twice, waved his head gently back and forth so that the suspended pipe swung in time, and drew his bow across the fiddle.

Before I could even start towards the dark young lady, four young swains swooped down upon her and bore her off. Then I noticed that the music was almost completely unfamiliar and, instead of the dancers embracing each other and shuffling around the floor as I was accustomed to do, they arranged themselves in groups of eight, facing each other. A big florid man had taken his place beside the organ and bellowed, "Two more couples wanted"; then, when a grinning farmer and his six-year-old daughter had responded, "One more couple wanted."

Then I noticed a determined, red-faced matron approaching me and, before I could duck, she had me by the hand. "Come on, teacher," she grinned. "Be my partner."

"Yeah, get in there and fight, Teach!" somebody shouted, and, as I looked around at their grinning faces, I knew that in some crazy way I was on trial. So I suffered myself to be led to the centre of the floor, which was by now so crowded that we could scarcely get through.

Then Grandma Wilson banged the organ, Orville Jackson sawed at his fiddle, the caller shouted in a great booming voice, "Places all!" and everybody began to move in different directions. Now, it may seem strange, but although I was born and bred on the prairies, I had in my whole life not only never participated in a square dance, but I'd never even seen one done.

As I recall it now, it was something like a football scrimmage and a basketball game combined. With women! As the music gained momentum and the caller bellowed louder and the stamping of feet became deafening, I became completely

31

and hopelessly lost. I was shoved and pushed and shivied about like a shopper at a bargain counter. Every so often one of the women would grab me and swing me around then drop me. As I stomped aimlessly about I would regularly meet a six-footer in a red plaid shirt and face to match who'd take me by the shoulders with two immense hands and literally lift me into place, like a mother lifting a child. But I never stayed in place for long.

I remember once seeing an ancient book in which the evils of "round" dancing were deplored and "square" dancing was approved. This square dancing was not only indecent, it was downright perilous. Those muscular lads grabbed their partners by the nearest handle and swung them off their feet. Their dresses half the time flew up over their heads, and flying feet narrowly missed other people's jaws.

On and on, faster and faster went the dance until each couple had its turn doing whatever we were doing and then the music stopped. The panting, sweating participants sat down. My partner never even spoke to me, nor did any other member of the set. Whatever test I'd been put to, I'd failed. Then the caller shouted his commands again and after a couple of "Two more couples wanted," the joint was jumping again. I can say this: that school house was mighty well built. Otherwise those dancers would have gone right through the floor and ended up in my quarters with their babies. At it was, the rhythm of the stomping feet shook the place till the desks rattled.

So it went on, and on, and on – square dance after square dance, with an occasional quadrille or schottische thrown in. Nobody invited me to dance again, and of course I didn't have the nerve to ask anybody. So I watched in a sort of terrified wonder as the others whirled and swung and pranced. Occasionally I caught a glimpse of my dark lady being pawed and patted and thrown about by raw-boned hands, but I realized that there was nothing there for me.

When not dancing, the half-dozen young fellows stood in a group in the corner and told dirty stories. I knew a few that I thought they might not have heard, but when I wandered over to join them they stopped self-consciously and said nothing. I asked them if they'd heard the one about the camel and the monkey and they looked at each other in shocked amazement. When I told it they didn't laugh but merely stared at the toes of their shoes ashamedly. What do you do when a joke falls flat on the floor like a piece of wet hay? I know what I did. I retreated awkwardly to a desk and perched on it. Shortly I was joined by a bewhiskered oldster who kept spitting tobacco juice on the floor behind the desks while he told me about his first experiences in school as a boy and gave me his philosophy on the art of instructing the young.

I again tried retiring to my own quarters, but found the kitchen filled with talking women preparing food. Since the bedroom was still full of babies, there was nothing for it but to return to the dance.

Around about midnight Mrs. Montgomery announced that lunch would be served and I felt like a besieged general when he sees relief coming over the hill. Big enamel pitchers of scalding coffee were brought up from the basement and served in thick, white kitchen cups. Chicken and pork sandwiches were passed around (there was virtually no market for chicken), followed by cake and cookies. I was waiting it out. Then each man rolled a fag or lighted up his pipe and the topic of economics was discussed in corners. Soon, I thought, even this will end. The kids will be cleared off my bed, everybody will go home and I'll get some sleep.

But I was greatly mistaken. Orville Jackson filled his pipe, hung it in place, and shuffled over to the organ again. Grandma Wilson draped her ample bottom over the organ stool. They struck up the music and the dance began again. And if I'd thought it lively before, now it was downright frantic. There was one slick little number where four men and four women joined hands. Then, with a quick manoeuvre, the men somehow had their arms behind the women's backs, hands clasped tight. They began to skip around in a circle, faster and faster. As the men gained momentum, the women's feet left the floor until their legs were straight out, their bodies parallel to the floor. I'd have sworn that if one had broken loose she'd have shot clean through the window.

Another feature of the after-supper session was what might be called the specialty numbers: dances performed by certain members who had become famous for them. "Dip and Dive," for instance, led by Uncle John Henry who weighed 275 pounds and was about five foot eight. Yet he had the grace and agility to lead the dancers, all holding hands, through an intricate series of dips and dives that was beautiful to watch. "Little Drops of Brandy" followed this, and a waltz quadrille.

But the specialty of specialties was when Orville Jackson and Grandma Wilson temporarily surrendered their instruments to an acne-afflicted youth and none other than our own Violet Sinclair. Then a reverent hush fell on the assembly as the two musicians took their places. Orville had set aside his peaked cap and pipe, revealing a head so bald and shiny it gleamed beneath the gas lamp. As the music began, the bald-headed man and the fat grandmother embraced each other for the only round dance of the evening. While the others formed a circle and clapped lightly and rhythmically to the tune of "Till We Meet Again," those two danced as smoothly and gracefully as any couple I've ever seen.

And the dancing went on. One o'clock, two o'clock, three o'clock plodded by and there was no sign of a break. At six o'clock a faint glow of light began to show outside and the dancers reluctantly began to make preparations to leave. They had been waiting for daylight to make the long, long sleigh ride home just a little easier.

Sleeping babies, wound in their cocoons of blankets, were carried up the basement steps and laid gently in the straw in the bottoms of sleigh boxes. Horses with steam shooting from their nostrils were brought out from the barn and hitched to the sleighs. One by one they pulled out of the gate and I was left alone – with a school room littered with cigarette and cigar butts, pipe ashes, and tobacco juice. I thought it would never be clean again, but I was too tired to care.

I stumbled down the steps and into my bedroom, which smelled strongly of babies neglected for ten hours, peeled off my clothes and climbed beneath the covers. For half an hour the throbbing in my ears kept me awake, but then I sank into the deep sleep of the just.

Not for long. At nine o'clock I heard a heavy banging above me, feet on the stairs, my door being opened and somebody looking into the stove.

"It's only me," Mrs. Hamilton's voice announced cheerfully. "A few of us have come to clean up. We'll need to heat water on your stove – some of that tobacco juice is hard to get off the floor." Then she added, "But you don't need to get up. I can find everything."

She thumped back up the stairs and, with four other ladies, tore into cleaning up the place. All morning they swept, scrubbed, scoured, and, it seemed to me, played shuffle-board with the movable desks. Then, for good measure, they gave my kitchen-living room the same treatment and left.

Thus ended the one and only social event I attended during my stay at Willowgreen School.

We Mean Business

Since being liberated from the "hungry thirties" I have written radio plays, magazine articles, and books about that unique period in Canadian history.

I remember the Aberhart days well. In Saskatchewan we were fascinated by this big, rotund man with the thick lips through which poured the most unorthodox theories we had ever heard. Give every man, woman, and child twenty-five dollars a month just for being a consumer? It made a lot of sense to us. That was half as much as I was earning as a full-time school teacher and more than many were earning. A school teacher, a Bible class teacher, and a preacher of the gospel, William Aberhart used all the skills he had honed to persuade the Albertans that he could lead them out of the valley of dust and poverty into the promised land. And he damned near succeeded.

He talked to the electors the way he'd talked to his students, using illustrations, parables, skits, and every other good teaching device that could be used to instruct them in a new brand of economics that he himself didn't quite understand. Since none of the other politicians had any solutions at all, the electors believed Bible Bill and elected his party to power with the man himself as premier. It was a typical western Canada thing to do, and Bible Bill was a typical western Canadian – full of confidence, arrogance, disdain for convention, zeal, and courage, fighting against fearful odds.

The following piece is taken from my book in Canada's Illustrated Heritage Series, *The Hungry Thirties*.

*You can't talk religion to a man who
has had nothing to eat for three days.*

William Aberhart

"We mean business!" the man on
the platform shouted. He was large and his face flushed as he
spoke. "People on the platform, what do you say?"

"We mean business!"

"Ladies in the audience, what do you say?"

"We mean business!"

"Men in the audience, what do you say?"

"We mean business!"

"All together, say it!"

"WE MEAN BUSINESS!"

"And I mean business! Tell your friends and neighbours
when you meet them that Aberhart means business!"

Few Canadians stirred up more controversy, attracted more
devotion, or incited more hatred during the thirties than
William Aberhart. Some people called him an emissary of God;
others said he was a tool of the devil. Actually, he was a practical man of good morals and intentions, a teacher and a
preacher, a rather shy and self-effacing man in private life. On
the public platform or in front of a microphone, however, he
was a rootin'-tootin' spellbinder of the old school. Almost single
handedly William Aberhart founded a new and successful political party, became the first Social Credit premier of Alberta, and
changed the voting patterns of the Canadian West.

William Aberhart was not the only politician born of the
Depression. In 1934 Ontario elected the most colourful and
flamboyant leader that conservative province had ever seen.
Mitchell Frederick Hepburn was an onion farmer and he spoke
the farmers' language. "Our Mitch" called the millionaire Prime
Minister Bennett, who owned the controlling interest in the
E.B. Eddy Co., "Lord Matchbox." His quick and corny wit de-
lighted the farmers and he hit the rural areas like a cyclone,
drawing larger crowds than the Liberals had seen in decades,
clowning, parodying, and mercilessly castigating his opponents.

He believed in the "big show." He met the people, talked with them, argued with them, and swore with them, and the desperate farmers gave him their confidence. Hepburn carried the province in 1934 and became its first Liberal premier in almost thirty years.

At first the new premier lived up to his election promises. He passed legislation to protect farm prices and, at the same time, to safeguard the rights of trade unions. Like most other government leaders of the thirties, however, Hepburn became alarmed by the "agitators" among the unemployed and union ranks. His carefree and careless personal behaviour, his pragmatism, and his susceptibility to big men with big money eventually led him into the camp of big business – the very enemy that he had attacked so successfully in his pre-election speeches.

His true colours were revealed when he mobilized the Ontario Provincial Police, nicknamed "Hepburn's Hussars," to smash the Union Auto Workers' drive to unionize the province's automobile factories. He finally locked swords with the cautious and cagey Mackenzie King, against whom no politician ever won a battle. It was the end of Hepburn's political career and, for more than a generation, the end of the Ontario Liberal party.

In Quebec, Maurice Le Noblet Duplessis would be luckier in his political machinations. The Union Nationale party was founded in 1935 in protest against the unemployment and severe economic hardships resulting from the Depression. The next year, the party succeeded in ousting Quebec's forty-year-old Liberal government on a platform of extensive economic, social, and electoral reform. Shortly after the election, Maurice Duplessis gained absolute control of the party.

He too attacked the corruption of the Liberal government. He too promised the farmers that he would end all their ills. Once elected he became the defender of the Catholic faith, the enemy of radicals and non-conformists, and a white knight who would save his people from Communism.

Duplessis quickly consolidated his political position, stepping hard on the toes of all who dared to oppose him. In 1937 he passed the notorious Padlock Law, by which he could close and padlock any premises where men gathered to further Communism. "Communism" meant anything that he decided was dangerous to him or his party. Although Duplessis was defeated at the polls in 1939, he would return to power in 1944 to hold undisputed and absolute control of Quebec until his death fifteen years later.

The political story of the decade, however, belongs to William Aberhart. He was born on a farm near Seaforth, Ontario, December 30, 1878, and raised strictly in the Presbyterian faith. He obtained his early education in small rural schools, then continued to normal school and studied for a Bachelor of Arts degree through correspondence courses. During his student years he could never quite make up his mind whether to become a teacher or a preacher, and so he finally became both.

Aberhart went to Calgary in 1910. Teaching alone could not begin to use up his tremendous energies, however, and at night and on Sundays he taught a Bible Class. In 1927 he organized the Calgary Prophetic Bible Institute. His first student was a young, lean Saskatchewan boy named Ernest Manning. Manning studied for three years and became the Institute's first graduate. After that he never left Aberhart's side.

With the advent of radio Aberhart realized that he could reach hundreds of thousands of listeners and he used it to the fullest extent. Financed by donations from his listeners, he began regular Sunday afternoon broadcasts in which he preached good, old-fashioned, down-to-earth, no-nonsense fundamental religion. He was one of the first of the radio evangelists so plentiful during the thirties, and he was certainly one of the most powerful.

He came to the people of Alberta when they were most vulnerable, beaten down by the Depression, disillusioned, frightened, and confused. As one desperately poor farmer expressed it: "When things are hopeless, your mind goes back to childhood and the simple scriptures. When Mr. Aberhart's voice came over the air with his scripture lesson, something clicked in our minds."

Aberhart taught the virtues of honesty, self-reliance, responsibility, moral behaviour, and forbearance, quoting the scriptures endlessly to back up his arguments. Ernest Manning was always at his side, helping with the broadcasts, leading the prayers, conducting the singing, exhorting the listeners to send in more money.

Everything might have continued this way, with Aberhart doing little more than urging people to turn to the Bible in their hour of need, if he had not happened to read a certain book. It was called *Social Credit, Unemployment or War*, and it was written by an Englishman named Maurice Colborne.

The book outlined the economic theories of a Scottish engineer named Major Clifford Hugh Douglas. It pointed out that the trouble with the economic world was that there was never enough money or credit to buy the goods available. Since price was made up of wages plus interest on money plus profit, there was never enough money in the wage envelope alone to pay it. This vicious system, Douglas maintained, was created and perpetuated by a world-wide conspiracy of bankers. Political parties, he said, were merely the tools of the bankers.

Aberhart borrowed the book from a friend while he was marking examination papers in Edmonton during the summer of 1932. His direct, mathematical mind seized on the salient points and believed it was a divine revelation. God had shown the way to rescue the people from the worst Depression of all time and it was up to him to spread the divine word.

The Social Credit doctrine, according to Aberhart, had three basic components – the Cultural Heritage, the Basic Dividend, and the Unearned Increment.

The Cultural Heritage was the stake that every bona fide citizen had in the wealth of the province. Aberhart estimated Alberta's total potential wealth at $2,406 million, which gave each citizen a share of $3,518.

Each bona fide citizen would be issued a certificate, which was as good as money, with which to buy food, shelter, and clothing. This was the Basic Dividend. Each citizen would get this over and above any salary he or she might be earning. The figures proposed were twenty-five dollars a month for each adult over twenty-one years of age, twenty dollars for those age twenty, fifteen dollars for those age nineteen, ten dollars for ages seventeen and eighteen and five dollars per month for children from one year to sixteen.

To most Albertan families, many of whom had no cash money at all, the idea was wildly attractive. A family of eight, for example, could collect more than one hundred dollars a month. There would be no more relief and no more degrading dole, Aberhart said. Each person would merely be getting what he was entitled to. The certificate had to be spent; it could not be loaned or invested. If there was anything left over at the end of the year it could be used to buy Alberta bonds.

In the event that a farmer, businessman, or any other citizen might get money through an increase in the value of land or stocks that he owned, Aberhart proposed that the government would tax away this money, because it required no work and was unearned. This aspect of the scheme did not bother the average Albertan, because nothing was increasing in value. So far as he or she could see, the plan had a lot more to give than to take away.

Aberhart brought his great teaching skill, organizational ability, and oratorical powers to bear on expounding the Social Credit doctrine. He used diagrams, pamphlets, folk-songs, humour, sarcasm – he was a master of them all. Everywhere he went he took his teaching aids, including immense coloured charts. One of these showed the bloodstream of credit compared with the bloodstream of the body. The flow must be uninterrupted and steady.

One favourite platform stunt was to stand before a live audience in a coat completely covered with old patches. It represented, he said, the old, worn-out, economic theories. As he expounded the virtues of Social Credit, his voice rising and his round face flushing, he ripped off the patches one by one and hurled them aside. Finally he stood there in a new, well-tailored, modern coat. "This," he thundered, "is Social Credit!" It brought down the house.

William Aberhart was not a politician. His goal was to convince enough people of the truth of Social Credit that he could force one of the political parties to adopt his plan. He tried this with the governing United Farmers of Alberta party. He appeared before their convention and answered questions for them, but they took no action. He had no more success with the Liberals or Conservatives. They all tended to look upon him as a crackpot.

William Aberhart was being forced into politics. The tide of feeling he had begun in the province had swelled to a great wave. His disciples were mostly school teachers, preachers, and farmers, given to the same oversimplification as he himself, but his organization was magnificent. He did not campaign, he taught. The province was organized into study groups – as many as 1,600 at the peak – and classes were conducted in school houses, town halls, and church basements. They were always packed. People came from ten, twenty miles in Bennett Buggies, jalopies, cutters, or on horseback. Many trudged through the snow in below zero weather.

A provincial election had been called for August 22, 1935. With incredible speed, the new party nominated a candidate for each of the sixty-three ridings, many of them Aberhart's personal choices. The local meetings increased. The lessons became more convincing. The radio thundered the message. The voters came out 300,000 strong, a far greater percentage of those eligible than had ever before voted in Alberta. When the votes were all counted, the new party had swept like a prairie fire across the province and elected fifty-six members.

Aberhart himself had not been a candidate, but a seat was soon found for him in the Okotoks-High River riding. On September 3, 1935, he was sworn in as premier of Alberta.

As an evangelist and teacher he could talk and persuade and convince. Now he was the head of a government with a tremendous debt to be paid and civil service salaries to be met, and neither he nor any of his fifty-six members had ever sat in a legislature before. In addition, there were powerful forces working against him.

Until the day of the election, newspaper editors outside Alberta had no more interest in Aberhart than they had in any other evangelist. When he became head of the first Social Credit government in the world, however, he was news. In no time Edmonton was full of reporters who watched the premier's every move, recorded every gesture, analysed every comment, and ridiculed every joke.

In his office in the Parliament Building, the new premier worked tirelessly. He had always considered education due for reform, and he appointed himself minister of education. He passed legislation to ease the burden of debt on the farmers, and he hired a financial expert to advise him on the best means of cleaning up the mess left by the previous government. Social Credit, he decided, must be introduced gradually.

Here he learned his first devastating lesson. To the voters, an election promise is an election promise, and they wanted their money. In their jubilation over the election, farm wives pored over the mail-order catalogues picking out the things they would buy with their share of the cultural heritage. Some quit their jobs, convinced they could now try something more compatible.

Aberhart reminded his people that he had specifically stated that no dividends would be paid for eighteen months. He was not used to making excuses, or explaining, and he didn't know how to placate. His relations with the reporters were abominable. He scolded them and called them "creatures with mental hydrophobia." Speaking on the national radio network, he stated ruefully that he felt like the young woman who, in the throes of having a baby, cried out, "If this is what marriage is like, you can tell my young man the engagement is off!"

Some of the new government members, alarmed by the unrest in their constituencies, began to demand action from their boss. Some even held clandestine meetings in the basement of the Corona Hotel and talked openly of dumping the chief. When finally, in January of 1937, after months of hard work, a sound orthodox budget was brought down calling for over $1 million in increased taxes, the howl from the people, the editors, and the insurgent members was heard across Canada.

Aberhart found himself in the middle of his own prairie fire and he got badly burned. He was accused of betraying the voters, double-crossing the caucus, and financing the government on "the pennies of the poor." Out-of-town reporters made the most of his misery, reporting to the world that Social Credit was a dismal failure.

In 1937 Aberhart set up a Social Credit Board, chaired by insurgent Glen Maclachlan, with power to go ahead and introduce Social Credit by the quickest means possible. In the parliamentary session beginning August of the same year, the board came out fighting. In three days the legislature passed three bills controlling banking in Alberta. Within a short time the federal government, acting through Governor General Lord Tweedsmuir, ruled that the three acts were contrary to the Canadian Constitution.

Aberhart accused the financially powerful and industrial East of stepping in to prevent an honest attempt by Alberta to improve itself. "Those plotters, those money barons, those sons of Satan – they shall not oppose the will of the people of Alberta!" he roared.

Now the people were with their prophet again. The real enemy had been identified. The wrath that had accumulated over the years because of high tariffs that prevented them from buying cheaper in the United states, banks that would not lend them money, implement companies that reclaimed their farm machinery, wheat speculators, and Bay Street manipulators – it all burst forth. The people stood like rocks behind their leaders.

Bolstered by this support, the Alberta legislature held another special session and re-stated its position. The controversial bank-licensing bills were re-enacted and another bill was passed imposing heavy taxes on the banks.

Goaded by what they considered to be irresponsible reporting by the press, the legislature passed the Accurate News and Information Act, which stipulated, in effect, that newspapers had to print what the Social Credit Board told them to print. This only served to increase the animosity of the newspapers, from the powerful Edmonton *Journal* to the lowliest weekly in the province. The *Journal* won the prestigious Pulitzer Prize for its part in the fight against the act.

No one was actually arrested or punished under what was popularly known as the "Press Gag Act," although there was a threat to send one reporter to jail. The controversial legislation was fought all the way to the Supreme Court of Canada, which overturned it.

When Canada declared war in the fall of 1939, the fight between the province and the federal government ended. The war united the nation, put money into circulation, and ended the Depression in the West.

In the election of 1940 Aberhart was again in a strong position. His study groups were as powerful as ever. He broadcast every Sunday night from a public meeting in Edmonton, he and Ernest Manning, the man who, upon Aberhart's death three years later, would become the second Social Credit premier of Alberta. Despite the fact that he had not given a basic dividend to one single person, his government was re-elected with thirty-six of the fifty-seven seats.

In many ways, William Aberhart *was* Social Credit. Without any zeal, energy, fanatical enthusiasm, organizational ability, and persuasive power the movement never could have succeeded. Certainly this makes "Bible Bill" – whether one considers him as a sincere honest man or an "evangelistic racketeer," as he was described by one editor – one of the most colourful and important Canadians.

Why Shoot
the Teacher

Why Shoot the Teacher is far and away the most important
book I have written and, I believe, the best. I wrote it during a
period when for some reason I had no pressing assignments
and, most unusual, some free time.

We had moved from Streetsville to Orangeville, Ontario,
and this was the period of my closest contact with Farley
Mowat, who lived about ten miles away at Palgrave. His
marvellous book *The Dog Who Wouldn't Be* had been published seven years earlier and I had enjoyed it immensely. It
was not that Farley urged me to write of my first teaching experience, because he knew nothing about it, but his book certainly had a lot to do with my decision to do so.

The experience at Willowgreen School in the winter and
spring of 1933 was still rankling. I was mad as hell that
anyone should have been treated so badly, and I wanted to get
back at the people who did it (a surprising number of books
are thus motivated). But when I got going on it I soon realized
that these damned farmers and their kids had been even
greater victims of the Depression than I. They were stuck in a
rotten situation and I wasn't. So, as I wrote, the self-pity and
anger quickly dissipated, and I saw the situation objectively
as an essential bit of Canadian history. And as I began to
describe my condition, the humour of it struck me so I embel-
lished the incidents to give them form and punch.

The book was an immediate success, and it changed my
writing life. I cried a little when I received the good news that
a magazine had bought three chapters at $500 apiece and I
still cry a little and laugh a lot when I read parts of the book.

In 1976 *Why Shoot the Teacher* was made into a movie,
with Fil Fraser of Edmonton as producer and Bud Cort and
Samantha Eggar playing the leading roles. The screen-play by
Jim DeFelice faithfully followed the book. It was shot on loca-

tion at Hanna, Alberta, just a few miles west of where the story took place. A windswept, desolate area still. The supporting players were Canadian actors and farmers and townspeople of the district. The children, who all but stole the movie, except for a couple of semi-professionals from Edmonton, were also locals.

After the usual vicissitudes of film making, the movie finally opened in Ottawa, Toronto, and Edmonton to rave reviews. I have reviews in my files from France, England, Australia, the U.S., and have yet to see a bad one. It is difficult to find a Canadian who hasn't seen the film.

The success of the movie and the success of the book have brought me a great deal of satisfaction, as well as being proof of Shakespeare's contention that "sweet are the uses of adversity."

1

At twenty-five minutes after two on the afternoon of the third of January, 1933, I stepped out of a frost-covered CNR passenger car onto the worn, wooden platform of Bleke, Saskatchewan. Since then, when I've permitted myself to think of it at all, I've been convinced it was then and there that I began to lose my mind.

The train that fetched me was what they call a "mixed." This means it was made up of freight cars carrying articles of some value such as farm machinery, rock salt, pigs, or gopher traps, and one passenger car tacked like an afterthought on the tail end, carrying what seemed to have no value on the prairies then – people.

To be accurate, since leaving the town of Mantario where the clergyman I'd been talking to got off, the car had carried only me. This was my first real experience with loneliness, the most desperate and deadly of all conditions. For the whole of my stay in this desolate district I was to fight against it with every stratagem I could devise, and I was to lose.

A couple of frost-bearded trainmen, with earlugs tied under their chins and gauntlet mitts on their hands, tipped my heavy trunk out the door of the baggage car and wrestled it onto the platform. They slanted perfunctory glances my way, perhaps wondering if, from its weight, it might contain a dead body. Actually it contained the only thing worth more than twenty dollars I owned in the world, a brand new, never-opened ten-volume encyclopaedia.

In point of actual fact, I didn't even own those books. I'd stolen them before leaving home. But that's another story.

Having also unloaded a carton of canned goods, a half-dozen empty cream cans, and a small sack containing a part for a harness, the men pushed the door shut. The "mixed" puffed off down the track, and with it went just about every vestige of the twentieth century I was to see for a while. For, although I didn't realize it then, I had stepped out of the world of electricity, automobiles, radios, and well-marked streets into a world where few of these existed and where nature's old law of be tough or perish was still very much in vogue.

Pulling my face down behind my thin overcoat collar, I looked around the settlement. It consisted of two grain elevators, a coal shed, a ramshackle building that served as a store, one frame house banked high with snow, and nothing more. A tiny oasis of futility on a barren sea of despair.

The storm door of the store opened; the wind caught it and banged it back. A big man buried in a ragged buffalo-hide overcoat and with a scarf tied around his neck and over his head advanced across the road towards me. With a shock I noticed that around his feet, in lieu of overshoes, he had wound ordinary gunny sacks, two for each foot.

"You the teacher?" he mumbled when he came within earshot. Nothing more. No pleasant introduction, no smile of welcome, no hearty handshake. He obviously resented me on sight, and somehow I'd expected him to. For one of the peculiarities of the Depression on the prairies, and one I'd never had satisfactorily explained, was the way that older people resented the young. It was as though they blamed them for the drought and poor prices and the death of their hopes. Probably not. More likely the long series of hopeless years, culminating in these near-starvation conditions, made them mad at everything, including a city boy standing alone on a bare platform wondering how he'd got there and why.

"Name's McDougall," the big man mumbled. "Secretary of Willowgreen School District." His small, wind-worn eyes scanned me from head to foot before he added, as though realizing belatedly that even an idiot was entitled to some kind of warning, "It's a twelve-mile drive out to the district."

A twelve-mile drive. Although I'd been born and had spent my entire twenty years in Saskatchewan, I still didn't fully understand the terrible meaning of those words. For I had lived most of my life in the city of Saskatoon, and life in a Saskatchewan city is little different from that of a city anywhere. Oh, the weather gets colder – an average January temperature of minus one degree – that's true. But the houses are well insulated and warm, streetcars comfortable enough, automobiles well equipped with heaters. Young people dress much the same as their counterparts in Toronto or New York: light overcoats, lined leather gloves. On my feet I had one pair of socks and a pair of oxfords with toe rubbers. I had never been in rural Saskatchewan in the winter in my life. I didn't know that the words "twelve-mile drive" were the equivalent of "trial by frost-bite."

Without another word Dave McDougall bent over and took hold of the leather handle at one end of my roped-up trunk. I took the other. He inclined his cloth-swathed head towards the end of the platform where a team of lean, shaggy Clydes stood, heads low against the wind. We staggered to the sleigh and slid the trunk over the side onto the thin layer of straw in the bottom. McDougall hunched himself down into the bottom of the two-deck sleigh box and pulled his buffalo coat tight around his knees. Then he clucked to the team. Demonstrating some sort of city-wise flamboyance that I suppose I thought necessary, I perched myself on top of the trunk exposed to the biting wind and snow.

The team wheeled slowly and plodded along the one short street. A black and white farm collie with fur like that of a winter wolf made a few jumps at the noses of the team and then began ranging after rabbits.

There was no straight road. In those days highways and township roads weren't ploughed clean of snow in winter. Rather they were abandoned entirely, and the first farmer to come along with a sleigh established a trail that followed the line of least resistance across the fields, winding around hills, snow drifts, and brier patches. Those farmers who were lucky enough still to be driving cars simply put them up on wooden blocks for the winter and took to cutter and sleigh.

It was some trip. Twelve miles with a team undernourished on wheat straw takes at least three hours. The temperature was somewhere below minus thirty degrees Fahrenheit, and there was the usual persistent, biting wind out of the northwest, a wind that was getting stronger. It soon became perfectly clear to me that I had two choices: I could either sit in the sleigh box and freeze, or I could get out and run behind.

I ran behind.

And while this twenty-year-old, filled with restless vitality, arrogance, and frustration, plods along behind that sleigh box, puffing his breath against a skimpy collar to salvage some of its warmth, trying to keep his ears, cheeks, and nose covered with thinly gloved hands, let's consider where he is and how he comes to be there.

This is the semi-arid region that lies on the Saskatchewan-Alberta border just north of the South Saskatchewan River. Although it lies next door to the flat, heavy-soiled wheatland of the Kindersley plain, it bears no resemblance to it. This slightly rolling, treeless, curly-grass country should never have been broken up for farmland. No prosperous farmsteads with large, white L-shaped houses and big red barns are seen from the road. Rather the flat-roofed, unpainted barns and shack-like houses. And everywhere Russian thistle poking spiny twigs through the snow.

The people who lived here were the usual pioneers from Ontario, the United States, Britain, and central Europe. They had come, filled with hope and vigour, to the "Golden West" to make a home and a future. They remained in a gritty dustbowl, their souls scarred by a smouldering resentment and a keen sense of betrayal. They stayed on for the least attractive of all reasons – because they couldn't get out. In those days before family allowances there was often no cash money in a house for months at a time. This accounted for the gunny sacks on Dave McDougall's feet. He literally didn't have the $3.98 to send to Eaton's for a pair of overshoes.

I didn't know all this as I stumbled along behind that sleigh box. Times were hard, I knew. They had been hard in Saskatoon ever since the stock-market crash of 1929 had officially opened "the great Depression," and made it impossible for me to attend university. In fact, I'd had to borrow money to finish normal school.

That was the first big resentment. I'd never wanted to go to normal school. Then, as now, the better students in high school looked upon elementary-school teaching as a second-rate occupation, useful at best as a way to pick up a quick thousand dollars so that you might continue your education.

So, until prosperity would come bursting around that corner where President Hoover had said it was lurking, I went to the Saskatoon normal school. Since I didn't want to be there, I contributed little to that institution and learned nothing about teaching.

How do you teach a person to teach, anyway? A medical student can be instructed in where the vital parts of the body are located, and how to remove and replace them. A dentist practises with drill and chisel. But teaching, it has always seemed to me, is something that must be learned by trial and error and by the development of a subtle feel for it, like flying an aircraft by the seat of your pants. To be sure we learned about the theories of education (Dewey's progressive ideas were beginning to influence educationalists) and the methods of some great teachers of the past. We made charts and timetables and books of nursery rhymes and spent a confusing two weeks in urban and rural schools as "normalites." Then we were released on the unsuspecting youth of the province.

But nobody wanted us. During the ten months at normal school the teaching profession had degenerated frightfully. Now there were hundreds of applicants for every job. After carefully clipping the "Teachers Wanted" ads from the paper, I

began writing applications in my best handwriting and according to the rules laid down by our English instructor. At first I
was choosy, selecting only schools close to the city and in
reasonably sized towns. My original asking price was $1,000 per
annum, considered a good price for teachers in those days, and
corresponding now to an annual salary in the neighbourhood of
$4,000.

There were no takers.

After twenty-five letters I became less selective as to location and size of school and dropped my price to $800. Still not a
nibble.

From there my preference diminished until I was offering to
teach anywhere for whatever they'd pay. I wrote by actual
count over a hundred applications, but not one single reply did I
get.

Then I took to visiting school boards, borrowing my
brother's car or badgering a cousin into driving me. During the
hot, dusty evenings of August I interviewed school boards in
front of hardware stores, in the offices of lumber yards, and in
grain elevators. I trudged for miles over stubble fields to extol
my credentials to tired farmers sitting impatiently on binders or
manure spreaders. I swore I neither smoked, nor drank, nor
went out with girls (all lies). Depending on whom I was talking
to I was United Church, Baptist, Presbyterian, or Anglican. I'd
have been Hindu if that would have helped. I promised to teach
Sunday School, lead the Boy Scouts, coach softball, board with
the chairman, play catch for the baseball team, and start an
athletic club for older boys.

They yawned in my face.

When people talk of jobs being scarce now, I just don't
know what they mean. That was real unemployment. Of the
200 students who attended the normal school that year only a
handful got jobs. Many never taught at all. University graduates
fared little better. It was said – and I can believe it – that of the
entire graduating class of engineers that year one man got a job.
And that was a job driving a truck.

The desperation for jobs passes belief. Occupations such as
being a fireman, delivering milk or bread, clerking in the Hud-

son's Bay store, had a very high priority, because they were steady. They told a joke in Saskatoon about the man who fell into the Saskatchewan River and five men, leaning over the bridge, shouted questions to him concerning his name and place of employment. On learning this, they raced off in an attempt to get his job, leaving the poor fellow to drown.

I never laughed at that joke. It was too close to grim truth for humour.

As the fall wore on and advertisements for teachers disappeared, I resigned myself to being unemployed. I helped my mother with the weekly wash, waxed acres of floors, feuded with an older working brother about whether "non-paying boarders" had any bathroom rights, bought Turret cigarettes one at a time at the drugstore, and slowly degenerated.

Then, one day after Christmas, to pass the time, I went to a hockey game involving the newly built technical school, and decided to enrol in that institution. Since there was no thought of getting a job anyway, I selected a trade that I thought might be helpful one day – motor mechanics. I attended one class and learned how to solder a radiator. Then, when I'd given up the idea of ever teaching, the letter came from McDougall offering me the job at Willowgreen School.

So, I quit technical school, and the world lost a fumbling motor mechanic. I wrote McDougall that I would accept the job, although I knew nothing about the conditions there, and he replied, advising me to be at Bleke on the third of January.

I had no money and no decent clothing. For train fare I went to a former Sunday school teacher and hockey coach and begged a loan. From the attic mother resurrected an old steamer trunk that had a warped wooden tray covered with flowered paper and smelled of moth-balls. Into this I packed my meagre belongings and looked around for something else with which to fill it.

On the front porch of our house on Tenth Street sat an unopened cardboard carton containing ten volumes of an educational encyclopaedia. The manner of its being there was typical of Saskatchewan in the early thirties. The lack of regular jobs had forced many aggressive young men into the business of selling insurance, magazine subscriptions, and sets of books. Their favourite targets were the teachers in one-room rural schools who had a little cash and were usually so lonely they would talk to anyone.

My sister was one of these. The encyclopaedia salesman dropped in during morning classes when she was trying to keep eight grades busy at once. He insisted on giving his sales pitch, and, to get rid of him, she signed the piece of paper he placed in front of her. Then, after he left, she read it and discovered she had contracted to pay $159.98 for a set of the books. Since this was one third of her yearly salary, she immediately wrote to the company to cancel the order. They wrote a crisp letter on crisp paper saying that a deal was a deal and the books would be delivered.

They were delivered. But my sister, who had her own way of dealing with such contingencies, simply refused to remove them from the verandah. There they sat. The company wouldn't take them back; my sister wouldn't take them in. I noticed them when I was packing my sparse belongings and dumped them into my trunk. When the company billed my sister for the books, she could truthfully say she didn't have them. When they billed me, I ignored them, secure in the knowledge that no one would follow me to Bleke, Saskatchewan.

And so, with my trunk and books riding, I walked or trotted most of the twelve miles from Bleke station to Willowgreen School District. Now and then, when I was taking a breather, Dave McDougall would mumble a question at me. But mostly he just sat with his broad rump against the side of the sleigh box and his knees pulled up in front of him, so that everything was covered by the buffalo coat. He didn't need to glance sideways at the team. They knew the trail and followed it home.

I didn't actually get frost-bitten during that drive, but merely did the kind of "freezing" I had been doing all my life. That is, my ear lobes became stiff and white and, when I rubbed them, red and sore. The same with my nose, fingers, and toes.

It was pitch dark when we reached the collection of shacks

that made up the McDougall homestead. All I could see as we approached over the flat field was a dim yellow glow flickering through a patched windowpane. When McDougall pulled up to the door, I noticed that the unpainted frame house was banked to the window sills with manure.

"You go in," he said. "I'll unhitch. No use in taking your trunk out of the sleigh until we figure out where you're going to live."

He shouted "Ha-low!" and the door was shoved open by a short, shapeless woman in a worn dress and long cardigan sweater. Behind her crowded four small children. I entered a small square room that was dominated by an enormous kitchen range and cluttered with outdoor clothing and a set of harness somebody had been mending. A shaggy farm collie got stiffly to its feet from behind the stove and growled a welcome. Mrs. McDougall held out a worn, rough hand, and muttered a greeting. Then, pushing the children forward, she said, "These here are some of your class, Teacher. Mary and Heather and Myron and Charles. Of course Mary don't go to school yet, but she'll be starting next year."

So, there I was, face to face with the raw material of my trade. The boys were smaller duplicates of their father, manure-stained moccasins, patched overalls, ragged home-made hair-cuts, and all. Of the girls I remember only skinny legs, much-darned brown stockings, faded cotton dresses, long stringy hair, and pinched white faces. In those hungry years, even farm children were undernourished.

Somewhere along the line I had formed a mental picture of my first public appearance as a pedagogue. Children and adults alike, I supposed, would be awed and deferential. I would be suave and rather jolly. There would be laughter and warmth.

It wasn't like that at all. Mrs. McDougall and the children just stood and stared at me with a mixture of resentment and hostility. I was a nuisance to one and all. To the children, because it meant beginning school again. To the elders, because they had to do something about me and, as a stranger, I accentuated their wretched condition. I smiled weakly and made an attempt at small talk, but their inscrutable stares got to me, and I gave up.

Then Mrs. McDougall took a coal-oil lamp from the table and led the way to a back bedroom with wooden walls and a slanted ceiling. There was a wash-stand and an iron bed covered with a thick feather tick. I learned later that the bed normally held two of the McDougall children who for this night were sleeping with the two others crosswise on a bed. I put my coat on the bed, rinsed my hands, and returned to the kitchen, carrying the lamp with me.

Supper of roast pork, potatoes, turnips, and preserved saskatoon berries was eaten in silence. Afterwards there was nothing to do. The light was too poor for reading, and besides there wasn't a book or magazine to be seen. Nor was there any radio. So we went to bed.

Before going, McDougall nodded to me and stepped out the back door. I followed him, not knowing what he wanted. But I soon found out. As the two of us stood and aimed our streams into the snow on opposite sides of the path, I looked up where the stars shone like lamps and the northern lights slithered about in the sky.

The prairie sky has been described with fine terms like "majestic," "inspiring," and "awesome." To me it just looked big and unfriendly. I picked out the Big Dipper and the North Star, not realizing that before I was through with this place I would be using them as my only guides across snow-covered fields, and that when they weren't visible I would be hopelessly lost.

McDougall grunted something. We shook, buttoned, and went in.

2

I didn't sleep well that first night in Willowgreen School District. The McDougall house was small and cold. There was no insulation in walls or ceiling and the house was heated, as were many prairie homes, by the kitchen range and a round ornate heater in the living room. Neither was kept burning all night. It just wasn't practical. McDougall had no coal to burn, and he couldn't be expected to stay up all night to shove wood into a stove.

Besides, who needs a fire at night? McDougall and his wife could certainly keep each other warm. The children slept together in their long, fleece-lined underwear and cuddled spoon style, generating enough heat for them. No provision was made for a visiting school teacher. Why should there be? He was something foreign in the body of this culture.

When I awoke in the morning it was pitch dark. I heard somebody in the kitchen clanging stove lids. Then I heard the kitchen door open and the sound of stamping feet. I knew it must be time to get up.

I slid my feet out from under the covers and onto the floor. Then I quickly slid them back again. The floor was like a block of ice. By fishing around on the floor I found my socks, wiggled into them, and made another try at the floor. This time I made it.

I found my pants, got a match from a pocket, and lit the coal-oil lamp. In the pale yellow light I could see frost clinging to the inside of the wall. Hurriedly I scrambled into my underwear and pants and picked up the big white pitcher to pour out some water. None came. A quarter of an inch of ice covered the surface. It was the first, but not the last, wash and shave I ever had in ice water.

And now I became acutely aware of the most practical, universal, and insistent of all problems. I opened the door on the front of the wash-stand. It was empty. I got down on my knees and looked around under the bed. Nothing there.

I sat on the bed and shivered. Where was it? I knew the house had no plumbing, but surely there was some sort of inside convenience. I could hear children's voices in the kitchen, and to march past them on such an obvious mission seemed a most unteacherish thing to do. Besides, I didn't know where to go when I got outside. I scraped the frost off a small patch of window pane and peered out. In the pre-dawn dusk I dimly made out a little cluster of outbuildings, half buried in the snow. One of them had a slanted roof. Maybe that was it.

The situation had deteriorated, as they say, to the point

where something drastic had to be done. I pulled on my shirt, sweater, and boots and tiptoed over to the door. Gently I turned the knob and eased it open.

My timing couldn't have been worse. At that very moment McDougall came past the door, braces pulled over grey underwear top. "Oh, you're awake then," he grunted. "Come on. Breakfast is just about ready." I was trapped.

The four young McDougalls were already in their places against the wall. Feeling I should do something friendly, I smiled broadly and said something asinine like, "Well, well, how is everybody this morning?" They neither smiled nor nodded nor spoke. Just stared.

Since I couldn't outstare them, I looked at my plate and breathed a silent prayer for strength. Mrs. McDougall came into the room then carrying an immense white platter covered three deep with greasy fried eggs and salt pork. A plate of thick toast made from crumbly, home-made bread was already on the table. There was no butter.

Mrs. McDougall handed me the plate of eggs and I gingerly manoeuvred one of them onto my plate and passed the platter to McDougall. He grunted, tipped the platter over his plate, and slid off half a dozen eggs together with a pile of the pork. The children did the same when their turn came, filled their glasses with milk, and began to eat.

My appetite was poor. I shoved the egg around in the grease with my fork and took a few tentative nibbles at it. The coffee and milk I left strictly alone.

As McDougall shovelled the food into his mouth and washed it down with coffee, he seemed to be preoccupied. "Don't know where you're going to live," he finally mumbled, wiping the grease from his lips with the back of his hand.

This stunned me. I hadn't even thought of it, considering that, since they had brought me here, they would see to it that there was a home for me. "Where does the teacher usually board?" I asked.

"Smithwick's," McDougall grumbled. "Used to, before the trouble."

The kids began to giggle, and McDougall glared at them; they stopped.

"There's a teacherage in the basement of the school," Mrs. McDougall hurriedly explained.

"Fixed it up for Sado and that wife of his," McDougall grunted in disgust.

Again the kids giggled. Again he silenced them with a look.

It was like a game of missing words or missing sentences. You fill them in. Obviously there had been some trouble at Smithwick's, and there was something odd about Sado's wife, too. But I had troubles of my own.

"The teacherage is really quite nice," Mrs. McDougall went on. "There's a table and a cupboard and a range heater in one room and a nice big bed in the other."

I didn't know what a teacherage was, but I was getting the idea that I would be expected to live alone there and do my own cooking. Even that seemed insignificant to what I was enduring.

Then I had an inspiration. The kind of desperate inspiration a man about to be executed might get. "The teacherage sounds nice," I gasped, putting down my fork. "Could we go and see it now?"

"Now?" McDougall raised his eyebrows. "I thought we'd better talk about your money first."

"No, no. Never mind the money. Let's go and see that teacherage!"

McDougall stared at me for a minute in disbelief, then pushed back his chair and heaved himself to his feet. "All right, come on," he said. "I'll hitch the team."

While he was hitching the team, I'd reconnoitre the outdoors for the "thing." Quickly I got into my hat and coat and rubbers and followed him out the back door. The snow on either side of the path was a yellow-stained skating rink where Mrs. McDougall had been throwing the slops for the past three months. I hurried along towards the barn and spotted my little square house with the slanting roof. There was no path, and so I floundered through the snow and pulled the door open, frantically kicking away the snow to do so. Finally the door came open, and I saw inside. A drift two feet high lay on top of the seat.

By now my situation was critical. I turned and dashed

through the snow to the barn door. This would have to do.

As I entered the barn I heard a voice, a small feminine voice. Mary McDougall had followed me. "Do you want to see our colt?" she asked. "We had two, but the other one died. Dad said it was just as well because there wasn't enough feed anyway."

Blast the kid! Why did she have to become communicative at this particular moment? I went and looked at the colt. And, by the time I'd seen it and the calf and the baby pigs, the team was hitched, and McDougall was waiting for me.

There was absolutely nothing in what we'd learned at normal school to cover this most vital of all problems.

We drove along the winding trail away from McDougall's house. The sun was shining in a blue sky. A flock of tiny snowbirds flew past, looking like an undulating wave; they landed on a nearby fence and went to work on the seeds of the brown Russian thistle stalks piled against it. In the distance I could see the square school house sitting up on a cement foundation in the middle of a school yard that was in the middle of nothing. There wasn't another building or even a tree in sight in any direction.

McDougall stopped the team, produced a key, and let us in. "This is the main room here," he explained, opening another door, but I wasn't with him. I'd spied the cellar steps and taken them two at a time.

At the bottom there was an indoor chemical toilet. My agony was past.

The school was typical of many that had been built in the post-war, pre-Depression years when the price of wheat had been good. It was about twenty-five feet square with windows all along one side. Except for a small cloak room and closet at the entrance, it was all classroom. A blackboard, made of wall board covered with shiny black paint that was chipped off in places, extended across the front and part way down the side. In the right front corner stood an ancient organ, brown walnut with its top scarred round the edges by hundreds of butts of roll-your-own cigarettes left there during dances by organists, fiddlers, and dancers.

A tattered map of the world, its oceans frilled with bright pictures of candy bars, products of the company who supplied it free, was on the side wall beside the blackboard. Above the blackboard at the front a two-foot-long Union Jack was held in place by thumbtacks. On the back wall was a picture of King George V. Below it was a hole in the plaster where it had been hit by a flying book or body. In front of the hole was a large glass water cooler, fitted on a stand so as to make a drinking fountain. I didn't know it then, but this thing was to haunt my dreams.

The seats and desks arranged in six rows were of the kind that can be adjusted up and down, forward, back, and slant-wise, but, no matter how you adjust them, never fit the sitter. They could also be moved, either by the occupant kiddie-car style, or over to the side wall when the room became a dance hall or political auditorium. As desks they were of doubtful value, but as noise-makers they were without rivals. The large drawer underneath each seat, for instance, always stuck, so that it could be opened only with a mighty heave. Then it came all the way out with a thump and a clatter that could wreck the strongest nerves.

At the front of the rows of desks, dead centre, was the teacher's desk with a small shiny hand bell on top of it.

McDougall waddled over and tapped the bell with a chubby finger. Then he pulled open the flat top drawer where I could see the brown cover of a register book. He fished around with his hand and finally located a piece of belting about two feet long and three inches wide. "Strap," he grunted. "Better get used to using this, because there's some pretty big kids in grade ten."

I stood behind the desk, looked down at the empty ones in front of me and the gaping hole in the plaster, and for the first time felt absolutely alone, helpless, and scared. I'd taken the bleak station, the long, frost-bitten ride, and McDougall's cold house, and even the strain of my bladder with a certain aplomb. But the sight of this bare, untidy, desolate room where I would spend most of my waking hours was almost too much.

McDougall hunched his ragged mackinaw around his shoulders, muttered something about nothing being colder than an empty building, and led the way through the door at the back of the room and down the basement steps. They were steep and narrow with a right-angled turn half way down. "Watch your head," he warned, ducking his own to miss the floor joist as he went past.

I'll never forget that basement. In retrospect it has become the Black Hole of Calcutta, the Moose River Mine, and a bottomless pit, all rolled into one. I think it was the darkness of it. The school had no electricity, of course, and I rarely took a lamp into this room which was dominated by a huge galvanized-iron coal furnace with an enormous hot-air pipe going out the top and an enormous cold-air pipe coming in the bottom. The chemical toilets, one for the boys and one for the girls, were under the stairs (those indoor toilets made up for a lot), and the coal bin was at the other side.

This was half the basement. The other half was partitioned off to make the teacherage McDougall had mentioned earlier. It consisted of two rooms, each twelve and a half feet long and about eight feet wide, and each with a tiny basement window near the ceiling. The living room had a table, a kitchen chair, and a heater-range, which was a Quebec heater with a kitchen-range-type top and an oven on the side. A coal-oil lamp with a dirty chimney sat on the table, its long grey wick curling down into the oil in the glass bowl like a grey tapeworm. The other room had a bed of sorts, without head or foot, and a wash-stand with a blue and white porcelain basin with a crack running across its bottom and up each side, and an immense water pitcher of the same design with its handle broken off, sitting in the centre of it. There was no other furniture.

McDougall stood in the middle of the room, hands in mackinaw pockets, shoulders hunched. "Well?" he asked.

"Is there a boarding place?" I asked. "Besides Smithwick's, I mean?"

"Well, not exactly. Nobody else wants to take the teacher full time, but some has agreed to take you month about."

"How would I get to school?"

"Walk. Or ride with the kids, if there is any."

"Why can't I stay at one place instead of moving around?"

"Well . . ." he looked around for a place to spit, found none, opened the door and splattered tobacco juice out on the floor of the basement proper. "It's a question of taxes. Work 'em off that way."

"I don't quite understand."

"They's not enough cash money around now to buy a gopher trap. But the work of the municipality's still got to be done . . . roads graded . . . weeds cut . . . coal hauled to the school here . . . miserable jobs like that. Everybody does some. Get a tax credit for it."

"I see." Then I grinned as though we shared a secret joke. "And boarding the teacher is one of the miserable jobs."

He didn't grin. "Some folks might call it that."

I gulped and sat on the one chair. "Perhaps we'd better discuss salary after all."

He heaved his big rump onto the corner of the table. "Can't pay much, and that's a fact. I hear they's getting teachers – experienced ones, too – in the other districts for four and five hundred. One south of the river got a teacher for three. You ain't got no experience, I understand."

"No. Except, of course, practice teaching at normal."

"Yeah. Well . . . in a sense you're sort of learning on the job, as they say. We'll provide you with a place to live, grub to eat, and a little cash money besides. It's a hell of a sight more'n a lot of farmers with thirty years' experience are getting right now."

"If I decide to stay here, how can I buy food?" I asked.

"People in the district will bring it. We got plenty eggs. We can send them over with the kids. Haven't any extra milk though, so somebody else will have to provide that. Maybe MacLean. He had a cow freshen last month. We'll see you don't starve."

I was thinking of my thin overcoat and riding to school every morning in a cutter or even walking. Besides, with the pride of youth, I was thinking of my limited wardrobe and my inability to buy more. Living alone here, I wouldn't need to disclose the state of my underwear or to buy the new suit I'd planned with my first pay cheque.

"I guess I'll stay here then," I mumbled.

McDougall turned and started out the door. "I'll let the

others know," he said. "The women'll come over on Saturday and clean up the place and bring stuff."

I followed him up the steep wooden steps from the basement and out the door into the clear bright sunlight. While he untied the team from the gate post, I looked around. Not a house or a tree visible in any direction. Just the rolling prairie land covered with snow, broken here and there by a barbed-wire fence clogged with Russian thistle.

A lead weight settled in the middle of my stomach. This desolate, wind-swept barrens was to be my home. Here I would learn what isolation means and what it can do to the soul.

Father's Day

In the fall of 1959 Aileen and I bought a piece of property on the shore of Brandy Lake in Muskoka, then, as now, one of the most beautiful spots I've ever seen. Colin was six years old at the time and Sylvia nine. Here they both learned to swim and paddle a canoe and dive off the rocks and investigate the squirrels and raccoons and chipmunks and porcupines that had been living there long before we came.

At first we camped there in tents, the only permanent structure being a one-hole backhouse. Often during the summer holidays I had radio writing to do and I set up a desk of sorts under a pine tree on a huge rounded rock. If it started to rain I had to quit work and haul everything to the car; if it kept on raining we'd go back home to Orangeville.

Then I had Alf Penny and Harold Foulkes build a wooden shelter near the lake. Later we had them convert this into a cozy cabin. Then in 1969 we built a house and moved here permanently. We are still here. And now I am seventy-two, like the man in the following story.

It was the second summer after his wife had died and he was beginning to get a little bit used to it. Not much, really. There were too many things to remember.

He drove the old car along the winding road through the bush, up the steepness of Shingle Tree Hill, sounding his horn as he always did to avoid a head-on collision with a car coming up the other side. He slowed almost to a stop, staring hard through the top half of his bifocals for the entrance to the driveway. There it was, almost completely covered with wild raspberry, weed maple, and grass. He was there.

He drove the fifty-foot length of the sand road and stopped under the tall oak tree. This was where they used to put the camping trailer. God, there was a rusting can of mosquito repellant that he'd left on the small shelf nailed between the oak and the maple. Nobody ever touched anything at Brandy Lake.

He opened the door and got out slowly with care. At seventy-two you don't jump around.

Then the old feeling came over him, as it always did in this particular spot. Just standing there, looking up through the green, green leaves . . . oak, maple, basswood, ironwood, rock elm . . . at the tiny patches of blue sky waving back and forth, brought a peace he knew nowhere else.

He unzipped his pants and wet on the dry leaves and twigs. That was another good thing about this place. You didn't have to always be keeping your eye peeled for some convenient place. Just let her go when you get the urge, and with an old man that's pretty often.

Then he went around the big oak and along the path, cluttered with dead twigs and growing ferns but still discernible. Past the big sprawling hemlock he went and along the edge of the big rock. For a moment he stopped and looked up towards the rounded top of the rock covered with greying moss and staghorn sumach. This had been her favourite place for the sun always shone there and she loved the reflected heat from the rock. Like a knife in his guts he remembered one hot afternoon on the moss of that rock when the kids had gone blueberry picking, so they were alone and they took advantage of it . . . right there on the rock.

Better not go up there. Not just yet, anyway. Since his heart attack the doctor had warned against steep climbs. Damn infirmity!

The path began to dip then, curving around the rock and going between two big ironwood trees with a decaying trunk lying on the ground between them. When they'd first come the trunk had been round, but by constantly stepping on it the kids had worn it down so that the roots of new trees growing in it stood out like varicose veins on an old man's leg. The young, feeding off the old.

From here on the path led through small white birch trees. White Birch Stretch, Sheila had called it. She had to have a name for everything. And it was she who had insisted they not bulldoze a road through the trees so that the car could come down to the camping area.

"It will ruin everything, Daddy," she'd pleaded. "Knock down half the trees. What's the use of buying a place full of trees if you knock them all down?" The logic of it was irrefutable. And now Sheila was married to an engineer and lived in San Francisco and had a summer place that was magnificent . . . so he'd heard.

The path turned again, past the big white pine. Stumps of sawed-off branches stuck out like horns of a dehorned cow. He'd left them that way so Darwin could climb the tree. Dar sure as hell wasn't much of a climber. His bad foot put a crimp into everything he tried to do in an athletic way. That damned club-foot.

"Don't worry about it," Doc Beaton had said the day Darwin was born. "They have a new kind of splint they put on in the first weeks. Turns the foot out. Doesn't bother the baby and in a year the foot is as good as anybody else's." But the foot never became completely normal. Always a size and a half shorter than the other, with a bump on the instep. Dar never exactly limped, but he never won any foot races either, and he was always cautious in matters requiring footwork. And here the path turned into the camp area.

The shelter was as good as the day Del Penny built it. And the cedar picnic table beneath it with its many coats of varnish. Each year they'd varnished the picnic table and put a fresh coat of Rez on the cedar posts of the shelter. And they'd never got around to building the cottage. Well, the kids liked sleeping in tents and he liked the sky above him and the leaves. His wife liked not sweeping floors. Besides, money was always just a little tight. And so the cottage was never built.

The old man sank wearily onto the summer seat he'd built between three maples. Small trees when he'd first pounded the nails into them, a good size now. He looked through the dapple of leaves and branches out to the lake. God, it was beautiful. The pre-Cambrian rock, here smooth, here straight-faced where frost and moisture had sliced off a piece. And the pines along the point reflected in the clear water. Is there anything as beautiful as a northern Ontario lake? Anything at all?

And he heaved a mighty sigh, as old men will. His breath came fast. That damned emphysema. He shifted his thigh and blew wind. Those piles were itching again. He'd never again dive off those rocks, that was certain. Or feel the cold water close around his body. Or pull himself up on the rock with a shout. Or take the canoe and race Sheila across the bay. Or splash back and forth along the beach pulling water lilies and arrowhead weeds.

No more of any of that. All gone.

Then a day sprang into focus. Father's Day, June 21st, longest day of the year. He and Dar had come up to the lake alone, his wife and Sheila being absorbed in the coming wedding of a niece. He'd needed the rest and his wife urged him to go. So he'd got the camping gear ready and away they went. Just the two of them.

Let's see, he'd been fifty-two then and Dar eleven. Dar was his last child, last of three families, so to speak. His oldest girl – child of the First World War – was grown up by then and married and living in California. The next two – children of the twenties – had both graduated from school and were more or less on their own. Then after a gap of seven years had come the last two – Sheila and Darwin.

So he and Dar had come to the camp alone. Vivid images popped into his mind. Dar sitting on a rock shooting his BB gun at a log in the water. Raking the beach until his muscles pained, then running into the water. A splashing fight with Dar, who dared him to come and get it. The boy didn't seem to mind being alone with his dad. He loved swimming and played for hours on the green air mattress, diving over it and under it, pretending to be a scuba diver impeded by crooks while seeking the sunken device that would blow them all to bits. The crazy things kids think of. A big fire on the beach under the moon. Just sitting there telling each other lies.

More and more pictures, leaping like frogs on the brain cells of memory. A long paddle around the lake, poking into little rocky bays to inspect cottages. No serious thoughts, but plenty of gags. "Do you know 'The Road to Mandalay'?" "Sure, do you want me to sing it?" "No, take it." Some questions: "Dad, why do those dragon-flies land on the water?" "That's where they lay their eggs." The weather had co-operated beautifully, he remembered. So they'd stayed over Monday, too.

Something else happened that day that he hadn't thought of in years. Dar had taken the hunting knife that he carried on a sheath at his belt and begun to carve on a tree.

"What will happen if I carve my initials here?"

"They'll never go away. The cuts form a sort of scar tissue. As the tree gets older, they raise up in bumps."

"Gosh. Think I'll do it."

So, while he'd puttered around on the beach the boy had worked with his knife.

"Come and see, Dad."

There on the young maple he'd carved the initials D.O. "Those are mine . . . Darwin Osborne." And below them W.O. "William Osborne, that's you." And below, June 21, 1945.

The boy had grinned up at him in one of those rare moments of life. "See, Dad. Sort of a remembrance of this day. If we come back ten or fifteen years or even twenty years from now, they'll still be there. Maybe we'll come back then, Dad. Just the two of us."

Twenty years. Nineteen forty-five to nineteen sixty-five. By God, it was twenty years to the day! Shaking with excitement, the old man got up on his feet. Where was that tree? It had been just below the camp towards the beach. He hadn't thought of it in years. He stumbled across the camp and picked his way down the bank, using the exposed gnarled pine roots as a foothold. He slipped and almost fell, but plunked his hand against the tree and saved himself, puffing hard. And there they were . . . the spread-out ridges of black on the rough brown bark of the maple. A tangible bridge to the past.

Slowly the old man ran his fingers over the roughness. Twenty years. Damn old age, damn it, damn it, damn it to hell! He picked up a dry stick, broke it violently, and pitched the stick towards the water. What a dirty, miserable trick to play on a guy! Then, panting desperately, he sank down, sat on a ridge of rock, and leaned against the maple. A tear squeezed from his eye and he cried. Cried because it was all over so soon, so soon. Like the fallen trees around him, he lived out his span. But he didn't want to go. Damn it, he didn't want to. Too soon, too soon!

Then there was a noise from above him. A car door banging. A cracking of dry sticks as younger feet pounded down the path. He shook his head, wiped a blue-veined hand across his eyes and struggled to his feet.

"Dad!" The voice was familiar. "For God's sake, is that you?"

"Yeah, yeah, it's me. Who . . . Dar!"

"Yeah, Dad, it's me. What are you doing here?"

"What am I doing here! I come here every year. But what the hell are you doing here?"

The young man threw back his head and laughed. "Well, I'll be damned. There's an architects' convention at the Skyview Lodge on Lake Muskoka. I'm driving up. And then . . . I came to our turn off . . . and I thought . . . by God, I'll just go in and see the old place. But I didn't expect to find you here!"

The old man held out his hand and the young man helped him back up the bank and they sat together on the summer seat.

"We'll just sit here and tell a few lies," the old man chuckled, and the young man laughed aloud.

"Remember when you said that, Dad? By God, it was twenty years ago."

And they sat and talked. And the young man went back up the path to his new convertible and opened the trunk where he kept an electric cooler and took out a case of beer and brought it down. And they had a couple of beers. And the young man told his father that his wife and children were fine.

"Let's see, when was it we saw you last? Christmas! No! God, how time flies. Anyway, Suzie's had the measles since then, but she's all better now. Christmas? God, I didn't think it was so long."

And the young man told the old man that he'd had a promotion in the firm. And they were taking on that big lake-shore reconstruction job that would mean a lot to them. Oh yes, they were going to move. Build this time. Kathie has the house all planned, swimming pool and all.

"How have you been, Dad?"

"Me? Oh fine . . . fine."

And he felt fine, too. Better, in fact, than he'd felt for years. He got up and hurried about the camp ground lighting a fire, putting on the steaks, making coffee. And with every step he felt younger, better. Maybe after lunch they'd go out in the canoe. And in the evening a fire on the beach.

The youth in tight jeans and sweat shirt, carrying a fishing-rod, came pounding down the path to the camp site. Then he saw the old man slumped against the maple tree on the ledge below. He spoke to him, and approached cautiously.

"What is it, George?" his companion called from further up the path. "Who's down there?"

"Just an old guy all alone, May," the youth yelled back. "Don't come down."

"Why not?"

"Just don't, that's all. I'll be right up." Then he turned and peered searchingly at the figure against the tree. "For Chrissake," he muttered, "the old bugger's dead!"

I've Quit Quitting
or The Thing to Do
Is Not Taper Off

The following piece was written back in the 1950s when we
had a house full of young kids and I was working my butt off
writing magazine articles and radio plays. At that time we
lived just outside of Streetsville, Ontario, a sleepy little village
that had no idea of ever becoming part of a megalopolis. We
had a circle of good friends, all about our own age with the
same number of kids as we had. We got together to play
bridge and have parties and we had a hell of a lot of fun.

I had a little trouble with this piece, although editors
seemed to like it. In fact, it was paid for twice but never used.
I think it made them nervous. Most of the editors I knew were
chain-smokers and always talking about how they wished
they could quit. Maybe this piece cut too close to the wind-
pipe. Anyway, I liked it, mostly because it was basically true.
And it is just as true now as it was then.

This is the age of the quitter.
People are always boasting privately or publicly about how they
have quit eating rich foods or smoking or drinking and how
abstinence has improved their complexions, personalities, and
sex appeal.

I say bunk! And I know because on three separate occasions
I have quit eating, smoking, and drinking. And each time I
started up again. Not because the craving for fatty foods or
tobacco or alcohol overcame me but because I discovered that

without these habits life becomes complicated, dangerous, and dull.

Take eating.

Ever since I can remember I've enjoyed stuffing myself with good things regardless of what they did to my shape. As a kid I was pudgy and went by the nickname of "Fat." But that didn't matter. I could still lick any other kid in grade five and move to my left as fast as the skinny kids. And I once learned through the grape-vine that one of the girls had said that she thought Fat Braithwaite was the cutest kid in the room. She wasn't the belle of the room . . . but she was a girl.

As a young man I continued to eat and that didn't stop me from winning the love of a beautiful and talented girl and making her my wife. I had friends, too. They said I was a jolly chap, full of chuckles and droll sayings.

Then one day I took one of the free medical examinations my insurance company was passing out. After the doctor had prodded me and listened to my insides and tied a rag around my arm and blew it up he stated that I was in pretty good shape but if I'd take off about twenty-five pounds I'd live to pay a lot more premiums.

So I quit eating. At table I nibbled away on raw carrots and biscuits made of sawdust and vitamins. Between meals instead of walking around munching salted peanuts I sat and chewed my nails. My stomach felt like the inside of a blast furnace.

While playing bridge I concentrated on not eating candies instead of how to finesse the king of hearts. Once, in response to a demand bid I shouted, "Two caramels!"

On top of that everybody became so mean and cantankerous. The kids loaded their plates with mashed potatoes and gravy just to annoy me. The butcher got sore just because I said I didn't see why he couldn't make sausages without fat. My wife changed, too. She had always been such a jolly, carefree type but one night at bridge club when I was explaining how crazy it was for anybody to eat butter I noticed her looking at me out of the corner of her eye as though I were something that had come up a drain. It began to look as though instead of living longer I'd soon end up with a stiletto in my back.

But I kept my mind on the day when I would emerge like a lean dragon-fly from a bloated cocoon. What a surprise I would hand my friends. How they would clap their hands and shout what a brave, resolute fellow I was.

Finally I did manage to lose the twenty-five pounds and I headed for the city. On the street I met a chap I hadn't seen in four months. I pulled in my abdomen, in a fair imitation of Kirk Douglas, and approached with lean jaw out-thrust. He took one look at me, held out his hand and said, "My God, man, you look terrible! Have you been sick?"

"No," I lied. "I never felt better in my live. Been on a . . . heh, heh . . . diet."

"Well, get off it," he said, "before it . . . heh, heh . . . kills you. You just aren't the thin type."

He seemed to resent my being thinner than he, as did practically everybody else I met that day. Gradually I realized that being thin and trim does not bring popularity. The way to make people love you is to be a little fatter than they are. Then they can say . . . "Gosh, fellow, but you're putting on weight." This is the most popular sentence in the English language, bar none. Using it makes people feel fine and superior. Deprive them of a chance to use it and they'll hate you.

So I started eating again and soon regained my front porch, my chins, and my sense of humour. People liked me; I liked them.

All went well then until I happened to read an article called "Are You a Man or a Smoke-stack?" in which the writer stated that after years of slavery he'd finally freed himself from the smoking habit. He claimed that now he slept better, looked better, tasted better, and could look himself in the eye and say, "Bully for you."

He pointed out that smoking was an expensive, annoying, repulsive habit, completely without justification. He said that it was easy to quit. All you had to do was throw away your pipe or your cigars or your cigarettes (never try tapering off) and in a few months you would be a man and not a smoke-stack.

But he didn't tell what happens when you go out into the world of smokers. I will.

I won't bore you with the struggles, heartaches, and hallucinations suffered while quitting; suffice it to say that in a few months' time I went out to face the world fresh of mouth, clean of breath, all traces of the foul weed gone. I was on my way to see a producer with an idea for a radio series that I'd been working on for a long time and that was going to boost me right into the big time.

When I got to his office he was in good shape for me. He had the look of a man who has shaved without cutting himself, enjoyed his coffee, and got out of the house without arguing with his wife. He beamed on me, called me by my first name, and urged me into a chair. It was going to be like shooting fish in a basket.

With a happy gesture I brushed away the image of fat cheques floating before my eyes and started to work on him.

He nodded his head in wise agreement, reached into his pocket and came out with a blue package, opened it, leaned towards me with a kind smile, and said, "Smoke?"

I shook my head and said, "Uh . . . no thanks . . . don't use them."

He looked as though I'd thrown a handful of ashes in his face. Surprised and a little hurt. "Didn't you ever smoke?" he asked.

"Yup . . . up until a couple of months ago. Then I quit." I didn't want this to sound self-laudatory and brave . . . but it did.

He looked at the package the way a pickpocket looks at a watch he's just been caught lifting. He started to put it away then sneaked out a cigarette and tried to light it without too much fuss. I went back to my sales talk but he wasn't listening. His head was hanging low and he was sad.

"God how I wish I could quit. How did you do it?"

Like a fool I said, "It's quite easy, really. You just quit. Never taper off . . . just quit."

Now he was getting resentful. I could see he was thinking, "Sure, easy enough for you young guys who are full of stamina and self-control, but what about old wrecks like me." The resentment grew to dislike to hatred. He didn't like the kind of suit I was wearing, or my haircut, and most of all . . . my idea.

Stopping smoking ruined my social life, too. I didn't know what to do with my hands and face. In the first place I suppose human beings were provided with hands to work with, eat with, fight with, scratch themselves with, and comb their hair. In early times man had enough of those things to do to keep his hands occupied. But nowadays machines do most of the work, we fight with our mouths and atomic bombs, soaps and hair oils have cut down the need for scratching and combing and we can't eat all the time. That left me with a couple of hands hanging out of my sleeves and nothing to do with them.

Picture me in a gathering where everybody is sitting around hugging their pipes, rolling their cigars between their fingers, or dispersing cigarette ashes with dainty gestures. I try shoving my hands into my pants pockets but the chair is too narrow. I lock them behind my head but I get a kink in my neck. Finally I run my fingers along the arm of the chair and gather little ridges of dust to play with. The hostess watches me as long as she can and then screams, "Stop dusting!" I mumble something about a sick budgie and go home.

It's the same with your face. Smoking gives you a chance to make faces and something to do with your mouth. I tried chewing broom straws and tossing salted peanuts in the air and catching them in my mouth but they were always bouncing off my teeth and getting under the rugs.

I know a fellow who gets along socially just on his ability to blow smoke rings. When the conversation gets too involved or boring for him he leans forward, puckers up thoughtfully, and emits a blob of smoke the size and shape of a truck tire. He always gets attention. I once saw him settle one right over his hostess's head. Then he spends the rest of the evening teaching the girls how to pucker up and blow smoke rings.

So I started smoking again. I don't know exactly what, but it seems to do something for me. I'll admit that . . . like eating . . . it costs a bit and I may never win a seven-mile marathon, but at least I can talk to people without squirming around like a nervous teenager with hives.

And that brings us to drinking. Here again I got into trouble by reading too much. In this article the guy said he'd been an occasional drinker until one night at a cocktail party when he happened to catch sight of himself in a mirror. The sight of his bloated face and vacant expression convinced him that he'd better quit. Then he went on to tell about how much money he'd saved on booze and the things he done with it and the places he went. When he got to Bermuda I was a dead duck.

I dashed to the kitchen and shouted at my wife, "Darling, I'm going to quit drinking."

She said, "Fine. Here's a tea-towel. Dry the silverware."

"This is important," I said. "You want a new evening dress. Well, maybe . . . after . . . ."

She flung her arms about me and shrieked, "Darling, I've got just the one picked out. I'll phone for it right now!"

That's how I started saving money.

Quitting drinking was easy compared to quitting eating and smoking. I was pretty busy that week, anyway, and never even missed the one or two martinis I sometimes have before dinner.

Then came the weekend, the time for relaxation and enjoyment. Saturday night we went to our regular poker party. This is a little thing where a group of us neighbours get together to exchange pennies and forget about our kids and our taxes for a while.

When we arrived at this one our hostess came bouncing up with a devilish gleam in each eye and a tall glass in each hand. "I can't wait for you to try this," she burbled gleefully. "It's something special Norman made from a recipe his cousin sent from Tanganyika."

My wife – the traitor – just stuck out her hand, grabbed the glass, said, "Thanks, dear," and headed for the chesterfield.

I stuck out my hand, too, but dropped it. "No thanks," I said. "I've quit."

My hostess looked a little puzzled and then burst into merry laughter. "Oh I know you," she said, "full of gags. Here, take this thing. I've got work to do."

I assured her that I had never been more serious about anything in my whole life.

"Doctor's orders? . . . an ulcer?"

"No, neither. You see, I figure . . . ."

"You don't have to drink this, you know. Have a beer."

"No . . . nothing . . . little lemonade maybe . . . ."

"Lemonade! All right, whatever you wish. But for heaven sake why?"

I started to mumble something about a mirror, but she had gone to the kitchen to find out how to make lemonade.

The other six guests liked the new drink fine and before long the conversation was, as they say, jumping. And then I discovered a funny thing about my friends. They couldn't stay on one topic. Just when I'd get started telling how much money I could save by not drinking they were talking about seal fishing off the Newfoundland coast.

I had another lemonade, but it didn't do much good.

When we started playing poker they took ridiculous chances and laughed about them. From where I was sitting I couldn't see a mirror, but when I was four dollars and sixteen cents down I went out into the hall and had a look. My face wasn't the least bit flushed, my lips weren't sagging, my eyes weren't bloodshot. I just looked sad. I looked at my watch and discovered it was only ten-thirty. In my drinking days it would be at least one-thirty by that time. I'd never been to such a long party or such a dull one.

I sat down on the telephone stool and began to worry. What if Sylvia pulled her sleepers over her head and smothered. Was that rain on the window? If water got into the ignition wires the car wouldn't start and there we'd be, five miles from home, and the house on fire!

I hurried back to the living-room to explain these things to my wife. She was on her second "special" and was completely relaxed, tossing chips into the pot as though they were free, trying to fill inside straights and giggling.

"Are you sure all the switches are turned off on the stove?" I yelled.

Everybody burst out into laughter and somebody said, "That Braithwaite, the longer the party lasts the funnier he gets."

My wife said, "Sit down, dear. I just thought up a new game. Eleven card stud with all the red cards and the one-eyed jacks wild!"

I said, "Don't you think we'd better be getting home?"

She said, "Sure," and started to deal.

We finally got home at two and of course everything was fine. I didn't sleep very well though, thinking about the money I'd lost, and in the morning I felt terrible.

Usually when I wake up after a weekend party I feel pretty good. I have just enough sense of guilt and remorse to be a dandy, understanding father. The kids seem more agreeable than they did Friday night and their voices aren't so loud. I have a few jokes with them and maybe take them out skating or tobagganing and we have fun.

But this morning I decided I really should get into my office and take another look at that manuscript I'd finished Friday night. Monday morning I felt worse.

So I'm back to moderate weekend drinking again. I need it. I realize that I misunderstood the whole point of that other article. It wasn't liquor that guy needed to keep away from . . . just mirrors.

Now when the pressure is too great before dinner and the kids are wrestling in the living-room and the baby is cross I mix a couple of martinis and my wife and I relax for a half-hour before attempting dinner. Sometimes in the evenings we sneak off to a pub down the road and watch the television. It makes us easier to live with.

Yep. I intend to keep right on eating and smoking and drinking until the end. I'll try to be moderate, but I'm damned if I'll quit. Maybe I won't last as long as George Bernard Shaw did, but Winston Churchill is doing all right, too.

The Rise and Fall of the Dumbells

The *Maclean's* flashback I wrote in 1952 on the original Dumbells was a labour of love. In the twenties and early thirties we all went to their shows in the old Empire Theatre in Saskatoon, Saskatchewan, and I'm sure that the Dumbells had a lot to do with my becoming stage-struck and, indirectly, with my becoming a writer.

Meeting Capt. Merton Plunkett, even after all those years, was somewhat akin to meeting Bing Crosby or Frank Sinatra would be today. I was as excited as a stage-struck teenager. Meeting Charlie Jeeves, whom I've always considered to be the greatest straight man of them all, was also a thrill. He didn't know if the great comic Fred Emney was still living but gave me the address of his London club. I wrote and received a little note from the great man himself saying that he was very much alive and still working.

I got the material for the history of the Dumbells straight from Merton Plunkett, who was living in Collingwood, Ontario, at the time, and I've always considered it to be as accurate an account as one could possibly get. Not long after my interview with him Capt. Plunkett died, and I'm glad that I had the chance to talk with him.

The year was 1927, the time seven P.M. A group of us from Nutana Collegiate were jammed with a hundred other breathless fans into the lobby of the old Empire Theatre in Saskatoon. We'd been standing there since six o'clock and we'd gladly have our feet walked on for another hour and a half, just to be sure of getting a front seat in the "gods" from where we were to watch what was to us then – and still is – the greatest show on earth, the Dumbells.

And deep inside us was a wonderful warm glow of anticipation. This was the night we'd waited for all year. The night when Fred Emney and Charlie Jeeves would kill us with those unbelievably funny skits, and Red Newman would render one of his rowdy raucous numbers like, "We're Getting It By Degrees"; and suave sleek Al Plunkett would stand near the wings in opera cape and top hat and have every woman in the house sighing while he sang a sentimental ballad. This was *it*. This was our annual brush with the wonderful world of show business – in the flesh!

No one who saw them forgets those fabulous frolicsome Dumbells who started their show in the muck and mire of World War One trenches and for a decade had Canadian audiences shouting for more. They toured Canada from coast to coast not once but a dozen times, packing big and little theatres alike. During their first three years they played the Grand Theatre in Toronto for a total of fifty-six weeks. They were a hit in the Coliseum, one of the biggest vaudeville theatres in London, England. They were the first "all-Canadian show" to play on Broadway and they were a hit. They made more than half a million dollars for their pudgy pugnacious originator, Capt. Merton Plunkett, and his associates. To thousands of Canadians over forty the word Dumbells still stands for the slickest, fastest, funniest revue they have ever seen.

The story of how this phenomenon of Canadian show business was born, thrived, and died is a story of rare courage (Plunkett once filled an engagement ten days after all but two of his cast had walked out on him), luck, superb showmanship, bad judgement, and a concentration of some of the best talent ever seen in Canada.

It wouldn't be hard to find a hundred First War vets who claim to have been connected with the Original Dumbells in France. Actually the cast of that first show, staged in a ramshackle shed near where the fighting was thickest around Vimy Ridge in 1917, consisted of exactly ten fighting men including a property man and pianist, Jack Ayre. Eighteen-year-old Al Plunkett was there and Ross Hamilton, Ted Charters, Alan Murray, Bert Langley, and Bill Tennent. (Later Dumbell stars, Red Newman, Pat Rafferty, and Morley Plunkett, were entertaining other soldiers in other sections.) The ten sang and danced and clowned so adeptly and the war-weary audience ate it up so avidly that shrewd producer Capt. Plunkett was convinced he had a million-dollar entertainment idea.

Merton Wesley Plunkett, like his brothers Fred, Syd, Morley, and Albert, was born in a red brick house on Barrie Road in Orillia, Ont. There he learned to play the piano slightly, did a little local entertaining, took a flyer at the grocery business, and in 1913, at twenty-five, went to Toronto to study singing. When war broke out he joined as a YMCA entertainment director with the honorary rank of captain and early in 1916 landed in France with the 3rd Division.

His job was to boost morale. He would come into a battle area and set up a piano on a small stage in a tent as close to the front lines as possible. As the men came out of the trenches, tired, dirty, often hurt, and always very sick of war, they would wander in to see what was going on.

According to those who saw him work the captain was terrific. A short blond roly-poly figure, he'd bounce out onto the stage, grin an infectious grin and start fooling around on the keyboard with songs like, "Tipperary," "Pack Up Your Troubles," "Smile a While," and "Mademoiselle From Armentières." Gradually he'd get them going into a rip-roaring sing song. Then he'd shout for volunteers to come up and entertain in any way they wanted. And he'd get them – singers, monologuists, endless satires on trench life and chorus lines featuring knobby-kneed privates in floppy hats and outlandish dresses. Female impersonators were always popular with these women-hungry men.

From these performances Plunkett learned two things which he never forgot and which accounted for much of his later success: soldiers like to clown and their friends like to watch them do it.

As he travelled from unit to unit Plunkett saw a surprising number of really good acts. A tall handsome private with the

9th Field Ambulance Corps named Ross Hamilton, for instance, who when properly made up had the grace and manners of a striking brunette and who could get his voice into a falsetto that sounded like a trained coloratura soprano. Sgt. Ted Charters whose mock sermon on the battle of the Somme left the boys helpless. His own kid brother, Cpl. Albert Plunkett, who had lied about his age to get into the 58th Battalion at sixteen and who was developing an engaging singing style that was later to make him the most personable singer who ever climbed onto a Canadian stage. Private Alan Murray who could look and dance like a pretty girl. Singers like Ptes. Bill Tennent and Bert Langley, and character actors like Pte. Frank Brayford and Cpl. Leonard Young. Most important of all he found a first-rate pianist in Cpl. Jack Ayre. He knew that if he ever got the chance he could get together a really good show.

Then, early in 1917, the chance came – an order from headquarters authorizing the use of fighting men for entertainment duty. Capt. Plunkett requested and got permission from divisional commander Maj-Gen. L. J. Lipsett to form the 3rd Division Concert Party. Because the unit's insignia was a red dumbbell they called themselves the Dumbells.

Of the ten originals none except Capt. (honorary) Plunkett ranked higher than a sergeant. They had an average of sixteen months' front-line duty, but even at that Plunkett had a tough time getting authority to keep them as permanent entertainers. They staged their first show in the military theatre at Guoy-Servins, just outside of the town of Poperinghe, Belgium. This was in the Passchendaele sector, centre of the bitterest fighting of the 1917 campaign.

Plunkett still remembers every detail of that historic production. Except for the "Dumbell Rag," written by Jack Ayre, they lifted their musical numbers whenever the lifting was good – mostly from English music-hall hits like "Zig Zag" and "Yes, Uncle." Al Plunkett had scrounged a white cape, silk hat, and suit of tails and was the envy of every khaki-clad man in the audience. His suave manner and smooth delivery made them think they were at the Ritz and the song he sang – a current U.S. hit, "Those Wild Wild Women are Making a Wild Man of Me" – hit every soldier where he lived.

Ross Hamilton, in a long, clinging gown with appropriate padding, was a knock-out as Marjorie. He represented every soldier's girl friend back home when he sang over the telephone to the dreaming soldier in the trenches (Bill Tennent) in that Dumbell classic, "Hello My Dearie."

Right after that in true Plunkett tradition ("make 'em cry one minute and laugh the next and you've got 'em") came Ted Charters dressed in a long Prince Albert coat, a plastered-down wig with a centre part and a sanctimonious look. He folded his hands piously and announced in a sepulchral voice: "My sermon is Be Ye Prepared, For No Man Knoweth When Inspection Cometh." It was full of references to stolen blankets and other soldier shenanigans and it had the boys rolling in the aisles.

Alan Murray and Al Plunkett danced, there was a chorus line and numerous broad skits on army life. The show was clean and fast and well filled with ingredients that never missed with soldiers or audiences anywhere – what Merton Plunkett calls sentiment and hokum. It was a smash. Gen. Lipsett was pleased. The Dumbells were in.

After the first show the Dumbells increased their cast to sixteen and from then until the end of the war they travelled in trucks to wherever the troops needed them most. They picked up and made what scenery and props they could, used horses' tails and rope for wigs, bits of cowhide for beards and moustaches. In an area where there were no buildings they'd set up seats on the side of a hill and give an outdoor show. Often their shows were interrupted by enemy action and, as Al Plunkett remarked recently, "Some of the men we entertained at five o'clock were dead at seven-thirty." When the fighting was too close and tough the Dumbells doubled as stretcher-bearers.

But they had a lot of laughs, too. One evening a young English officer was so smitten by Marjorie's rendition of "Some Day I'll Make You Love Me" that he turned up at the stage door with a bunch of flowers and a certain look in his eye. To save his feelings Capt. Plunkett explained that Marjorie wasn't feeling well and the next day the show had moved on.

There was no doubt the Dumbells were good under the rough-and-tumble conditions of the trenches, but how would they go over in a regular theatre? Plunkett saw a chance to answer this in the fall of 1918 when the troupe was on a two-week leave in London. He went to see a Mr. Johns who was manager of one of the city's biggest vaudeville houses, the Coliseum. But Johns told him through a secretary that he wanted no part of any soldiers' revue. So Plunkett booked his whole show in at the lowly Victoria Palace at sixty pounds a week and obtained a two-week extension of leave. When Johns heard of the effect the Dumbells were having on London audiences he sent for Plunkett and offered him two hundred pounds a week for the show. (All profits went to the YMCA entertainment fund.)

They got a further leave extension and played the Coliseum for four triumphant weeks. Johns cancelled all his vaudeville acts and put the Dumbells on ahead of the feature attraction, the famous Diaghilev Ballet. But the Londoners cheered the Dumbells so long and so heartily that after a couple of nights the Diaghilev manager came to Johns and demanded that his ballet precede the soldiers' show instead of following it.

When the Canadian army moved into Mons on November 11, 1918, Plunkett was ready for them with, of all things, a full-dress production of Gilbert and Sullivan's HMS *Pinafore*. To give the show more zip he had picked up some entertainers from the Princess Pats' Concert Party (Jack McLaren, Fred Fenwick, and others) and fitted them into the show as a comic guard for Sir Joseph Porter and an American reporter (McLaren) who was aboard the good ship strictly for laughs. This was the troupe's first chance in a legitimate vehicle in rented costumes and they gave it all they had. With the RCA fifty-piece band in the pit and young Al Plunkett in the Capt. Corcoran role the show ran for thirty-two days, two shows a day, with a battalion crowding in for each show.

Capt. Plunkett returned from France in June 1919 and immediately began work on a show that would capitalize on the wartime popularity of the Dumbells. He gathered together all of the original cast he could get, persuaded his uncles, Albert and Sam Kerr of Orillia, to put up six thousand dollars and, after a couple of try-outs in Owen Sound, Ontario, approached the biggest man in show business at the time, Ambrose Small, manager of the Grand Theatre on Adelaide Street in Toronto. Small was sceptical but said that maybe if Plunkett could enlarge his cast, get more numbers and more money he'd give the show a try.

Plunkett hurried back to the uncles and persuaded them to throw another twelve thousand dollars into the kitty. Then he lined up Red Newman, Charlie McLean, black-face comedian Ben Allen, baritone Tommy Young, and female impersonator Jock Holland. These with old-timers brother Al, Ross Hamilton, Fred Fenwick, Alan Murray, Jack McLaren, Bill Tennent, Jimmy Goode, Jack Ayre, Bert Langley, and Frank Brayford made up that first Canadian troupe.

They opened in London, Ontario, on October 1, 1919, with a show called *Biff Bing Bang*. Their audience was made to order – veterans, who knew them from the trenches, and their families and friends. Red Newman sang "Oh It's a Lovely War." When he came out in his old dirty bedraggled uniform with web gear askew, puttees undone, and red wig sticking out under a battered helmet, they cheered just to see him. When he started "Up to your knees in water, up to your waist in slush," there were lumps in a few throats and when he went into that never-to-be-forgotten routine of pitching his clothes and gear on the stage as he sought an elusive cootie, it just plain stopped the show.

Plunkett was in Small's Toronto office at ten the next morning, his face wrinkled in the I-told-you-so grin that was becoming a habit. Small offered him his usual deal – a fifty-fifty split with a one-dollar top. The show went straight into the Grand Theatre where it played eight weeks to capacity crowds and only left because of Small's previous commitments for Christmas. It opened again in January for eight more weeks, took a swing around to Hamilton, Ottawa, and Montreal, and then headed out for the first of its twelve cross-Canada tours. Everywhere they were met by enthusiastic veterans and their friends. The show is believed to have made a profit of about eighty thousand dollars that first year.

The next fall they had a brand-new show, bigger and better than ever. So much so that in May of 1921 they invaded Broadway, the graveyard of so many successful shows before and since.

Merton Plunkett tells a story of how they were almost scuppered before they opened at the new Ambassador Theatre. In the Princess Theatre in Montreal they had used a joke about Gen. Douglas MacArthur's famous Rainbow Division being the one that "came out after the storm was all over." Although this "killed" the Canadian ex-servicemen, it drew such violent and vociferous protest from a group of American convention wives in the audience that comedian Ben Allen didn't dare appear again that night. Then, in New York on opening night when everybody was tiptoeing around with fingers crossed, two stern females with blood in their eye caught Plunkett and demanded if this was the Canadian show that went around insulting American fighting men. Plunkett assured them that the foul joke was in another Canadian soldiers' revue and managed to get rid of them. "If they had ever made a public fuss," he says now, still shuddering at the memory, "we'd have closed that night instead of running twelve weeks."

As it was, they loved them on Broadway and the reviews were flattering.

With their New York notices plastered on advertising bills the Dumbells again hit the road. Crowds and reactions everywhere were satisfactory but travelling back and forth across Canada was rough. About 75 per cent of the stops were one-night stands with pretty primitive living conditions and theatres. In Pincher Creek, Alberta, they had to use the house next door to the theatre for a dressing room and climb a six-foot fence on their way to and from the stage, while out in the audience the manager was selling orange crates for seats at three dollars each.

Then late in 1922, Capt. Plunkett faced his greatest test as a showman. Ten days before the Dumbells were to open the fall season in Hamilton a group of the original cast presented an ultimatum – either they get more money or they would quit and form their own show. Plunkett told them to leave if they weren't satisfied and with only ten days and two stars left (Al Plunkett and Ross Hamilton) set about building a new show.

Other ex-service entertainers soon provided replacements (Pat Rafferty, Sammy Birch, Bert Wilkinson, Glen Allen,

Morley Plunkett) and the Dumbells opened as advertised in Hamilton with what Al Plunkett describes as "the best show we've ever had." The captain went into the act introducing a song he'd written himself called "Come Back Old Pal" and, according to him, some of the strikers who had come to scoff and remained to marvel confessed to damp eyes while this was being sung. Red Newman rejoined the show later and the rest of the rebels tried their luck with a show called *The Originals* which folded within the year.

The captain, Al Plunkett, Ross Hamilton, and the backers then organized a limited company and the Dumbells went on to even greater triumphs. They became an annual habit with Canadian theatre-goers from the Atlantic to the Pacific and the names of their stars were household words.

As the war faded in men's memories the Dumbells' sketches (mostly bought from English music halls) and songs got farther and farther from the trenches. Professional entertainers like tenor Harry Binns, bass Cameron Geddes, and violinist Howard Fogg joined the show. Many people believe the Dumbells hit an all-time high for Canadian comedy with newcomers Fred Emney, Charlie Jeeves, and Scotty Morrison and old hands Pat Rafferty and Red Newman. Emney in particular, a silly-ass Englishman in plus-fours and monocle, has been called "one of the funniest men who ever got on a stage anywhere."

But they kept to the Plunkett formula of few encores ("if they want to hear it again they can come back the next night and pay for it"), clean family-type humour, and a fast mixture of laughs and tears. The personable Plunketts continued to make friends, money, and whoopee up until 1929. Wherever they went they were wined and dined and lionized. It was easy to turn a buck in those days. The show was making big profits and every city had brokerage offices where bigger ones could be made. Al Plunkett tells of a small investment in oil in Calgary that earned him twelve thousand dollars by the time the show had gone to the west coast and back.

But it was easy to lose a buck, too. Merton Plunkett said recently: "If I hadn't been greedy and had stuck to the Dumbells instead of getting into other ventures I'd be worth a quarter of a million today." On the theory that if one soldiers' revue made money two should make twice as much, he launched the Maple Leafs, also full of ex-army entertainers, hokum, and sentiment. It lost thirty thousand dollars. At a cost of fifteeen thousand dollars he built the Merrymakers open-air theatre at Sunnyside in Toronto where he used some of the Dumbell stars when they weren't on the road. It made money for awhile but then went into the red and the Toronto Harbour Commission took over the property. He brought out the famous English comedian G. P. Huntley and took him on the road with a little thing called *Three Little Maids*. It flopped with another forty thousand dollars of the Dumbells' profits. But the clincher came in 1929 when the stock-market crash just about cleaned out both the captain and Al.

The Dumbells had introduced girls into the show with the tenth annual revue, *Why Worry*, in 1928. Some diehard fans still insist that the girls ruined the show; others say they improved it. The girls remained with the show from then until the end in 1932.

But whether the girls helped or hindered, the handwriting was on the wall for the Dumbells. Transportation costs had gone up, musicians and other workers were unionized and, worst of all, talking pictures had arrived. Theatre managers who were packing in crowds couldn't afford to rent their houses to the Dumbells for the short end of a seventy-thirty split. Stars like Al Plunkett, Newman, and Emney, travelling in special cars lugging costumes, props, and technicians with them, just couldn't compete with the Jolsons, Tibbetts, and Marx Brothers, travelling on movie film in little tin cans.

Merton Plunkett didn't give up easily. In 1931, without any money, he tried a comeback with "the biggest dollar's worth in show business," a variety show with a cast of two hundred, in the Victoria Theatre, Toronto. It played to good houses for a week but had to close when the creditors moved in too soon.

In 1932 he tried one last, disastrous tour. With many of the smaller expense-paying stops eliminated, the show just couldn't pay its way. It got as far as Edmonton and on the way back was stopped at Winnipeg by union officials who slapped a fine on musicians and stage hands for accepting half-filled pay envelopes and put Plunkett on the black list.

Plunkett went into the insurance business until 1939 when he again went overseas as an entertainment supervisor for the Canadian Legion Auxilliary Services. He wrote a song called "We're on Our Way," which the soldiers sang on the ship going over, and which later caught on in England where it is still occasionally sung. Invalided back in 1941 after a car accident, Plunkett worked at a number of jobs, including secretary-manager of the Albany Club in Toronto, and recently retired with his wife to Collingwood, Ontario. Now, at sixty-three, he is a grey-haired little man, slightly crippled with arthritis but not unhappy.

Al Plunkett had fair success in radio and night-club work in Montreal and the U.S. during the thirties. Now he works for the Ontario Department of Highways and helps his wife run the Plunkett Nursing Home.

Red Newman, who made three hundred dollars a week with the Dumbells and saved his money, owns a hotel at Wasaga Beach on Georgian Bay.

Ross Hamilton, the female impersonator, has been entertaining off and on ever since he left the Dumbells in 1930. When he joined the Army Medical Corps in Toronto in 1940 he dumbfounded the clerk by giving his occupation as actress. Now he lives in Brookfield, Nova Scotia, and is retired.

Jack McLaren has a display advertising business in Toronto.

But the days of the travelling revues are over. The old Empire Theatre in Saskatoon is now the Victory movie house. The high-school kids in that city rarely see a live professional on the stage. But their fathers still tell them about the Dumbells, the like of which may never be seen again.

Irish
Immigration

This article is another of the famous Flashback series on Canadian history that *Maclean's* magazine ran in the 1950s. All my ancestors were northern Irish, some by way of Scotland and some by way of England. My maternal great-grandmother, Elizabeth Edgerton, after her husband, Hugh Copeland, died, immigrated to Canada with her nine children, whom she raised on a farm in Ontario. She died at the age of one hundred.

Her second son, James, my maternal grandfather, born in County Fermanagh in 1820, married Arabell Timmins, whose family had also come from Fermanagh, and settled in Winchester, Ontario. They had eleven children, the third youngest of whom (Mary) was my mother.

The Braithwaites came from County Armagh in northern Ireland to which they had come in the distant past from Ambleside in Westmorland County, England. I don't know when they came to Canada, but my father was born near London, Ontario, in 1868.

So I have a natural interest in these Irish immigrants. When reading this account of their hardships I like to think of Elizabeth Edgerton Copeland and her nine children, all of whom survived and lived to a ripe old age.

The brig *Midas* sailed into the harbour at Saint John, New Brunswick, and anchored at Partridge Island quarantine station on the sunny afternoon of May 5, 1847. That was an important date in Canadian history, for after it the young country was never quite the same again.

An immigration officer went aboard for routine inspection. What he saw has been described as "the most horrible, the most ghastly, the most pitiable sight ever seen in a Canadian port." Port officials in those days were hardened to boatloads of squalor from across the Atlantic, but they'd never seen anything like this. Hundreds of filthy, ragged, starved immigrants from Ireland were packed in the hold like blacks in a slaver. Between rows of wooden benches that served as berths were piled boxes, sacks, pails, barrels, and bundles containing the wretched worldly goods of the passengers. Neither floor nor berths nor passengers had been washed since the ship left Ireland six weeks before. The straw ticks hadn't been aired and were filled with "abominations." The ship gave off such a fetid stench that longshoremen demanded bonus wages to board her.

Men, women, and children huddled hollow-eyed in their berths, too sick with typhus to stagger on deck for their first glimpse of the land of promise. Eight children and two adults had died on the way over, and many more were to die and be buried on Partridge Island in the next few days.

The *Midas* was no isolated hell-ship. She was merely the first of the "fever ships" from Ireland, the forerunner of an armada of misery that in the next seven years was to fill Canada's Atlantic ports, bringing the biggest single wave of immigration in our history. After witnessing a similar arrival at Quebec a Dr. Douglas declared: "I never saw people so indifferent to life. They would remain in the same berth with a dead person until the seaman dragged out the corpse with a boat hook."

Nine days after the *Midas* docked at Saint John, the sailing ship *Syria* made her way up the St. Lawrence to the quarantine station at Grosse Isle, below Quebec City. By May 20 no fewer than thirty more ships were anchored at the island unloading or waiting to unload their cargoes of death, disease, and incredible wretchedness. By the end of the year similar ships had dumped more than a hundred thousand destitute Irish men, women, and children in Canadian ports. By 1854 Canada's population was increased by nearly 350,000 Irish.

For 1847 was the year of the typhus epidemic, the blackest year in Ireland's sad history, the worst year of the potato famine that within one decade reduced Ireland's population from 8,500,000 to just over 5,000,000. An estimated one million of these actually starved to death or died from typhus. A total of 1,656,044 emigrated to North America, 1,300,000 to the United States and the rest to Canada.

Ireland's loss was Canada's gain, although Canadians did not see it that way at the time. The newcomers were referred to by some editors as "Irish trash" or "boatloads of indolence and poverty." The Governor General, Lord Elgin, called the influx a "terrible scourge" and petitioned the home government to "stem the tide of misery." Still they came, and the survivors went to work to build railways, roads, bridges, canals, sawmills, and factories. They cleared the land for farming. They were largely responsible for increasing Canada's population from just over one million in 1831 to 3,689,257 in 1871.

The census of that year showed 846,414 Irishmen or their descendants in Ontario, Quebec, Nova Scotia, and New Brunswick out of a total population of 3,485,761 – or 140,000 more than those of English origin and 200,000 more than those of Scottish origin. So during the period when Canada was changing from colony to nation almost one person in four in the settled area was an Irishman.

Whether their influence was good or bad is still a subject of argument, but there can be no doubt that the Protestant and Catholic Irish who came to Canada in the nineteenth century brought new and lively issues into Canadian politics.

And their influx was almost entirely due to potatoes. Without a superabundance of spuds there never would have been so many Irish in the first place, and certainly not nearly so many eventually in North America. Potatoes are supposed (by one theory) to have been introduced into Ireland from North Carolina in 1585. By 1700 they were being grown all over the country. Irishmen thrived so well on them that between 1700 and 1800 the population jumped from 1,250,000 to 4,500,000. In the next forty-five years potatoes combined with early marriages and the discouragement of emigration to increase Ireland's population to the unprecedented high of 8,500,000.

That was almost exactly twice as many Irishmen as there are at home today – and about twice as many as the economy could support. Fully one-third of these Irishmen lived almost entirely on potatoes. Tenant farmers, cotters, and farm labourers subsisted on patches of potatoes varying in size from a quarter-acre to five acres. They ate spuds three times a day, made flour out of them, fed them to the pigs, and even turned them into whisky. When the crop was good they had nearly enough to eat; when it failed through floods or drought or frost or insects – as it did in 1739, 1821, 1831, 1835, and 1839 – they lived on charity, starved, and emigrated.

In the first half of the nineteenth century overpopulation and one-crop dependence caught up with the Irish. The cotters and labourers were desperately poor. Their thatched-roofed, clay-walled huts barely kept out the weather. Speaking in the British Parliament in 1838 the Duke of Wellington stated: "There never was a country in which poverty existed to so great a degree as it exists in Ireland." Early in 1845 an Irish member of Parliament admitted that there were four and a half million paupers in his country.

On this sorry situation in the summer of 1845 a fungus growth called late blight fell like a headsman's axe. It had ruined potato crops in North America in 1844, but since there was plenty of other food it caused no great distress. There was heavy rainfall in the spring of 1845 in Ireland and the praties came up lush and green. Weeding their fine patches the cotters noticed little purple blotches on the leaves. They'd never seen them before, and so ignored them. More rains came and the blotches got larger, leaves began to droop. By midsummer the whole potato patch was a rotten soggy mess giving off a stench that carried for miles. In some regions in the west and south the entire crop was wiped out. That winter many Irish were hungry, but few actually starved.

The spring of 1846 was six weeks early and the potato growers hoped for an early harvest. They got no harvest at all. By now the blight had spread all over the island and gaunt famine stalked in its wake. Early in 1847 typhus fever, spread by lice and thriving on overcrowding and undernourishment, broke out everywhere.

The first reports of starvation came from the counties of Cork in the south and Mayo in the west. By February people were dying everywhere. In one townland near the city of Cork seven hundred of the eight hundred inhabitants were starving.

On April 17 the *Roscommon Journal* reported: "Deaths by famine are now so frequent that whole families who retire to rest at night are corpses in the morning and frequently are left unburied for days for want of coffins."

By the middle of March fifty thousand deaths from starvation and disease had been reported to the constabulary office in Dublin. During March and April two thousand died every week in the workhouses alone. Thousands more perished on the roadsides and in ditches. Coroners stopped holding inquests for lack of juries. Hungry men became crazed criminals. One broke into a house in Cork and murdered two children just to get at some scraps of cake. Food riots broke out at the ports, for although the peasants starved the regular export of oats, flour, beef, pork, and mutton to England continued.

The British government distributed forty-five million dollars' worth of corn in the first six months of 1847. Supplies were shipped from the United States and Canada, but it was not enough. For hundreds of thousands the choice was: emigrate to the unknown wilds of North America or stay at home and die.

In March the great exodus began. Help was forthcoming but not all of it was disinterested. Some landlords, eager to consolidate the peasants' plots into larger farms, invoked a provision of the Poor Relief Act, which enabled them to pay the passages of tenants and take over their land. Parish officials often decided it was shrewder to put up money for fares than to attempt to feed the destitute. But in many cases friends and relatives already established in North America sent money. Philanthropists helped others. One of the most remarkable of these was Vere Foster, an English diplomat and author. In 1847 Foster visited Ireland and was so shocked by what he saw that thereafter he devoted most of his time and money to the relief of Irish suffering. In all he helped twenty-five thousand single Irish girls emigrate to North America. Of these, sixteen thousand came to Canada. Foster even braved the horrors of the refugee ships to learn conditions at first hand.

The refugees swarmed to the ports of Ireland carrying their

pitiable belongings on their backs. And immediately new troubles beset them. Unscrupulous agents often bought up the entire steerage space of a vessel and then fleeced the destitute passengers. They forced the price of passage up from three pounds to five pounds and then to seven pounds. They sold the travellers useless junk as "essentials in the New World," they gave false information – "New York is directly on the route to Quebec" – and sold passages on ships not due to sail for several weeks.

The emigrants were jammed into the holds of old sailing tubs once used to transport timber and potash across the Atlantic. According to a description of one four-hundred-ton vessel, pigs on their way to slaughter had it better. The hold was seventy-five feet long and twenty-five wide. On either side of a five-foot alleyway were double tiers of wooden shelves each ten feet wide and five feet long. Each shelf was supposed to hold six persons, allowing twenty inches each, but since two children under fourteen or three under seven counted as one adult, and infants didn't count at all, sometimes as many as a dozen were jammed into one ten-foot space.

Since each family must take care of its own feeding arrangements the passageway was jammed with chunks of meat, sides of bacon, pots and pans, in addition to settlers' effects. Often the only ventilation was through the hatchways, and these were battened down in rough weather. "We were shut down in darkness for a fortnight," one survivor related.

By 1850 a few improvements had been put into effect (one regulation stipulated that "adult passengers of different sexes, unless husband and wife, shall be separately berthed"). But when Vere Foster in that year took a trip incognito as a steerage passenger in the *Washington* he found little actual change. The medical examination, he reported, consisted of a series of staccato questions: "What's your name? Are you well? Hold out your tongue. Pass on . . ." rattled off in one breath without pause for an answer. Only thirty of the nine hundred passengers received any water the first day out. Some were "cuffed and kicked" by the mates. To get near the cooking fires the passengers bribed the sailors. Those with no money didn't cook. Twelve children died of dysentry and starvation.

The ships were dirty beyond belief. The only cleaning below decks was scouring with soft sandstone. An immigration official reported that the ship *Elizabeth Grimmer* was so filthy that "after she'd been discharged from quarantine persons could not be had to go near her for three weeks and then only by extraordinary wages." Rats scurried about the holds, biting children and stealing the passengers' meagre supplies of food.

Many emigrants had typhus when they came aboard and the lice soon spread it to others. Few of the ships carried doctors. One hundred and thirty-six persons perished aboard the ship *Avon* on the way over. Of the four hundred and eighteen aboard the *Alderberon* thirty-four died before they reached Canada. In April 1847 alone seventy-five fever ships cleared for Quebec carrying twenty-two thousand Irish. Many of them never made it.

North Atlantic storms took additional toll. Many ships were blown off course or wrecked. Vessels headed for Quebec finally docked at New York or even New Orleans. Many piled up on the rocks in the Gulf of St. Lawrence. Lonely stone monuments are still to be seen on desolate beaches, such as the one at Cap des Rosiers, Quebec, in memory of "Those Who Were Shipwrecked." The passengers who managed to make shore were taken in by the Canadian fishermen. To this day there are residents in these areas who speak only French but have names like Reilly or O'Flaherty.

When the ships reached port the dead were lowered over the side by ropes (one account states at one dollar a head), stacked up like cordwood and buried in hastily dug trenches on the beach. The living fared little better.

Most of the quarantine stations had been built in 1832, the largest previous immigration year, when 51,746 immigrants came from the British Isles following a minor famine and brought a cholera epidemic to Canada. Facilities were hopelessly inadequate. Grosse Isle, for example, was built to accommodate two hundred persons. A report for the week ending July 4, 1847, lists 1,817 in hospital, 144 deaths, and 42 bodies (chiefly children) brought ashore from ships. The authorities managed to round up fifty extra beds and a quantity of straw. A shed was built to hold sixty persons. Many of the sick and dying were sheltered under tents made from old canvas and spars borrowed from the ships.

One eyewitness described the fever sheds as "miserable affairs . . . most of the patients had dysentry and the stench was terrible. It was impossible to separate the sick from the well or to disinfect or clean the bedding. I have known poor families to prefer to burrow under heaps of loose stones near the shore than to accept the shelter of the infected sheds."

In view of the terror of epidemics in those pre-antibiotic days, officials and citizens of the Canadian ports were often heroic in their treatment of the immigrants. Doctors, nurses, clergymen, and laymen risked and even lost their lives tending the sick. Most notable of these on Partridge Island were two brothers, Doctors W. S. and J. H. Harding, both of whom caught typhus. Twenty-three-year-old Dr. James Patrick Collins rowed out to the island to help his countrymen, caught the disease, and died within a few days. At Grosse Isle twenty-two of the twenty-six doctors tending the sick contracted typhus. Four died. Twenty-two nurses and four priests also lost their lives.

An official report which states that "a large mass of indolence, pauperism and destitution and disease has been thrown into the Province," gives some significant figures. Of the 89,738 British immigrants (mostly Irish) in 1847, 30,265 had typhus while 10,037 died in quarantine or in immigrant hospitals in Quebec City or Montreal.

Eastern Canada has many stone and metal reminders of this greatest mass suffering in Canada's history. At Saint John harbour a Celtic cross marks the burial grounds of hundreds. At Point St. Charles in Montreal a huge rough stone with an iron fence around it was erected by the workmen on Victoria Bridge "To Preserve from Desecration the Remains of 6,000 Immigrants Who Died of Ship's Fever AD – 1847-48."

What happened to the Irish after they got off the fever ships? They became part of the Canadian community; some with comparative ease, others with almost as much hardship and suffering as their crossing had caused them. But wherever they went they had a considerable influence on Canadian ways and affairs.

Most of those who landed in New Brunswick stayed there and found work on the docks. In winter they went into the forests to cut trees for the thriving timber and ship-mast trade. Irish benevolent societies assisted those who wished to go farming by providing basic provisions – usually a bag of salt and pepper, a sack of flour, and an axe. Most of these settled along the St. John River valley. A group of unemployed mechanics from Dublin built a lumber mill and established the community of Mechanic, New Brunswick. The mill, built entirely of wood except for the saw blade, was powered by water and operated for almost a century.

Many of the Irish who landed at Quebec and Montreal remained in Lower Canada where work was plentiful. A report on the arrivals of passenger ships during 1851 states: "Employment is abundant in almost every section of the province. A thousand labourers are now required in the St. Lawrence and Atlantic Junction Railroad to whom contractors offer from four shillings to a dollar per day. Domestic servants and farm labourers are also much sought after."

Many of the immigrants stayed in the cities. The 1851 census puts the population of Quebec City at 42,052 of whom no fewer than 6,344 were native-born Irishmen. By the census of 1861 that number had increased by more than a thousand. Even today the English-speaking population in the lower town is predominately of Irish origin.

Some newcomers found shelter with relatives already established in Quebec villages. Steven Broderick, for instance, and his eighteen-year-old bride, Bridget, arrived from Galway at the home of their uncle, John Ford in Compton, with exactly forty cents to their name. They prospered in the friendly community and one of their daughters, Mary Ann Broderick, later married a local merchant named Jean-Baptiste Moise St. Laurent. Their son Louis has since made quite a name for himself in Canadian politics.

Montreal had had a considerable Irish community since the beginning of the century and the new immigrants added greatly to it. In 1851 one-fifth of the population of 57,715 was Irish. Still more came until in 1857 those of Irish origin claimed to make up one-third of the total population of Montreal.

Many of the Catholic Irish girls married French-speaking Montreal boys. Hundreds of orphans from the ships were adopted into Canadien homes (one priest reported bringing thirty orphans ashore and having them "taken up" within half an hour). Advertisements in Montreal newspapers indicate that the Irish were prominent in the wholesale and retail trade. Between 1851 and 1864 about a dozen Irish lawyers and doctors were advertising in each issue of one newspaper alone.

About half the immigrants – mostly Protestants from the north of Ireland – kept right on to Upper Canada. Many travelled up the Ottawa and St. Lawrence rivers by flat-bottomed boats while others made their way as best they could on foot, by oxcart, or by stagecoach. But still hunger and want pursued them, as this item from the *Kingston Herald* in June 1850 reveals:

"What is to be done towards relieving the numbers of immigrants who, having arrived here, are unable to proceed further for want of means? Every evening numbers are left on our wharves who know not how to provide food for themselves and their families . . . . We call upon some wealthy citizens to step forward and take a lead in devising some means of relief for those truly unfortunate people." The 1851 census shows Kingston to have 4,396 Irish-born inhabitants out of a total population of 11,585.

An account from Ottawa tells how between June 1847 and May 1848 hundreds of Irish were arriving each week at the landing place at the juncture of the Rideau Canal and the Ottawa River opposite where Union Station now stands. They were in a frightful state and found what shelter they could under bushes, old tents, and upturned boats. The area was described as being "knee-deep in filth." Typhus spread through the city causing hundreds of deaths. The population of Ottawa, then Bytown, showed 2,486 Irish-born out of 7,760 in 1851 and in surrounding Carleton County more than one-third of the residents were from the Emerald Isle.

Toronto got a supply of Irish to the extent that in 1851 more than one-third of the population of 30,775 was Irish-born. Hamilton had about the same proportion of Irishmen. In these and other cities the newcomers picked up what jobs they could as ditch diggers, domestic servants, and coachmen. Many got into the traditional "Irish occupations" of policeman and bartender. A number of families followed the old-country tradition that one son enters the priesthood. Before long many Irishmen established themselves in the trades, in business, and professions.

Some newcomers sought out relatives and friends on farms. One man named Cooper visited his brother near Brampton, Ontario, and gave him typhus from which he died. Many hired out as farm labourers. A letter from John Clark, of Peel County, describes how a man could work for three years at twenty-five pounds, about a hundred and twenty-five dollars, and then buy land for himself. According to a publicity brochure put out by the Ontario government in 1883 many of these did exceptionally well. Patrick Gaerty from Monaghan, Ireland, worked as a farm hand in Peel, set up for himself, and within a few years had land and equipment worth twenty-five thousand dollars.

Many of the Irish trekked north in groups to the less settled portions of the province where free land was offered. Simcoe, Victoria, Renfrew, Grey, Huron, and other counties received thousands. Peterborough County which had been pioneered by earlier Irish immigrants (principally the Peter Robinson settlement of 1823-15) had 4,216 Irish-born out of a population of 15,237 in 1851 and gained a thousand new Irish before the 1861 census.

Such a predominance of settlers from a country always noted for political strife and religious upheaval naturally had a tremendous influence on Ontario. But unlike many of their countrymen in the U.S., the Canadian Irish did not try to fight the old country's battles by remote control. The Fenian movement, founded by Irish-Americans to support the cause of Irish independence, never got anywhere in Canada. When zealots from south of the border visited Montreal to stir up trouble they spoke to empty seats. In a speech in 1866 that great Irish-Canadian booster D'Arcy McGee stated: "I venture to say that they (Irish-Canadians) yield a larger aggregate of sterling worth, character, and influence than the millions of our countrymen in the U.S. put together."

On the other hand they did bring their religious discord with them. About half the immigrants were Protestants from the north of Ireland and about half were Roman Catholics from the south. They opposed each other in everything.

Most of the Protestants joined the already large and powerful Orange Lodge and voted Tory almost to a man. The Catholic Irish usually took the other side. One community in Victoria County was typical of many. Just north of the town of Omemee is a concession road known as the "Orange Line." North of it in Downeyville lived the Catholic Irish while south of the line was solid Orange. It wasn't too safe for a "papist" to show his nose south of that line unless accompanied by friends well armed with shillelaghs.

On the Glorious Twelfth of July the Orangemen from L.O.L. 646 and other lodges got out their drums, white horse, peaked caps, ribbons, and sashes and paraded through the streets. The boys from north of the Orange Line naturally came down and tried to break it up. Old-timers recall street fights that lasted for days. One story from nearby Peterborough (a city full of Irishmen) tells how a rash individual snatched the orange ribbons from a pretty lass during the parade. The Orangemen chased him downtown where he took refuge in a hotel. Then they brought a two-wheel cannon, old but still usable, trained it on the hotel, and threatened to blow the place to pieces if the miscreant wasn't delivered into their hands. He was delivered.

Politics were considerably livelier then than now, for which some historians give the Irish full credit. On election days both sides filled the town with banners and bands. Many landholders suspected of intending to vote the wrong way were forcibly prevented from getting near the polls. One old-timer described how a white chalk mark was put on the coattail of a man who voted "wrong" so that he could later be beaten up.

Some historians consider the Orange Lodge to have been the most potent force and the toughest pressure group in Ontario politics. They claim that vital political questions were apt to be decided along strictly religious lines. Orangemen deny this and take credit for keeping Canada loyal to the British crown through trying times. Whatever the political significance of it, certainly between 1845 and some time in the 1890s there were more Irishmen in the country than any other English-speaking group.

But the Irish predominance was short-lived. By 1854 economic conditions had improved in Ireland and the population had shrunk to numbers the land could support. Emigration stopped. By 1901 there were more Englishmen in Ontario than Irishmen. Few Irish came to Canada between 1901 and 1911 when the opening of the west brought thousands of English and Scots into the country. By 1941 the 846,414 of Irish origin in 1871 had increased to only 1,267,702 – or just over 11 per cent of the total population, compared with 25.8 per cent of English origin.

So the Irish influx was as brief as it was violent. And if it hadn't been for spuds it never would have happened at all. The abundance of spuds produced the surplus Irish; the lack of spuds drove them here. Nobody can say exactly what their influence has been. But one thing is certain – without them our nation would be a lot less melodious, humorous, rugged, and lively. For whatever else the Irish may be they are rarely dull.

Never
Sleep Three
in a Bed

I have chosen this chapter from *Never Sleep Three in a Bed* because it describes a most important aspect of prairie farm life that is now gone: the threshing gang. This gang, numbering up to twenty men, that gathered each fall to cut, stook, and thresh the immense crops of wheat, has been replaced by a huge combine that cuts and threshes all in one operation and is driven by one man. The other nineteen are mostly unemployed. Progress.

Threshing time was an important ritual on the prairie farm. Everybody took part: men, women, children, horses, dogs, and cats. Many of the men came from far away on special harvester trains. It was a time of hard, hard work and great fun. Of early frosty mornings and hot fall noondays, of monstrous feeds prepared by the farm wife and her helpers. It was a time for swapping stories and comparing the year's crop to all the other crops that had preceded it. Along with the long, lonely whistle of the steam locomotive, the pride in good work-horses, and the bustling prairie hamlets, this ritual is gone. Whether this is a good thing or a bad thing I'm not prepared to say, but to me it is a sad thing.

The best thing that happened to me when I was seventeen was that I went harvesting. And the best thing about *that* was that I got to know my brother Morley.

Morley was rarely home. Oh, in Prince Albert I remember him being with us for a while in the winter, but he got back to

Nokomis as soon as he could to work on a farm. In Saskatoon, he occasionally showed up in the winter and drove a delivery rig for the Hudson's Bay Company department store, but he'd be gone again come seeding time.

Whenever I think of a prairie wheat farmer I think of Morley, for he was as good a prototype as you'll ever find. Religious, practical, and straightforward, with a loud, resonant laugh, he loved to tell stories, he loved horses, and he loved the land. Everything about farming was a joy to Morley, even milking cows. Long after he stopped raising his own food he still kept a cow – just for the fun of milking her.

Aside from all this, Morley could fart better than any man I ever knew. All the Braithwaite boys were good farters, but Morley was the best. "A farting horse will never tire; a farting man is a man to hire," he would say, and he believed it. It was his boast, and he wasn't given to idle boasts, that he once stopped a six-horse team by farting at them.

I don't know the anatomical explanation for farting, but I know that it can't possibly do any harm to the practitioner's health. His social standing perhaps, his love life maybe, but not his health. It can, however, contribute tremendously to sibling discord. I remember one winter in Saskatoon when Hub was working at Bob Gordon's fruit store and eating as much fruit as he could hold. All night he released the vilest farts of all time. I was sleeping with him, and I know.

He was playful about it, too. "Heads under cover place!" he would shout, after releasing a putrilaginous sneaker, and then he would yank the covers up over both our heads. Whereupon I would let out a pitiful scream, "Ma – Hub's making smells again!"

After which I'd leap out of bed, pull all the covers off, shake them violently, and throw open the window to the thirty-below-zero cold. It didn't do any good. The vileness of those fruit-farts would seep up through the folds of the covers all night long, and haunt my every dream.

But back to Morley and farming. As soon as a Braithwaite boy was ready for the harvesting, Morley was waiting on a farm somewhere in the Nokomis area to give us our ordeal by pitchfork. First, there was a couple of weeks of stooking, followed by pitching bundles. You earned the fabulous sum of four dollars a day, and board, and you came home hard as nails, and full of wild tales about the things you'd done and the people you'd met.

It was a sort of coming-of-age thing, like puberty rites among the Watusi, or a belated bar mitzvah. After going harvesting you were a man. Hub went, and was reported to be "better than most grown men" in the harvest field.

So, late in August, I packed my belongings into a cardboard suitcase, and set off for Nokomis. It meant that I would miss at least a month of grade twelve, but I was confident I could make up for it. Besides I needed the money so badly for clothing and books that I absolutely had to go, whether I could make up the time or not.

I arrived in Nokomis and looked around fondly. It was the first time that I'd seen it since leaving there twelve years before. It had changed some, but the old stone house was still there. And the school we'd all dashed away from, to see our first aeroplane, looked much the same. The Chinese restaurant hadn't changed much either, but the little building on Main Street, where Dad had his office and where I used to go for nickels, was gone.

It's a peculiar thing. I've been back to the old town many times since that spring day in 1919 when we drove out of it in the Russell and, of course, there have been many changes. But, to this day, the only picture of Nokomis that comes into my mind is the one that was impressed upon it when I was six years old. Whenever I think of the town, that memory, and that alone, is what I see. The back lanes where we played run-sheep-run in the autumn dusk, the vacant lot where we played prisoner's base. The ditch beside the railroad track, called "Shunkies," where we swam nude and showed off for the passenger trains roaring by.

Morley met me at the station with the pick-up truck, and we drove down the dusty road between the fields of ripening grain to the farm of Wick Thompson. It was a good farm. The immense frame house was painted white, and the huge barn a bright red. Numerous well-painted granaries and other out-buildings were scattered about the yard, including a bunkhouse which was to be my home for the next month.

There is a smell in a bunkhouse that is like none other. It's composed of dust, dry straw (the mattresses are stuffed with it), body odour, horse manure from the men's boots, horse sweat, and another smell, which I can only describe as the essence of the oh-so-dry prairie in the fall.

There were half a dozen others sleeping in the bunkhouse, mostly transients. The other harvesters, like Cap McLaren and Bowser Jardine, were Nokomis residents who took holidays every autumn from their jobs in town so that they could work in the harvest. They loved it, and they were good. The professionals of the trade, you might say. They could handle a fork with the same skill and dexterity as a painter handles a brush. They never seemed to be working hard, but they got an incredible amount done. And they drove me almost crazy.

"We're going to begin cutting tomorrow morning," Morley informed me. "You'll go with Blooming 'Arry. He's around here somewhere. Probably reading. He's always reading. Anyway, I'll call you in the morning."

He did. At four o'clock.

"Rise and shine. Rise and shine!" he shouted, rattling the wooden door of the bunkhouse. "Time to get up!"

It was pitch-dark and cold. I groped my way into my clothing and out into the frosty, damp morning, down the path towards the house where a pale yellow light was showing. Inside, the house was warm and smelled of frying pork and eggs and hot bread. Breakfast was ready.

Morley was already at the table with a couple of others, while Mrs. Thompson and her daughter, Marion, hurried back and forth from stove to table, fetching plates of eggs and pork and fried potatoes and toast and cups of scalding hot tea.

Hunched over his food, paying no attention to anyone, was Blooming 'Arry. He was an Englishman, and that meant he'd had a rough time on the prairies since his arrival there as a young man, forty years before. For just about the favourite sport of prairie dwellers in the twenties – and maybe still, for all

I know – was Englishman baiting. They were fair game because they talked funny. They dropped their "h's" or added them to words where they didn't belong, so that they were usually greeted by some local comedian with " 'Ellow 'Arry, 'ave you 'eard of the 'orrible things that are 'appening?" After which, everybody would burst into loud guffaws and slap their knees, while the Englishman would grin good-naturedly, and wonder why that was so funny.

They also had a peculiar way with "a's," and another good laugh was "I hawf to lawf to see the cawf go down the pawth to tyke a bawth on Sunday awfternoon."

I have never been in a small town or on a prairie farm where there wasn't at least one wag who could imitate the resident Englishman to perfection.

Blooming 'Arry – whose name was Harry Bloomington – had long since ceased to be visibly annoyed by this foolish teasing, and had closed more and more into himself. Whatever hopes and schemes he'd had when he first came to this "golden land of opportunity," as the early brochures had described it, had long since been blighted by plain bad luck. Gradually, I pieced together his story. He'd been a gentleman's gentleman in London, and had come to Saskatchewan on a buffalo-hunting expedition in 1879, when Saskatchewan was still part of the District of Assiniboine. Seduced by the offer of free land, he left his employer, took up a homestead, and remained to fight it out with wind, drought, early frost, grasshoppers, blizzards, and loneliness. And he had lost.

He'd put up a good fight for a while, though, building himself a sod hut, surviving off the collection and sale of buffalo bones, which he hauled thirty miles to the railway at Lumsden by oxcart. It was rumoured that he'd once been married to a half-breed girl, and that there were children, but they all died of smallpox around the turn of the century. Since then, Harry had been a drifter, a hired man, working wherever he happened to be needed, carrying in his little pack all his belongings. And it was one of the items in that pack that enabled me to get closer to Harry than anyone had been in years.

On that first morning, I ate only a little breakfast, since I wasn't very hungry. Besides, it didn't appear appetizing. I'd never had fried potatoes for breakfast before, and the idea didn't seem right somehow – potatoes were for dinner. "Better eat up," Morley warned. "Lunch is a long time away." How right he was!

After breakfast, when a rosy glow was showing in the east, I walked with Harry, our shadows long before us, out into a field behind the barn. Wick Thompson, Cap McLaren and Morley were already in the field cutting the grain with binders. I can still see them following each other down that long, long field, each binder pulled by four horses, cutting the tall, almost ripe grain, binding it into sheaves, and dumping the sheaves out in rows as they went. Our job was to follow them on foot and stand the sheaves up in stooks so that they would further ripen and withstand any rain that might come before threshing time.

Harry didn't bother to give me any instruction, but by watching him I soon caught on to how it was done. He walked over to the first sheaf, which was between three and four feet long, picked it up, and tucked it under his right arm. Then he picked up another and bounced it up under his left arm. Then he went into a sort of squatting position, jammed the butt end of the sheaves hard into the stubble and leaned the heads together. There they stood as he piled other sheaves around them until he had a little teepee of eight or ten sheaves. Then he moved on to the next pile of sheaves, and built the next stook in line with the first, so as to make a straight row.

It looked ridiculously simple. I picked up a sheaf with my gloved hand, grunted at its weight, got it up under my arm, picked up another and squatted to stand them up. They fell over. I picked them up again and jammed them harder into the stubble. They fell over again, sliding off each other like a couple of drunk companions. The next time I picked them up by the binder twine that bound them together and it slid off the butt end, spreading the straw about me. It took me about four more tries to get two sheaves to stand up by themselves, and to build a very ragged-looking stook that looked as though it might topple over at any moment. Beside Harry's neat, firm stooks it looked disgraceful.

Then and there I began that part of my education that commences outside of school. Like most high-school seniors, I was insufferably arrogant and self-assured. Why an old bum like Blooming 'Arry could never teach *me* anything. Not very likely! What I hadn't realized until then was that Harry was a skilled workman, and I wasn't. Everything he did, he did well, with dexterity and speed. In the harvest field it didn't matter a tinker's damn how much history or literature a man knew; it was how well he could do the job in hand that counted. I was to learn this lesson many times before I went back to Saskatoon.

There was a rhythm to the way Harry worked, I soon discovered. Every move used the amount of energy required for it and no more. He never took an unnecessary step, or moved an arm where it didn't need to go. His squat, gnarled, lean figure functioned like a machine.

And, like a well-oiled machine, Harry never stopped – sheaf after sheaf, stook after stook, row after row down that flat field that stretched endlessly before us. On and on he went. Since we each took the next pile of sheaves available, he never left me behind, but he surely did tire me out. When it seemed that we'd been working about six hours, when my back was aching and I was so hungry that my stomach thought my throat was cut, and the sun was riding so high that I thought it must be just about noon, I ventured to ask Harry the time. He hauled a huge turnip of a watch from the bib pocket of his overalls, peered at it, and grunted, "Ten past eight."

"What? I thought you said ten past eight."

"That's what I did say." He held the big watch up for me to see.

"Is it right?"

"Never been wrong in thirty years."

"But it seems so much later. Can't we sit down and have a rest?"

"We don't get paid for sitting."

"But I'm as dry as a board. I've got to have a drink."

"There'll be a jug at the end of the field. Come on, let's get going."

He began again to pick up the sheaves in that precise, neat

way that I had come to hate, and stand them up into those perfect stooks. Well no gawd-damned sixty-year-old Englishman was going to make a monkey out of me. So I creaked to my aching feet and went doggedly to work as everything became a blur of bending, lifting, piling. Four hours more of this before lunch. How could I stand it?

Finally we reached the end of the field and Harry stopped long enough to dig down into the deep grass and produce a glass jug, full of yellowish water. He unscrewed the top and handed it to me. I tipped it up and took a long, long pull of the worst-tasting water on earth. The wells of southern Saskatchewan are deep, and the earth is filled with numerous salts. So the water in many places has a sulphury, salty taste which is not improved by sitting in the sun all morning, sparsely sheltered by long dry grass. Just the same, I took a good swig every time we reached the end of the field.

"Better be careful with that," Harry advised. "It's physic."

(I found out what he meant later that afternoon when I could barely get a stook up fast enough to squat down behind it.)

Finally, when I had given up on lunch entirely, I saw a cloud of dust coming towards us over the dry stubble field. It turned out to be the pick-up truck, driven by Marion Thompson. She wheeled up beside us, jumped out, and announced, "Lunch-time!" Then she produced a huge basket of food and a blanket from the back of the truck, and set them down on the stubble. She looked so nice and fresh and pretty in her skirt and sweater that all my fatigue vanished.

"Hey, a picnic," I quipped. "The fondest thing I am of! You are an angel of mercy. You have saved my life." Then as she got back into the truck, "Aren't you going to eat with us?"

"Nope. This angel of mercy has other men to rescue." With a roar the Model-A pick-up bumped off and I was left with Blooming 'Arry and the dry, dry stubble.

Finally the day wore to an end, and the next and the next. For the first week I ached all over, but gradually I began to – as they say on the farm – toughen up. My arm muscles grew hard, and I developed one on each side of my spinal column that felt like broom handles. I even learned to set up stooks that wouldn't fall over, and I gained as much satisfaction from the acquisition of that skill as I have from any other. Harry remained as taciturn as ever, and to mitigate the loneliness and monotony of the long days I developed the habit of talking to him. I told him about our home and the kids I knew and what I thought of them, and I discussed the problem of making up one's mind about the future, and about Mary Patterson, who was currently breaking my heart.

Although he never answered – or perhaps because of it – I opened up to him completely, telling him things that I'd never told anyone. Apart from an occasional grunt or mumble, he said nothing in reply, and I thought he was totally uninterested in my youthful confidences. It wasn't until later that I discovered how wrong I was.

Finally the grain was all cut and stooked, and we were ready for threshing. While the rest of us had been finishing up the last few acres, Wick Thompson and an engineer from town had been working on the tractors and separator so that there'd be no breakdowns during threshing. It's hard for anyone who hasn't experienced it to realize how important time becomes during those fall days. All through spring and summer the farmer had helplessly waited for that wheat to grow, all five hundred acres of it. He'd watched the sky endlessly for signs of rain or hail. He'd poisoned grasshoppers and gophers. He'd stood many a night in late August looking at the clear, star-filled sky, dreading an early frost. The wheat had survived all these hazards, had been cut and stooked, but it wasn't worth a cent until it was threshed.

A drastic change in the weather, a long rainy spell, an early snow, could lower the grade of the grain and cost the farmer all his profit on the entire year's work. Every day that it rained meant hundreds of dollars lost. The sight of a dozen men sitting around on their tails eating their heads off was a nightmare to the farmer. He daren't let the men go during bad weather, because he might not be able to find others. So, every day that was good had to be used to the full.

The crop that year was what Morley described as "fair to

middlin'," which meant that it wasn't any "bumper crop" nor was it a "failure." It would run about twenty to twenty-five bushels to the acre, and since the price that year was about a dollar and a half a bushel there was "an awful lot of money sitting in that field."

The weather remained favourable. The sun shone every day and there was little wind. This is the best time of year on the prairies. The winters are too cold and too windy; the summers are too hot and too windy; the springs are too wet, or too dry, and too windy. But the fall is often gorgeous. The big sun sits in the sky, too low to cause much heat but warm enough for comfort. And at night the great harvest moon comes up and rests on the horizon like a round ball of fire, slowly rising in the clear sky to take its place among the endless stars.

Each night I sat alone in the bunkhouse except for Harry who lay in his bunk reading, so unobtrusive that I forgot he was there, and wrote a letter to Mary, describing the moon, making funnies about the other characters in the harvesting gang, and pouring out my boyish heart. My God – I wrote poetry – I quoted Shakespeare – I was inspired.

But then we started threshing. Threshing! I had thought that I'd seen the ultimate in back-breaking toil while stooking, but compared to threshing it was a game of marbles. There is no work in this world, I'm convinced, as difficult as pitching bundles. I mean, of course, for the beginner. It kills your back, ruins your hands, and fills you with dust and chaff. You're convinced that you'll never be able to walk another step. And along with all that there are the horses.

I don't know why, but there is absolutely no rapport between me and horses. They hate me. The first morning of threshing Morley took me into the steaming interior of the big red barn, walked up beside a nice, gentle horse, and showed me how to curry-comb and brush him, and then to put on the bridle and harness.

"After you get your team harnessed, you just run them out of the stall and they'll go to the trough for a drink and wait for you to come and hitch them up." He did it. His horses did it, and I tried the same thing with my two.

Their names were Gent and Lady. Believe me, she was no

lady and for that matter he was no gentleman. I walked up into the stall beside him and said, "Whoa, boy, whoa," as I'd heard Morley do, rubbed his nose gently as Morley had done, took the bridle off the peg as Morley had, and tried to put it on. But instead of nuzzling his nose down into it like Morley's horses, this damned fool tossed his head about eighteen feet in the air, where I couldn't possibly reach it. And he wouldn't bring it down. Finally I had to climb up on the manger, leap at his head with the bridle extended and, dangling there, work the bit between his clenched teeth. It took four tries, but I managed it. He was equally unco-operative when I put the collar and harness on him, leaning over against me and crushing me against the side of the stall, just for good measure.

After a half-hour struggle I got both horses harnessed, and turned them out into the barnyard as directed. Did they go to the water trough for a drink, as all the other horses had done, and as they themselves had done every blasted morning of their evil lives? They did not. No sooner had they got outside the barn door than they tossed their heads in the air, dilated their nostrils, whinnied, kicked up their heels, and galloped out of the gate into the field. How about that?

"I've never seen that team do a thing like that before," Morley averred when he could stop laughing. "They've caught on that you're a greenhorn. Horses'll sometimes do that to a greenhorn. They can always tell."

He jumped on one of the other horses and rode out after the runaways. They didn't avoid him. They came back calm as lambs, but I noticed that they were watching me from the corners of their mean little eyes, and I could have sworn one winked at the other.

Then came the hitching to the hayrack. This was a simple enough manoeuvre. You snapped one end of the neck-yoke onto each horse's collar, slipped the end of the wagon-tongue through an iron ring on the neck-yoke, hitched the traces to the single-trees, threw the lines up onto the rack, jumped onto it, shouted "Ha," clucked your tongue a few times, and the team proceeded in a forward direction, dragging the rack behind them. Nothing to it.

Nothing to it, that is, if one horse will step over the wagon-tongue to get on the other side of it and if both horses will stand still while you do your thing, and not swivel their rumps away out at an angle so that you can't get the traces hooked. They will do all these things just fine all year round until a greenhorn gets hold of them and then, like mischievous kids, they do everything wrong. Act as though they'd never seen a hayrack before in their misbegotten lives, and had never been hitched to anything.

At last I got Lady and Gent hitched to the rack and was ready to go. Morley had told me, "Just two things to remember: always go through a gate straight on, at right angles to the fence, or the ass-end of the rack will hit the gate post. And don't turn too sharp or you'll break the reach." (The reach is the long pole that "reaches" between the front and rear axle of the wagon.) I wish he'd never mentioned those two things.

I jumped onto the rack and clicked my tongue for the horses to begin. I was a little self-conscious because all the others who were aleady hitched hadn't driven off but, instead, were waiting for me to go first. I soon discovered why. I'd hitched the horses on the wrong sides so that the reins were reversed. Let me explain. At the end of each rein there are two straps, a long one and a short one. The short one snaps onto the outside of the bit of one horse, while the long one snaps onto the inside of the bit of the other horse. So, when you pull on a line, you are pulling on the same side of each bit. But if you get them reversed, it's the short straps that cross over to the other horse so that when you pull on the reins you pull the horses' heads together. They walk along like a couple of lovers, with heads tight together and rumps V'd out on each side. It looks very funny, and just about kills the old hands who wait around for the greenhorn to do it. I've never heard men laugh so loud.

Well, I finally got the horses reversed and out of that gate into the field, where the neat windrows of stooks stood waiting to be loaded onto the racks and hauled to the separator. Morley showed me how to drive the team along beside the windrow and fork the sheaves into the rack, building the load carefully so that the sheaves wouldn't fall off when it got high.

"Just two things to remember," he cautioned (him and his

damned "two things"), "you've got to keep your turn at the feeder. Cap McLaren goes in first, and then Bowser, and then you. Don't get behind or you'll have a hell of a time catching up. The other thing is to pull in good and close to the feeder, so you won't have so far to pitch the sheaves. Okay, you're on your own."

So I began pitching bundles. Very easy, actually. You have this long-handled, three-tined fork. You jab it into the sheaf and pitch it onto the rack. As the load gets higher you jam the sheaves down hard on the side, with their butt ends out and heads in, and keep pitching sheaves into the centre. When you are finished you've got a load that is a good seven feet high, and looks like a square box except that it's rounded at the top. While you are loading, the team, who are used to this work, walk along beside the row of stooks and you don't even have to drive them. Just shout at them.

So I began loading my rack in a good steady pace – one sheaf at a time. Felt kind of good. My muscles were hard from stooking, and I considered that this job wasn't going to be bad at all. I'd just nicely got the bottom of the rack covered when I looked over to see how Cap was getting on. He'd already built half his load. I watched him in awe. Working like a machine, in perfect rhythm, he jabbed his fork into the stook, picked up not one but *three* sheaves at a time, and pitched them onto the load. Right there he was tripling my speed. He had other tricks, unnoticed by me at first, that increased his advantage tenfold. There and then I quit dallying, dug my fork into the stooks, and heaved like a madman. And I never slacked that crazy pace.

It availed me little, however. Before I was half loaded I saw Cap perched atop his sheaves jostling his way towards the threshing outfit, which was now ready to start transforming those sheaves into wagon-loads of grain and huge stacks of straw.

The tractor started up, the long, sagging belt between it and the separator began to move, all the wheels of the separator whirred and rattled, the whirling knives of the feeder flashed in the sun. Cap moved his load in beside the feeder, stood up on it, and began tossing sheaves down into its hungry maw. Wisps of straw spouted out of the blower to drift leisurely to the ground, and the threshing had begun.

I was too busy pitching those bundles onto my load to watch it, though. Long before I was loaded I saw Cap driving his empty rack away from the feeder, and Bowser pulling his full one right in behind so that there would be scarcely a pause during the transition. Frantically I redoubled my efforts, and by the time Bowser pulled out I managed to limp up to the outfit with about two-thirds of a load.

Now I had to direct my fickle team up close to the feeder to pitch off my load. A threshing outfit was a noisy, dusty place, redolent with the clangs, squeals, rattles, and bangs of hundreds of moving parts. To me it was like running the gauntlet with sure disaster barely inches away. In order to see properly, I had to stand up on the load, precariously balanced on uneven and shifting sheaves. Somehow I made it, and there, four feet below me, was that awful feeder with its revolving canvas floor and its murderous chewing knives. Horrible stories were told of greenhorns who had fallen into a feeder and been mangled by those blades. It was a picture that haunted me.

The expression "separate the men from the boys" is a tired cliché but an apt one when it comes to a threshing gang. That is one place where you become a man, or you don't. You are judged by nothing save your ability to keep your turn, to build a good load, to pull your weight, to work like a man. Nobody to help you or to coddle you along or make allowances. You damned well do it or you don't, and you are forever pegged by the gang as a "good worker" or a "bum." Like most other aspects of life on the plains, threshing is ruthless, tough, and painfully revealing of character.

Not that I was thinking of any such things during my first day of threshing. I was too busy getting my load off, and urging my team back to the stooks for another. And inside me was developing a cold fury – such as invariably comes over me at times when I am feeling particularly inadequate. I would damned well show these hicks, I told myself, that I could pitch bundles better than they could. Of course I never did, but the fury kept me in there pitching. It wouldn't let me quit.

And I was to need all the backbone I could muster before that day was over. I never did catch up. Cap and Bowser and the others were constantly "working themselves into a rest." They'd pull into the threshing machine with a magnificent load while there were still a couple of loads waiting to get into the feeder. Then they'd lie in the sun and doze, or kid around with each other, thoroughly enjoying themselves. But me – I barely managed to get to the feeder as the empty rack ahead of me was pulling away, and then, immediately, I had to begin unloading.

When, at last, the long day ended I was in for one final humiliation from my benighted team of horses. Each of the other men, I noticed, unhitched his team from the rack when the outfit finally closed down, and left his half-filled rack where it stood. Then he simply leapt onto the back of one of his horses and rode the mile back to the barnyard. I tried this, too, but when I climbed onto Gent's back the damned brute bucked me off. Then I tried Lady, and she did the same. The first time I at least managed to hang onto the reins to prevent the team from running away. But the second time I had only one rein, and when I pulled on it the horses began to gallop around me in a wide circle, like circus horses in the centre ring. Round and round they went, with me in the middle hollering madly at them. Faster and faster they sped, until I became dizzy and let go. Then they galloped wildly across the field, trampling the reins to bits.

One half-hour later I dragged myself into the barn to find the team standing in their stalls. They still had to be unharnessed and fed. Outside the barn it was quite dark. I could see the lights of the house where I knew the rest of the gang were already eating, and probably regaling each other with tales of the greenhorn. Farther along I could see the dim, unlighted shape of the bunkhouse where I could collapse onto a bed. I was a terrible mess. My feet were swollen and sore. My down-at-the-heel oxfords were no good in the stubble field. My hands had blisters as big as twenty-five-cent pieces, and were so swollen I could scarcely make a fist. Finally hunger won out over fatigue, and I staggered to the house, washed up in the shed, and filled myself with roast beef, potatoes, corn, tomatoes, green peas, fresh bread, two kinds of cake, and two pieces of pie. After that I didn't feel quite so sad.

The next day was a little easier, and the next and the next. Gradually I learned enough to be able to function as a bundles-pitcher. I never managed to work myself into a rest as Cap and Bowser did, but I came to realize that it was futile to compete with those experts. They were professionals at their job; I would never be anything but a clumsy amateur.

For two full weeks all went well with Wick Thompson's threshing. The sun shone. The grain poured out of the spout and was hauled off to the elevators. Strawstacks grew on the stubble fields like great golden shaggy beehives. And then the rain came.

There was still about a week's threshing to do, so Thompson couldn't let all of his gang go. Cap and Bowser and Red went back to town, agreeing to return when again the weather was good. Morley had his regular chores to do, and that left old Blooming 'Arry and me alone in the bunkhouse.

There was no reading matter in the bunkhouse, and I envied Harry his private stock. Finally, in desperation, I asked him if he would lend me a book. He looked at me with his watery blue eyes, and then dug into his pack and produced a tattered volume. "Ever read this one?" he asked. "It's my favourite."

I took it from him and glanced at the faded title on the cover, *Three Men in a Boat*.

"No . . . I never have," I said, "but I'd like to."

"Don't know if you'll care for it or not. Kind of old-fashioned."

"That doesn't make any difference."

"About England, too."

"I've read lots of books about England. Hardy is my favourite."

"He is? Well then, you may like this." His attitude suggested a fond dog owner who is afraid that a stranger may not appreciate his pet. I took the book from him and began to read, conscious of his beady eyes upon me.

Well, anyone who's ever read the book can guess what happened. After about two pages I was giggling, two more and I was roaring, a couple more and I was rolling on the bunkhouse floor holding my sides. When I finally looked up there was old Harry beaming on me with a most beatific smile. "Well now," he said, "you're human after all."

Thus I was introduced to Jerome K. Jerome, who had died just two years before at the age of sixty-eight. I have re-read his great, funny book many times since that first time I discovered it by the dim, yellow light of a coal-oil lamp in Wick Thompson's bunkhouse. And every time it makes me laugh just about as hard as it did then.

Even more important than the pleasure I've derived from that book was the fact that it broke down the generation gap, the culture gap, the skill gap, and all the natural suspicion that had existed between me and Harry. He was to produce many more books from that pack – Proust, Thackery, Thoreau, Butler, and a couple by Eric Linklater, whom I also learned to appreciate. He was full of stories, too, was Blooming 'Arry, had a great sense of humour, and a fine feeling for beauty. And through all those years, in God knows how many threshing gangs and work parties, he'd been known only as "a funny old Englishman."

Quoting Proust, he taught me that "happiness is beneficial for the body, but it is grief that develops the powers of the mind."

Max Braithwaite's Ontario

The book, *Max Braithwaite's Ontario*, published by Douglas and McIntyre of Vancouver, was first written for another publisher, and it illustrates one of the difficulties that writers experience in their dealings with publishers. The book was contracted for in 1969 and written during that year and 1970. The editor was dissatisfied with the first draft but, for some reason, was unable to say exactly why. This state of affairs is common for editors, but the really annoying thing was that when parts of the book were rewritten they languished in the editor's office for months before I learned whether or not they were satisfactory. After my repeated phone calls, he finally gave me his reaction. He didn't like the new material.

After a year or so of this, we agreed to give up on the project. Later I learned that the man with whom I'd been dealing had wanted to write the book himself after he retired.

So I had a manuscript and no publisher. Some time later while talking to Jim Douglas, I mentioned the manuscript and he asked to see it. He liked it fine and with a few revisions published it. And it did very well for his company and for me.

It was Jim Douglas who, after reading chapter one, which is included here, decided to call it *Max Braithwaite's Ontario*. Other writers would write other versions of Ontario. This was mine.

I first saw Ontario when I was thirty-two years old, and I fell in love with the province immediately. I guess Ontario was in my blood, really. Both my parents had been born there and had emigrated to Saskatchewan while young, and Dad had told us all about the wonders of "Old Ontario," about stump fences, pitching suckers out of the creek with a fork, picking apples, making maple syrup, outings on the lake steamers. It was all wonderful to us who had been born on the southern prairies and who had never seen an apple growing, a creek running, a body of water larger than a slough, or a maple leaf.

Uncles and aunts who came to visit were all from Ontario. They looked a little different from us, somehow, and talked differently, too. One cousin of whom we were particularly fond, I remember, had a beautiful contralto voice and was a soloist at Timothy Eaton Memorial church. Eaton's . . . that was a familiar word, all right, because it was from there we got our long fleece-lined underwear and our shoes and even our kitchen cabinets.

After the Canadian Broadcasting Corporation went on the air in 1936, our house was full of Ontario. Every Saturday night in winter Foster Hewitt's thrilling voice described the action of everybody's favourites, the Toronto Maple Leafs. We hated the Argonauts and Balmy Beach teams that regularly clobbered our western football heroes. We heard the music of Horace Lapp and the comedy of Woodhouse and Hawkins, all from Toronto.

We were literally surrounded by Ontario. *Maclean's* magazine came into the house regularly and in it we read about the problems of Queen's Park, the growth of the mining industry, and the warnings of Grattan O'Leary that high taxes would ruin Canada. *Saturday Night* from Toronto was full of big glossy pictures of the city and portraits of famous Ontarians. Stephen Leacock, whose humour column appeared in the *Saskatoon Star-Phoenix* that I delivered for years, lived somewhere in Ontario, we knew, and the quaint people he wrote about lived there, too.

The book from which I received my most vivid impressions, however, was *The Man From Glengarry* by Ralph Connor. He wrote about all the great Ontario things. Lumber camps along the Ottawa River where sturdy Scotsmen (always the good guys) thrashed conniving, drunken Irishmen and boisterous Canadiens (always the bad guys); and about strange practices such as sugaring off deep in the dusky maple bush, barn-raising bees, logging bees, and box socials.

At school we got Ontario from all sides. That was where Champlain fought the Iroquois and made lasting enemies of them so that they burned up missionaries. Toronto was where Mackenzie marched down Yonge Street to fight our battles as well as his. Ottawa was where responsible government was finally granted, then Confederation. And all of it happened in Ontario.

In common with most westerners we had a mental picture of Ontario as fat, prosperous, and selfish. When weird things happened to the stock market or the price of grain, Bay Street was to blame. There was sophistication such as didn't yet exist on the plains. Terribly rich people dressed up in fancy clothes and attended horse shows at the Royal Agricultural Winter Fair, and very fancy balls at the Royal York Hotel. There was even a castle called Casa Loma.

Ontario was the place I yearned for. The publishers of magazines and books were there, and the producers of radio shows. People there would actually pay money for writing, and writing had become the focal point of my life. As I sat at my old upright Remington at five o'clock in the morning, indulging in my one-sided love affair with words, I directed my efforts to Toronto.

So, when the navy transferred me to Toronto in 1944, my wife and I approached the province with the wide-eyed delight of two kids going to their first fair.

Before we crossed the border from Manitoba the fun began. We were in the rock country, the spruce-tree country, the lake country of the vast, rugged Canadian Shield that covers nearly all of northern Ontario. As the train rattled over a river bridge or curved along the rocky shore of a beautiful lake we hugged ourselves and each other with pleasure. We were here. This was it. From now on life would be different. And it surely has been.

It took a long time for the train to cross northern Ontario, for it is very wide, as wide as southern Saskatchewan and Manitoba combined. Along the side of the track we saw the swaths of black and white spruce being hewn out of the forest for pulp-wood, and streams plugged tight with the floating logs. We saw mine shafts through the trees, too, and at Sudbury the great nickel smelters and the barren waste they have created.

By the time that rock and trees and lakes were becoming monotonous we left them and came into the rolling farmland of southern Ontario. Now we were in Dad's "Old Ontario." We were used to unfenced, flat wheat fields that stretched forever into the horizon. But these little garden plots of fields, neatly fenced, with beef and dairy cattle everywhere, were more like a story-book picture of farms.

The elm trees between the fields, too, were most impressive. Taller than any trees we had been used to and much bigger in diameter, they stood like huge umbrellas spreading their shade over the livestock below. Truly the most striking feature of Ontario farmland.

The barns surprised us, too. On the prairie farms the good farms had immense, domed-roof barns, painted red or black or white. But the Ontario barns were smaller, usually built into the side of a hill so that a hayrack could be driven into the loft and, most surprising of all, unpainted. Those unpainted barns almost offended us. They looked so out of place in the neat farmyards beside the big brick houses with lush fields on all sides, fields that obviously never lacked for rain.

The towns and cities became more numerous and as we continued south, we saw something we never saw in Saskatchewan . . . factories. Huge brick buildings with smoke stacks and names printed on them of familiar products we'd been using all our lives. I think the name that impressed me most was Neilson's chocolates. I'd gobbled up hundreds of their bars in my day but it felt odd to see an immense factory where they made nothing but chocolate bars.

Then we were in the Toronto area and the track was lined on either side with unbroken rows of dirty brick buildings like Massey Harris and Westinghouse and General Electric and Steele Briggs seeds. We went underground and pulled into the immensity of Union Station.

We had three children with us on that trip. Beryl was eight and pretty well able to look after herself, but Shari had just turned two and Chris had been with us only a couple of months.

So we had a child, a toddler, and an infant in arms, with all the extra gear and paraphernalia they require.

I was clutching a fistful of baggage checks for a baby carriage, a baby's basket and cart, two trunks, a couple of boxes tied with rope, and a number of suitcases. We found our way to the taxi stand. There we stood, unhappy, tired, hungry, and more than a little afraid of this city which, according to all reports, had none of the warmth and hospitality accredited to western communities.

Then a taxi driver came up to me. He was a small, wizened man with a squint and I knew I shouldn't trust strange taxi drivers in a big city, but he asked me where we were going and where our luggage was.

I handed over my tickets and watched as he scanned them.

"I can come back for this stuff. Get your kids into the car and I'll take you to where you are going."

We got into his cab and mighty glad we were to sit down.

"Could you please stop at a confectioner's store?" Aileen asked. "I have to get a bottle of milk for the baby's formula . . . ."

"In Toronto! On Sunday! Lady, nothing but the churches are open."

"But I've just got to have milk."

"I'll get you some."

And he did. When we got out to the residential area he spotted a milkman's rig clopping along the street and stopped it. So we had our milk and things looked better. The driver deposited us in front of the furnished house we'd rented on Bain Avenue for the summer and said, "Okay, you go in and get that baby fed. I'll go back for your stuff." He drove away with all my baggage checks and I didn't have his name or the licence number of the cab. Perhaps, I thought, I'll never see him again.

We carried the kids up onto the verandah and I reached into my pocket for the key. It wasn't there. It was, in fact, in the pocket of my uniform which was in one of the suitcases the cabbie had said he would fetch.

There was no way of breaking into a Toronto house. I tried

every window and door but they were all tight. A head poked out of the brick house across the street and a man asked me the trouble. Within a few minutes he appeared in his dressing-gown with an immense bundle of keys which he fitted and manoeuvred in turn. Finally he woke up another neighbour and it turned out that our landlady had left a key with him years ago. After rummaging through innumerable drawers and boxes he found the key and we were in.

Not long afterwards the taxi pulled up at the curb. Big, bulging boxes stuck out of the open rear trunk and suitcases filled the back seat, while the baby buggy and knocked-down crib were lashed to the top. The grinning driver was enjoying it to the limit. As we unloaded, he told me of his own kids and the exasperating move he'd once made from Kirkland Lake. Finally, after everything was in, I asked him how much I owed him.

He shrugged, "Oh . . . a couple of bucks?"

I gave him five and embarrassed him silly with my fulsome thanks for his services. He was glad to get out of there.

A few years later I wrote an article for *Saturday Night* in which I contended that Torontonians didn't deserve their reputation for aloofness and reserve, that I'd found it as easy to speak to strangers on the streetcar or in restaurants as I'd ever done in a western city. To help prove my point, I described these events of our arrival in Toronto.

Strangely enough the only person to take exception to this article was the late Frank Tumpane, a native Torontonian, who wrote in his newspaper column that I was obviously being more politic than factual. Torontonians, he maintained, were reserved and stand-offish and proud of it. It was one of their better qualities.

During the twenty-five years we've been in Ontario our enthusiasm for the province hasn't diminished. We still view the landscape with wonder. We've travelled to every part of the province where there are roads. We've camped in most of its provincial parks and swum in many of its lakes. Often on an afternoon we'll just take a drive through the rolling countryside and poke into old churchyards, peer through windows of old farmhouses, and inspect old roadside halls of the Orange Lodge that was once the most potent social and political force in the province. There is always something new to see . . . a small waterfall dropping down a limestone cliff, a deep gorge worn down by years of erosion, a drumlin to climb from which we can see for miles, a moraine cut by an old gravel pit where we can find fossils in the limestone, beautiful little rivers that wind through hardwood bush and have names like the Mad and the Noisy and the Pretty.

Or we go hiking along the Bruce Trail. We climb stiles over aged cedar-rail fences, fill our bellies with wild apples that grow everywhere, catch glimpses of shy warblers in the trees, and listen to the woodpeckers drumming. For the most heavily populated area of Canada, southern Ontario still has plenty of walking room and maple-lined back roads for driving.

Most of all, though, we love the rock country. When we reach the Severn River we are in it. Our kids have a song, "Rock countree . . . rock countree . . . we're getting into rock countree." The words aren't much, but the feeling with which they sing them is tremendous. There we see the big, rounded mounds of granite, pink and black and grey, or cut jagged where the highway has been blasted through. And clinging to it with often only inches of topsoil, the evergreen and poplar, white birch and hardwood trees. Fifty feet away from the highway you are in a forest, walking a carpet of leaves, stirring up chipmunks and red squirrels.

And the lakes! There is nothing anywhere like the lakes of the Shield. Their rock bottoms are scarred clean by the glaciers of thousands of years ago, and they are full of water so clear you can see ten feet down, deep and cool and inviting. Although many lakes are lined with cottages and noisy with roaring motor boats, thousands still have no roads to them at all. You have to fight your way through the bush carrying your canoe and gear, slapping at murderous mosquitoes and black flies. But when you get there and come out on a rounded rock and sit looking at the reflection of pines in that clear water, it's worth it all right. The peace and silence seep into your soul and you just want to sit. Some sit in boats pretending to fish, but other just sit and look.

That is Ontario to us. We admit to a tremendous prejudice for the province. We've become as smug and self-satisfied as we used to accuse the visitors from "Old Ontario" of being. We don't mind visiting other parts of Canada and being awed by the Rockies, astounded by the prairies, and captivated by the ocean, but we're always glad to get home to Ontario.

That's the place for us.

I Want
to Be Alone

This piece was written in the fifties for the now-defunct *Canadian Home Journal*, which at that time was edited by a fine woman named Mary-Etta MacPherson. Mary-Etta and I had what the psychologists call "good rapport," which simply meant that we vibrated on the same wavelength.

Looking back thirty some years I remember Mary-Etta as being quite old, but then in those days anyone over forty-five seemed old. She was a small woman with sparkling eyes, a ready smile, and a keen sense of humour. She helped me make a living and I helped her get material for her magazine. I liked her a lot.

What this country needs is not a good five-cent cigar or "unrunnable" nylons or disposable dishes, but privacy. We've solved all the problems except how to be alone. Every day we're getting closer together and hearing more and seeing more of each other. A school of cod on the Grand Banks has more room between individuals than a community of people.

For instance, the other day a friend (male) and I went into a restaurant for a quiet lunch and a chat. A pleasant girl in white teeth and dress said, "There's a table at the back . . . out of the way," and pointed over the heads of about a hundred eaters packed in like chickens in a feed yard. To get to our table we had to squirm and wiggle between people supposedly enjoying their lunch. We bumped into elbows, tilted chairs, dragged our coat-tails through bowls of soup.

Our table for two was in the middle of a row of tables for two squeezed up against the wall. Instead of individual chairs on the wall side there was a long leather-covered bench about nine inches wide that did for all the tables. If you spread your napkin a little wide you got it on the lap of your neighbour.

As I peered narrowly at the menu, a low, excited voice gasped in my ear. "Well . . . May says she's going through with it. The doctor's warned her but . . . and wait 'til I tell you . . . ." It was my neighbour on my left, a plump lady with a hat and a horrible secret to impart.

I didn't want to hear what the doctor had warned May against. I didn't want the ghastly details. I can't stand things like that with my lunch. Desperately I shouted at my friend. "You know, Jim, with a little more strength down the middle the Leafs might have a chance this year. It's this way . . . ."

I stopped in embarrassment because I wasn't looking at Jim at all, but at a thin brunette sitting closer to him than any woman has a right to sit to a man except her husband. The way that girl was looking at me made me blush . . . until I realized that she wasn't looking at me at all but at a red-faced boy next to me, whose arm got all tangled up with mine when either of us moved.

"I'm sorry, Harry," she breathed, "but I really didn't think you'd mind." These two very definitely should have been alone . . . with soft music and candles.

There was a time when restaurants provided separate rooms for separate people. Then they cut the walls down to partitions and then the partitions down to nothing. Now the idea is to get as many tables into a given space as possible. What does it matter if you take a forkful of your neighbour's combination salad now and then and listen to the most intimate details of his life. Privacy is expendable.

There's a fortune in it for the man who will arrange for people to be out of contact with people. Take the hotels now. Not long ago I was in a new hotel in Montreal. The rooms were small and neat and modern, but the partitions between them might as well not have been there.

I awoke in the middle of the night with a start. My room was full of people. Then I realized they were really next door, but I could hear them as plainly as if they'd been sitting on my bed. They were playing cards and telling stories about a convention they'd been at that afternoon and drinking beer.

Somebody called Gord, whom I judged to be tall with a moustache, was saying, "Did you notice Mildred's face when old George told the waiter to . . . ." The rest was lost in screams of laughter from the others. I might have laughed too if I'd known what old George said. They'd all been there and heard him, so that it wasn't necessary to repeat it. They could have had a little more consideraton for their neighbour, though.

It went on like that until four in the morning. I never got the point of one of their stories or, in fact, heard one in its entirety. Their laughter got louder, their remarks more ribald. It was all good clean fun. I'm no wet blanket. I just like to be in on the fun or completely out of it. Right then I wanted some sleep.

Everything nowadays is calculated to herd people closer together. The intimate little shop has given way to the jammed department store, where you rush for an elevator and battle thirty people to get into it. A fat man will walk on your feet and never bother to mention it. I said, "Excuse me," to a fellow in a revolving door once and he looked at me as though I were nuts.

The corner grocery has given way to the super supermarkets that hold thousands of people. The aisles are like highways. If you aren't fast on your feet you'll get run down by a cartload of tomato juice.

The thing is to get as many people into any given space and hang their comfort. The other afternoon my wife and I went to a movie. We went in the afternoon because in the evening the line-up reaches clear down the block and around the corner.

It was my favourite type of movie, featuring Gary Cooper and a South Pacific Island covered with palms and dancing girls. Throughout the news-reel, mostly about a dog show, and a sappy cartoon about a pig and a chicken who talked like Senator Claghorn and Jimmy Durante, we could see the screen fine.

Then came the dancing girls and the throng. An usher had said there were seats down front, but everybody who came down was sure there were at least two farther back. So they wandered back and forth in the aisles, peering through the dusk. Every time Cooper started swinging his fists or reached for a dancing girl, all I saw was somebody's hat and overcoat.

Of course, nobody expects privacy on a streetcar or bus, but in the privacy of your own car that you're only four payments behind with you should get some solitude. You get about as much as in a free picnic grounds on Wednesday afternoon. They've made the traffic lanes so narrow you can count the grey hairs on the motorist next you.

Not long ago I was in a line of rush-hour traffic. I wasn't minding the wait. I'd had something to eat downtown and, surrounded by steel and glass, I felt pretty much alone. Then I heard a tapping on glass, glanced out my window and there, about six inches from mine, was the dirty face of an ugly urchin. He stuck out his tongue at me and yelled, "Where'd ya think you're going, stupid?" His father reached over and clipped him, and for the next five minutes my ears rang with threats, howls, and a shrill voice from the back seat saying, "Stop beating the child!"

And our houses! We're building them so close together you can't get a dog kennel in between. We've knocked out the front wall and replaced it with a see-all picture window. And what's happened to all the partitions that used to separate the rooms? The first thing we do on taking over an old house is kick out all the partitions that aren't holding up the roof. We even saw doors in half so we can cut our privacy in half when they're closed.

Besides, telephones, radios, and television have made the phrase "privacy of your own home" as meaningless as a dentist's smile. Not long ago I sat down in my living-room to read a magazine. Presently I was aware of someone sobbing heartbrokenly. I looked up and saw a poor old grandmother clutching to her bosom a granddaughter whom she hadn't seen since the days of the underground in Italy. A TV program called *This Is Your Life* had flown that little tyke all the way to New York so that two million sensation-seeking yuks could watch the old lady cry on a seventeen-inch screen.

Intimate scenes of great sorrow or great happiness always

embarrass me. So I left the living-room and went into my study. From here I could hear my daughter's radio across the hall and a hearty voice asking a man to describe how he met his wife, while a studio audience howled.

I persuaded her to turn this down a little and started to read again. The telephone at my elbow rang. It was a cultured-voice female who wanted to know how I intended voting in the next election . . . as if it was any of her business. What in hell is the secret ballot for, anyway?

I went into the bathroom and took a shower. Just about the only private spot left.

Sometimes I get so tired of all this propinquity and prying and sharing of emotions that I feel like heading north to somewhere like Pond Inlet and living in an igloo with an Eskimo family. I'd do it, too, except that the place would probably be cluttered up with a National Film Board crew doing a picture on Eskimo life. Privacy, like the passenger pigeon, is extinct.

New Baby –
A Cure for
Middle Age

A writer may write about anything that happens to him or moves him. After rhapsodizing over rural life in "A Veteran Gets a Home" and then meeting head on the problems of living in the country, I countered with a piece titled "Ah Wilderness, Ah Nuts." Both were true; just another view of the same situation.

When our fourth child, Sylvia, was born in 1950, when I was thirty-eight and Aileen thirty-seven, I wrote an article for *Chatelaine* magazine about the joys of having a baby in middle age. When I read it now it does seem a bit syrupy, but I guess that's the way I was feeling at the time.

In any case, it enhanced my reputation for writing about anything that happened to me. A friend remarked laconically when he saw the story, "Max said to his wife, 'I've got a great idea for an article. Come on to bed.'"

Here it is.

While I am writing this, in the room across the hall from my office a four-week-old baby is yelling her head off. And I feel wonderful. Somewhere about the house my wife, Aileen, is bustling about with a can of baby powder in one hand, a diaper in the other, and a grin on her face like a horse player who's just copped the daily double. And this is a couple who are crowding forty and who for the past fourteen years have thought they were living for the day when no small people would clutter up their household.

Yes . . . a year ago we were ready to sink into a placid middle age . . . watching our family grow up and get married and produce grandchildren. Christopher, age six, started school this fall; Sharon, age eight, is in grade three, while Beryl, age fourteen, is in second year high. It looked like peace and quiet for the old folks at last.

But this little bundle of noise and irresponsibility has jarred us out of that, all right. We're right back into the formula, daily-wash, up-in-the-middle-of-the-night routine all over again. And we love it. We haven't heard any complaints from the kids, either. In fact, we'd say that this little twenty-eight day wonder is the best thing that could have happened to all of us. The whole family is involved.

We have discovered, somewhat to our surprise, that the second family is just as much fun as the first. In some ways a lot more.

In the first place, for some reason we're not going to attempt to explain, babies seem to be in style right now. Whereas a dozen years ago it was considered smart to have none or one child, now young married couples, and young people considering marriage, talk glibly in terms of three or four or even five.

Of the dozen women Aileen met during her stay in the hospital one was having her thirteenth child, one her eleventh (we're willing to admit these are exceptions), *five* their fourth, two their third, and only three their first or second.

A quick look at birth statistics confirms this. Last year the birth rate was up almost seven points above the Depression low of 20.4 and exactly three points above the wartime peak of 24.

All this makes it nicer to have babies. The announcement of a pregnancy – which used to be received like the announcement of a broken leg – now calls forth whoops of enthusiasm accompanied by offers of cribs, bassinets, clothing, and places for your other kids to stay during the crisis. Makes you feel ten years younger and right back in the swim again. Having a child is the "thing to do," and it's nice to be doing the "thing to do."

When we first realized that we'd contracted a severe case of pregnancy the old feelings of frustration, resentment, and terror momentarily descended upon us. This was a throw-back to the deadly Depression days and uncertain war days when our first three were born. Then it suddenly hit us. Why shouldn't we have another child? We could afford it – almost. We had a big enough house with lots of space around it and, who knows, maybe this little life cell just beginning was destined for big things. That kind of thinking gets you after a while and it wasn't long before we were pretty pleased about the whole thing and were throwing our chests out.

This attitude carried over to the kids, too. We told them early so they'd be in on the whole deal and we billed it as something supercolossal. Since it was getting on to Christmas, Aileen told them that this year we had a surprise present for them – something really extra special. Then we sprang the news Christmas morning, right after they'd opened their other presents and were standing in front of the tree knee-deep in wrappings. We'll never forget their reaction.

Beryl responded in what may or may not be a typical teenage way. "Mummie!" she screamed. "A flower girl for my wedding!"

Shari's face lit up like the Christmas tree. She hunched her shoulders, clutched her fists in front of her chest, danced from one foot to another and shouted, "Gee – a baby!"

Christopher just grinned all over his face. But he was pleased, too – largely because he saw everybody else was and wanted to get into the act.

Even after we explained that this would mean extra work for everybody, they were still all for it. We're not going to try to say that everybody pitched right in and worked uncomplainingly like eager little beavers. Nothing as Pollyanna-ish as that. But it is a fact that Beryl, who is a whiz around the house anyway, straightway began knitting little booties and sweaters, that Shari lost at least some of her allergy for the dish pan and Kiff became a pick-up man for his mother who was getting out of shape for much stooping. It convinced us that there is nothing to equal a coming blessed event to give children a sense of responsibility and appreciation for their home.

As further proof of this we offer two quotes – absolutely spontaneous and unsolicited. The first from Shari. Looking at her mother seriously one mealtime she suddenly grinned and said, "You know, somehow mothers who are having babies seem more previous than other mothers."

The other came from Kiff who showed that he appreciated – at least to some extent – that the state of pregnancy is no bed of roses when he thanked his mother quite seriously one day "for borning me."

And Beryl. When the going-to-the-hospital time conflicted with a long-planned and much-looked-forward-to vacation with friends at a northern lake, she insisted on calling off the trip. All through her mother's absence she kept the house in order and cooked the meals.

We may be wrong, but we think that sort of thing is good for children.

While we are on the subject of pregnancy, we can truthfully say that the older you are the easier it is. To be sure it's still an annoying, frustrating, tiresome business; but it fits in better with what you like to do when you are thirty-seven than when you are twenty-seven. Then we always had the feeling it was keeping us from a lot of fun – parties, dances, tennis games, and so on – which it was. Now it's not such a hardship to sit around and play bridge or charades or just talk with friends.

Instead of going away for a holiday last summer we stayed home and put the money and energy into the house. We got a lot of satisfaction out of having a new heating unit installed along with some much-needed plumbing repairs. And, surprisingly enough, we were just about able to pay for them on the money we'd saved through being confined to home.

We should report, too – and this is the experience of the other fourth-baby mothers we met – that this latest confinement was easier than any of the others. Aileen set something of a record for herself – out of bed on the second day and home helping look after a little Sylvia on the seventh. With each of the others the hospital stay was at least two weeks and the recovery much slower.

That brings us to the part about what it's like having a brand-new baby around the house again. And right here, at the risk of getting maudlin, we are going to get maudlin. We'd forgotten how much fun a small, helpless cuddly baby can be.

Beats a pup all hollow, or a trained seal, or a bowl of tropical fish or anything else you care to mention. Everybody is walking around with stars in their eyes. If you misplace a kid – or an adult, for that matter – you can be pretty sure to find them in the nursery just standing there beside the crib, staring at Sylvia, watching her make those silly little faces and talking the doggondest gibberish at her you ever heard.

It's true that Sylvia makes extra work, but there are five people around here just busting to do for her. In fact, we've had to work out a sort of sliding scale for the kids, based on age and proficiency.

Beryl is a whiz with babies and can do just about anything her mother can . . . including bathing Sylvia and changing her britches. And, what is more important, she is crazy about doing it. When she finally got around to going away for a holiday after the baby arrived she practically had to be kicked out of the house, and she left pretty definite instructions concerning the care of "her baby."

This provides us with the perfect built-in baby-sitter. We can slip out to a show or a bridge game feeling absolutely confident that all will be well when we get home. Naturally, we don't want to tie Beryl to the cradle either, but there are seven nights in a week and it doesn't take much organization to give everybody all the freedom they need. Besides, there are certain evenings when teen-age girls like to have the house to themselves.

Shari is permitted to hold the baby and give her the bottle. She is also pretty good at hanging diapers on the line. This chore she fits right into her cowboy games. The other day she was standing on the back porch pinning diapers like sixty and talking just as fast to Roy Rogers (Chris) who, with hands deep in jeans pockets and straw in mouth, was lolling against a tree down below. "These diapers aren't for my own baby, you know," she informed him. "I'm just doing them for Mrs. Blare who cooks at the Star ranch. Poor thing, she's been in bed ever since the baby came."

The old man takes care of the daily wash. One thing you can say for diapers – they at least have no buttons to rip off in the wringer.

Kiff gets into the act, too, by watching that the baby doesn't fall off things. He doesn't seem too disappointed that the baby turned out to be a girl instead of a boy, as he insisted all along it would . . . even though he did lose a two-bit bet to his oldest sister on the deal. We were afraid the girls might give him a bit of a ride, but Sharon's remark when he first came home from visiting friends during the time his mother was in the hospital more or less set the tone. Taking his hand she said, "When you see her, Kiff, you won't mind that she's not a boy. You'll just love her."

In fact, for one so small it's a marvel what Sylvia has done for family harmony, unity, and loyalty. She represents a project that everyone can whole-heartedly endorse. The kids are united in a common cause. Even Kiff, who is closest to her in age, has shown no sign of jealousy. Not long after Sylvia arrived his mother told him that the amount of love parents have for children depends on how long they've had them. At this he cracked back, "I guess that's because they can do more work for you."

For a while we fretted a bit lest, by having a fourth, we might be depriving the other three of some things they might want, but now we realize that was just another example of negative thinking. I don't know of anything we could have given the kids that would provide more fun, pride, and satisfaction. Shari and Chris have the drop on most of their playmates. Whatever the other kids may have, they've got something better – a real live baby sister. It's a rare evening after school that they don't lead a group of properly subdued, tiptoeing young sprouts into the nursery to show off their prize package. Watching the smug look on their faces is worth the price of the baby alone. Shari hit the nail on the head when she turned to a pigtailed moppet and demanded haughtily, "See, isn't that a lot better than any old rubber wettums doll?"

So far as we parents are concerned, we can truthfully say that we are getting more kick out of this baby than we did out of any of the others. We think that the reason for this is that older people like babies better than young people do. We used to marvel, when Beryl was a baby, how our grandparents seemed to get more fun out of her than we did. We put this down to the fact that they could have all the pleasure of the baby with little of the responsibility and drudgery. Now we don't think anything of the kind.

Young parents are inclined to take a baby too seriously. They are too tense, too afraid they may be doing something detrimental to the baby's physical or mental development. As you get older and have been through the mill two or three times you take things easier . . . are more relaxed about the whole business. You take time out to enjoy the baby. Besides, you are more self-assured. You've seen babies before, you know that they grow up to be children. And children don't frighten you any more, either. They're just kids, after all, not little monsters . . . almost as important as adults, but not quite.

At this point we can hear the screams of protest from some modern, science-ridden critics with the latest theory on child-raising at their tongue tips. "Those Braithwaites," they are probably saying, "will spoil that poor baby as no baby has ever been spoiled before."

Well, those critics can go climb a tree. We're not worrying, and we're betting that the kind of attention Sylvia gets here won't do her too much harm.

So, there it is, parents. If you find that you're getting a little bored with things, that you're growing old too fast, or if you just want to do yourself a big favour, we recommend the one-more-baby tonic. Producing a brand-new human life is still the most satisfying and exciting project two people can undertake. It is just about the only positive thing left in an otherwise pretty negative world.

And, we repeat, a new baby is good for a family . . . good for the kids and good for the parents.

Lusty Winter

Most writers, except those who write historical and science fiction, write from their own experiences. Of course, they create new characters, make up incidents, and devise plots, but the settings and time are often well known to them.

So it is with *Lusty Winter*. For some years Aileen and I have been living an isolated life in the Muskoka bush on the shore of Brandy Lake. We often go for days without seeing anyone else. Hence the Muskoka setting. And then, not too long ago, I visited a man who was living alone in a log cabin without benefit of electricity or plumbing and who had a lady friend who occasionally kept him company. Put the two together, add a career-woman wife and the menace of snowmobiles and you have the basis for plenty of complications and conflict.

Complications and conflict are the essence of all novels. Without them you have no story. Then add the "what if" element: "What if this or that had happened instead of what did happen?" Build the conflict and add to the complication and you are on your way.

The theme of this novel can be stated by quoting Robert Burns' "To a Mouse" – "The best-laid schemes o' mice an' men/gang aft a-gley,/An' lea'e us nought but grief an' pain/For promised joy."

Sunday morning. Just getting light. I go outside and look for the tracks of the snowmobiles. There they are all right. Just past my woodshed, where the old logging road runs. Maybe they think that's going to be their regular run. Well, they'll soon find out differently.

Old lumber from the woodshed. Long pieces of two-by-fours and shorter one-inch boards. I fix a trestle at each end and put the two-by-fours across. That does it. Now for a sign.

PRIVATE PROPERTY
NO TRESPASSING

Then I add, just to make sure that they understand:

SNOW MACHINES
PROHIBITED

It's quiet. Dead quiet. Off somewhere a burrrr against a tree, hard and echoing. A woodpecker drumming on a dead branch. The chickadees come and I feed them some sunflower seeds. They sit on my hand and look up at me before taking one and swooping off to a tree to open it.

I watch a black squirrel running through the trees. Along one thin branch and then onto another that bends and dips away down with him, but he clambers up and continues his running. Such balance. He stops, big tail curved back over his body in the classic pose. Away he goes again. A long leap this time – over six feet – grabs a skinny twig and climbs up. He's been at my bird feeder again. Got to figure a way to foil him.

A roar in the sky – away off. A jet plane goes over maybe seven miles up, leaving a long vapour trail. Going west. Vancouver, probably. In a few hours it will be there and the bored passengers will stuff their business papers into attaché cases and go to their meetings. They left Toronto at eight o'clock and will arrive there at ten. How long is it since it took a week to cross the country? And before that a month, and not so long before that it was impossible? And now a few hours. What have we gained?

A jay gives its squeaking-gate call from a hemlock thicket, then glides over to the step and looks around for scraps. Never tame that fellow. Doesn't trust anybody.

I put on my snowshoes and trudge the two hundred feet down to the lake. Snowmobile tracks. Abominations in the white snow. Half a mile out I find the track of my friend, the wolf. How long will he stay here, hunting for rabbits and mice on his island, with those damned snowmobiles around?

It will work, I tell myself as I trudge along. It will work. It's got to work. There has got to be some place where a man can find some peace and quiet.

This cocktail party in town now. Should I go? Do I want to become friends with those rich bitches in town? What have I in common with them? Nothing. I hate cocktail parties as a rule. All that talk without substance, Yatatayatatayatata. And somebody is sure to say, "Did you see Carol Burnett last week? She was so funny . . . ." American television deadening minds. The opiate of the people. Rising taxes on cottages. That will get a good going over. People getting tipsier, voices a little louder, opinions a little more inane.

To hell with it.

And yet. They are people. Women. And this funny feeling I have that something might happen at this cocktail party. What? Don't be a fool. Nothing will happen. But how will I know if I don't go?

So I decide to go.

I go in and shave, trim my beard, take warm water from the reservoir, and give myself a sponge bath. "I wash up as far as possible, then down as far as possible, and sometimes I wash possible." Where did I hear that? Oh yes. From Uncle Frank when I was visiting on his farm one summer.

My tweed jacket looks pretty good and the flannel trousers. Not a bad figure of a man at all. Still slim and trim and, thank God, not many wrinkles.

What else? Ah yes, the pipe. Don't often smoke a pipe these days, but it's good for the image. The retired English teacher image. Who ever saw a retired English teacher who didn't have a beard and a pipe? Makes one look intellectual. A man with a pipe is ten times as impressive as a man without one. Good hand prop, too. Gives you something to do with your hands – and your mouth. Definitely, the pipe.

I get into my parka and overboots, take the almost boiling kettle from the stove in one hand and the powerful oxide battery from behind the stove in the other. Go out into the snow and tramp the hundred yards to the road, where the Land Rover is parked in a shovelled-out space just long enough for it at the end of the driveway.

I pour a little boiling water on the engine's vital parts, attach the extra battery with the jump cable, and the engine responds immediately.

As I get into the Land Rover I notice over the trees to the left a big fat old raven soaring low. Don't see many ravens this far south. Probably hangs around the garbage dump down the road.

The air is crisp. The road winds in among the trees and rocks. Hardwoods, beech, maple, oak, with birch and poplar and hemlock and pine mixed in. The rock faces are all covered with waterfalls of ice. No cars at all on this part of the road.

Now and then the trees thin out to meadows. Farmland with farm buildings. Old Harve's place with its snug brick house and barn painted black. How like Harve to paint his barn black.

Then more bush again, the road going up and down following the contours of the rocky land. Twisting and turning. At the top of the hill I meet a big new sedan going about twice as fast as it should for this road. And almost in the middle of the road, too. I yank the steering wheel hard to right and miss him by inches, and barely avoid going into the high snowbank on the shoulder. Damned fool. City people always drive on country roads as though they'll never meet another car. Worst of all, it was pulling a trailer with two snowmobiles on it. Two, for heaven's sake. His and hers.

I catch glimpses of the lake here and there as the roads run along beside it. Deep bays and islands. Then I hit the main road, which is straighter and cuts through the rocks instead of going over them.

The town is like most towns in the Canadian Shield. About fifteen hundred people catering to hunters, fishermen, summer cottagers. A small sawmill doing its best to denude the country completely of trees. Filling stations, of course, plenty of filling stations. A couple of supermarkets and some small hardware, clothing, appliance, and variety stores. A new government liquor store that also sells beer, and churches of every denomination. Along the shore of a narrow bay of the lake (not Wolf Lake, but another larger and more fashionable one) are some big fine houses built by the lumber millionaires who opened up this country, and now owned by other millionaires who like to have a place in the country.

I drive up a winding driveway to one of these. At the end of the driveway is a parking area full of cars. Big sedans covered with chrome and low, wide sports cars with tires a foot wide and two exhaust pipes. Not a car among them, so far as I can see, that is over six months old. And, God help me, two black and white snowmobiles. Not much evidence of any gas shortage here, I can tell you. This is going to be fancier than I thought.

The house is big, with a verandah most of the way around it and two towers on the front with big windows that look out over the bay, and wide wooden steps up to the verandah. I can see through the big windows that the place is full. For a second I think of jumping in my Land Rover and getting the hell out of there. Then I remember Beatrice's prediction that I'll become so bushed I won't want to see anybody. So I shove my pipe in my mouth, straighten my cap, and go up the steps and ring the doorbell.

The door is opened by a boy of about sixteen whom I take to be the host's son. He wears a sweater and jeans and that inescapable air of confidence and self-assurance that comes from having money. He invites me in without looking at me, shouts to his mother, "Another one!" and beats it back up the wide stairway.

There are a few people in the entrance hall with cocktail glasses in their hands, talking earnestly. On either side are wide doors leading into two front rooms. From each comes the buzz of cocktail talk. I stand there with my cap in my hand waiting. Nobody even looks my way.

What in hell do you do when you are ignored? I desperately want to turn around and go out, but I can't do that. Mr. Sloppy-Sweater-and-Jeans has seen me and will report it to his mother sooner or later, and I will be put down as a rude fellow, which I am not.

A woman with a glass, a young woman with an elaborate hair-do and a long gown, looks up briefly and smiles tentatively.

I grin back, standing first on one foot and then on another. A big black Labrador bitch comes up and sniffs me. I reach down to pat; it snarls and I draw my hand back quickly.

That does it. I decide that, rude or not, I'll get out of here. Just as I turn a woman speaks to me.

"I don't think you're delivering anything. Or are you?"

I look down and there is a small, compact woman dressed in a very nice jacket and trousers. Man's clothing, but on her they look feminine. She has a blouse under the jacket and some lace about the throat. Above that is a small head with hair cut short and styled about her head. And on her it looks very good.

Hard to say how old she is. Somewhere between forty and sixty. Can't tell any more. Certainly not the prettiest woman I have ever seen, but from her comes warmth and friendliness and something else which I can only describe as sexiness. I want to put my hand out and touch her. Instead, she puts her small hand out and touches me on the arm.

I desperately want to be urbane and witty with this woman.

"Nothing but myself," I say.

Her eyebrows raise, questioningly.

"Uh . . . that's all I'm delivering."

She laughs and it's a nice laugh.

"Let me take your coat. I'm Susan Ridgeman, your hostess's sister. Gwen is somewhere around being hostessy."

"I'm George Wilson. I . . . uh . . . just got here." I hand her my parka and cap and climb out of my boots. My God, if I feel this much like a bumpkin already, how will I feel in six months of living alone?

She hangs up my things in a closet and, taking me gently by the arm, steers me towards the room on the right. "The bar is this way."

I was right. The women I see all look exactly alike, whether they are young or old. Each with the same careful fifty-dollar hair-do. Each with the same bored look. Each holding a drink and posing. The sixty-year-olds pose the same way twenty-year-olds pose. Why do they do it? Why do all women pose? Maybe they see so many pictures of models on television and in magazines that they can't help themselves.

The men are posing, too. Some with cigarettes, some with pipes, some with cigars. Old and young, they have that *Esquire* look. I think of Harve.

"Yahoots!" I murmur.

"What did you say?"

"Nothing."

"Yes you did. It sounded like yahoots."

"Please. I'll explain later."

"I should say you will. Here is the bar."

I order a scotch and water.

"Make it a double," Susan Ridgeman says to the man in the white coat behind the table, and then adds, "and I'll have a double scotch and water, too."

When we get our drinks, she takes me by the arm and guides me to a corner beside the fireplace.

"Now then, explain yourself." She has a most engaging smile.

"Well, I'm sorry. You see I've rather got accustomed to talking to myself, living alone as I do, and something about these people made me think of Harve."

"We'll come back to the part about you living alone later. Who is Harve?"

"A friend. A farmer who lives near my place. He's a wonderful guy, actually. Full of philosophy. He . . . uh . . . calls certain people yahoots."

Her laugh is even better than her smile. Not a big and loud, but genuine and pleasant. "I must meet your friend Harve. Where do you live anyway?"

I'm thinking now about her meeting Harve, or being at my place.

"I have a cabin on Wolf Lake."

"Wolf Lake? But nobody lives there. There's hardly any road and no hydro."

"That's right." I've had a couple of pulls at my drink and am feeling better.

She is looking at me with real interest. "You don't need hydro at all?"

"Nope. Big old cook-stove. Stone fireplace. Coal-oil lamps. They all work fine."

"Marvellous! I must see your place."

"And so you shall, I hope."

"Then let's go."

"Now?"

"This party is awful. Four politicians. Two doctors. A local artist. Two actors up from the city who admire each other. A writer who keeps saying he must find a place up here and keeps dropping names like Updike and Mailer. All yahoots." Then she frowns a pretty frown. "But maybe you want to meet all these people so that you won't be so lonely."

"I'm not lonely. And I've met all these people dozens of times at dozens of cocktail parties just like this one."

"Don't tell me you're a writer."

"Photographer. And you?"

"The sister of your hostess."

"And?"

"Oh, I have a job."

"Well?"

"Are you going to show me this marvellous cabin of yours, or stand here asking questions? If it's made of logs, I'll burst."

"It's made of logs."

"Come on." She takes me by the hand and electric sparks fly up to my elbow.

"But the hostess."

"Oh yes, Gwen and Eric. I'll explain. Don't budge, I'll be right back."

She is gone and I'm shaking my head. In a minute she's back with a tall woman with a fancy hair-do and a stately looking gentleman with a pipe.

"This is Gwen and Eric and they are very pleased to meet you and hope that next time you can stay longer."

"You must excuse Sue," says Gwen. "She's the impulsive one of the family."

I shake hands with Eric, who twinkles at me and says, "I have a feeling we will see you again."

Sue looks up at me and tilts her head. "I have a feeling you will, indeed."

Outside, the sun seems to be shining a little brighter. I know that sounds corny, but it is true.

"Shall we take my car?" She points to a low-slung Ferrari with wide tires.

"No, I don't like riding in those cheap modern cars; they might break down. Prefer my own." I point to the Land Rover.

"A Land Rover! I haven't seen one of those since the summer I was in Africa."

"You were in Africa? In a Land Rover?"

"Yep. Year before last. Before – " She stops with a grimace.

"Before what?"

"Never mind. Too early in this relationship for an exchange of confidences. Tell you what. We'll go in the Land Rover. I just can't resist. Then when you bring me back, maybe the party will still be on. These parties have a way of lasting. And you won't be able to escape."

"Okay, the Land Rover it is."

So we climb in. I'm not sure it's the drink, but I drive quite a bit faster than usual. No, it's just that I'm feeling young.

She loves it. And she loves the cabin even more. Stands in the middle of the room and keeps repeating, "I don't believe it. I just don't believe it." Somehow that phrase has always annoyed the hell out of me. Now I find it completely enchanting.

I light a fire with a flourish. And as I throw on one of my split oak pieces, I say, "Bucked by hand!"

Now why in hell did I say that? Trying to impress her? You're damned right I'm trying to impress her.

And it works, or at least seems to. "Do you mean you sawed that wood, and split it, too?"

"Yes, ma'am, my favourite hobby."

"And this?" She points to the camera set up at the window.

"My work. I'm photographing birds and animals. Trying now to get a shot of a flying squirrel with a flash I've rigged up. At night they climb up on that maple there and then fly down to the bird feeder."

"That's fascinating. What are the pictures for? I mean more

than the thrill of catching a delinquent flying squirrel filching food?"

"Thing I'm doing that I've always wanted to do. Now I've got the time."

"More," she said. "Tell me more."

"Wait." I go to the cupboard and get out the Chivas Regal. "You missed a party, so we'll have one here." I get down the glasses and then get some ice-cubes from the icebox.

"Tricky," she says, admiring the way I make ice-cubes from a block of ice by putting an ice tray on top and letting it melt its way in.

I hand her the drink. She sips it. "Umm good. You drink nothing but the best?"

"My one vice. What I save on hydro and rent and fuel bills, I spend on good booze. A habit I got from my father."

She takes a good big swallow of her drink, peering at me over the brim of the glass.

"Why are you living up here alone? Taking pictures of birds? Without even a television set? What are you, some sort of communist?"

My turn to laugh. "No. I live here because this is where I want to live. And this is the way I want to live."

"Alone?"

"Can't have everything. My wife is . . . well . . . . She's got her damned television show and . . . ."

"Television!" She sits up in her chair "Wilson! Beatrice Wilson! Your wife?"

"You know her?"

"No. But I've seen her on television. She's marvellous. Just what this country needs, a good, strong, independent woman!"

"Oh, Beatrice is all of those things. In spades."

"So I know you have children."

"Four. One born before the war. Three after. I was a little busy during those four years."

"Did you hate the war or love it?"

"Huh? How do you mean . . . love it?"

"Oh, some men did, you know. Oh yes indeed. It gave them freedom from family ties, adventure, a licence to letch." She scrinches up her eyes a bit and frown lines appear on her forehead.

"Like someone you know?"

"We're talking about you. Remember? Well?"

"I hated the war. Didn't particularly want a licence to letch, as you say. And the idea of shooting anyone . . . well . . . ." This is a subject I never get on.

"Let's forget that ghastly war. Tell me about your children. Boys or girls?"

"Two of each. The oldest boy . . . ."

She holds up a slender finger. "No, the girls. I know all about boys."

"Yeah, well, the oldest, Cindy . . . is . . . let me see – " Watch it, George, keep age out of this. "She's, uh . . . quite a girl. Has two kids of her own now." I motion to a picture of Cindy and kids that sits on my writing desk.

Susan gets up and takes the picture, studying it. "Nice. Don't you miss the grandchildren?"

"Yes and no." But I'm not thinking of grandchildren right now. Damn me, I'm thinking of how gracefully this woman moves and the curve of her ass as she moves – and what else?

"What does that mean?"

"What?"

"Yes and no."

"Well, it's great to see them come and great to see them go. That's the advantage grandparents have over parents. You can watch 'em go."

Her laugh is nice. I like a woman who laughs easily. I like this woman.

"And the other daughter?"

"Ah yes. Little Lisa. The baby of the family."

"And the favourite."

"Why do you say that?"

"Because, my friend, of the way you say her name. 'Ah yes, little Lisa.' You've probably spoiled her rotten."

Have I? Did I? I wonder. The youngest child. No doubt you're not so up-tight when that one comes along, having used up your up-tightness on the first three, especially the first one.

And yet she gave us the most worry. The drug scene. I hate to think of it even now. Nothing, but nothing can scare a parent like drugs. Thank God, we are past that. The sixties were a hell of a time for young people. No doubt about it.

"Is she married?"

"No. Lisa is a modern woman. She believes in her freedom. A product of the pill. Emancipated. Independent."

"How I envy her." Said with such feeling as to make me start. "God, how I envy her. Born thirty years too soon, that's me." An abrupt change. "But that's enough of that. To hell with the past. The future lies before us."

She stands up. Twirls around. "You know, it's getting hot in here." She removes her suit jacket. The blouse has short sleeves and her arms are white and plump. She walks around the room, running her hand along the varnished logs, looking at my best pictures pinned to the wall, picking up some of the carvings, and setting them down.

I watch her and know it is happening to me. I'm falling in love. Now. Right at this moment. This morning I didn't even know this woman. And yet here she is in my cabin and I'm falling in love.

That's one of the great advantages of experience. I know I'm falling in love. And I'm willing and eager to fall in love. No holding back.

What do I do?

If I were sixteen, the age when I first fell in love, I'd do lots of crazy things. Because love to me was something I knew nothing about except through the movies and magazine fiction and fairy-tales. Like everybody else of my generation, I thought it was something mysterious. And dangerous. Ah yes, dangerous. Because wasn't all true love ill-fated? Didn't its course never run smoothly? Didn't women who fell in love – Tess, Madame Bovary, Anna Karenina, Hester Prim – come to a sad and sorry state? And weren't all the men who fell in love the authors of their loved ones' downfall? Babies came from love. And babies belonged only in good established families.

My God, what a lot of junk I was brought up on.

Now all that is gone. Now the giving and receiving of love

can be natural and fun and doesn't have to last forever.

I stand up and she takes a small step towards me.

Then there is a banging on the door. A loud banging that can mean only one person. Harve! Crude, raucous, bumbling old Harve!

Harve doesn't wait for me to answer his knock, of course. He just shoves the door open and barges right in. That's good old Harve.

His glasses are steamed up from coming in from outside so he can't see too well. "Saw your rig outside and figured you'd be home." He doesn't have his teeth in, as usual. The tip of nose and tip of chin almost meet. "Jazuz Keeryst," he roars. "Cold enough to freeze the balls off a brass monkey!" Then he sees Sue. "Oh oh, sorry, didn't know you had company. Sorry if I've spoiled something."

That does it. Sue throws back her head and laughs.

"Harve, I want you to meet Susan Ridgeman."

"Sue," she corrects me.

"Sue, this is Harve Bright. My neighbour and closest friend. He . . . drops in from time to time."

"I'm very pleased to meet you, Harve," she says. "I know it sounds like a cliché, but I've heard a lot about you."

Harve just stands there like a big bear and stares at her.

"Hello," he says, finally. "I think maybe I'll run along."

I start to mumble something but Sue takes over. "Please stay. I really would like to talk to you. Mr. Wilson and I are refugees from a very dull cocktail party. He told me about his cabin and I insisted on seeing it."

"Yeah. Oh yeah. It's quite a place, all right." Harve is still staring.

I've recovered. "Take off your coat, Harve, and join us in a drink."

Harve mumbles something that I don't hear because he has his hands over his mouth. Something like "Dringawaddah." Then he sort of crab-walks over to the sink, bends down and fusses around some more, and when he turns around I don't know him.

For in place of that thin, grinning, toothless, often leering mouth are a set of the finest, whitest choppers seen outside a dentist's office. I realize I've never before seen Harve with his teeth in and I can only stand and stare stupidly.

Sue carries it off. Never lets on for a moment that she's just witnessed a transformation greater than Hyde to Jekyll.

"Please do join us," she says. And then I know that I love her.

What a difference teeth make. Harve's whole personality has undergone the complete reversal. He's now suave, urbane, and, God help me, atrocious. I'm embarrassed for my old friend. He sits straight in his chair instead of being that slouching, comfortable blob he usually is, and runs his hand nervously through his mat of hair to smooth it down.

He holds his drink of rum in his hand and, instead of slurping decently, sips daintily.

And his conversation. "Don't you think it's rather an unusual winter we are having?"

Sue allows that it is.

Then he adds, "But of course that's the outstanding characteristic of our Canadian weather, isn't it? Unusual."

I can't stand it. "What was it you said when you came in?" I ask. "Cold enough to what?"

But that doesn't faze the old fraud, and all I get is a disapproving glance from Sue. The little minx, she's encouraging this farce.

"I sometimes think that if it weren't for the vagaries of the weather, we Canadians wouldn't have any conversation at all," she simpers.

That's too much. "You damned betcha," I say. "It sure is a blue-assed sonofabitch the way we do go on about the weather!"

Unfortunately, I say this just as Harve is taking one of his delicate sips and the liquid goes down the wrong way. His face goes blue and he bursts out with a blizzard of half cough and half sneeze so violent that his beautiful teeth fly out of his mouth and land on Sue's lap.

"Goddamn those gum-pinching, side-slipping choppers," he roars. "I might as well put them in my ass and bite the buttons off the chesterfield!"

Soon after that Harve leaves.

But all the magic is gone, too.

"I really think we should get back to the party," Sue says.

"Yes, I guess we should."

She puts on her smart, embroidered coat with the cute little tuque to match. I watch her and there's a dizziness in my head. Something is happening to me here. Something has already happened. I don't want this woman to leave me, because if she does I may never get a chance to see her again.

Got to be careful, though. Don't frighten her off.

"Uh . . . Sue . . . ."

"Yes?"

"Uh . . . I'll drive you back."

She laughs. Relieved? Maybe. "I certainly hope so. It's a long walk."

Damn. Never was much good at talking to girls. "Yeah. Of course. Well, let's go then."

So I drive her back. All the way I'm trying to think of something to say, something that will make her want to see me again. But nothing comes. We reach the driveway and I'm desperate. I stop the car without parking it.

She turns a bright cheerful smile my way. Women! Don't they ever have these feelings? "You'll come in?"

"Uh . . . no. Look, Sue. Back there in the cabin . . . before old Harve barged in . . . ." It's not going well. "What I mean is . . . can I see you again?"

"If you wish."

"I wish. I wish. Will you come out to the cabin again? We can go skiing or . . . something."

"Yes, I think I will."

"When?"

"I'm not sure." And then she gets out of the car and I roar out of there.

Now what the hell does she mean by that, and what is happening to my vaunted freedom and independence? Anyway, I'm not dead yet. Not by a damned sight. But do I want to get involved? Hell, I am involved. It's a good feeling. Yes, it's a good feeling.

Chick

This story is about my youth in Saskatoon, which I remember
with some fondness and some sadness. That's where I went to
high school and normal school and saw innumerable movies
and played hockey and laughed my head off at the Dumbells
and finally got married. Both of my parents and my sister
Doris are buried in Saskatoon. Brother Hub still lives there, as
do most of his children and grandchildren.

I return to the city quite often, usually to flog a book or
make a speech, and I always take a walk along the river bank
where Chick and I fished for goldeyes and filled our bellies
with saskatoon berries and choke-cherries in season. The core
of the city hasn't changed much. There's a new library and
the *Star Phoenix* has moved to a new building and, oh yes,
they've torn down the Capital Theatre, which had stars on the
ceiling and represented the ultimate in cinema-house luxury.
I never see any of my old friends or class-mates but they are
all there, Jack and Bev and Peggy and Chick and Mac and the
rest, lurking in the shadows just out of sight.

I chummed with Chick in the
late twenties in Saskatoon, Saskatchewan. We both went to
Albert School and were in Sammy Trerace's room and then we
went to Nutana Collegiate Institute, but I was in A School and
Chick was in E School.

Chick was a skinny, wiry kid. He was a Norwegian. Chick
was a nickname, of course. His real name was long and hard to
pronounce, and I can't even remember it. Everyone had called
him Chick. His dad, the Reverend Oscar Thorwaldson, was the
pastor of the Norwegian Lutheran Church near the high school.

Chick was one of those kids who could do just about everything. In fact before he met with disaster, I considered him the

luckiest and best-adjusted kid I ever knew. He was far and away the best kid artist I've ever seen; his pen-and-ink drawing of the New York Woolworth Building, then the tallest in the world, correct in minutest detail, was the wonder of all his friends and teachers alike. It was done on a piece of white cardboard about two feet high and even the window sills were correct. He did it from a picture he'd found in the rotogravure section of a weekend edition of the *Chicago Tribune*, which was the most impressive picture supplement we got in Saskatoon. Chick was in grade seven when he did this picture, so that he couldn't have been more than twelve years old.

Another thing Chick used to do was make models of sailing ships. He'd get a piece of six-by-six pine about two feet long from Wentz's lumber yard and with a plane and a draw knife he'd shape it into the hull of a ship, which he'd hollow out. Then he'd get a piece of thin cedar and make the deck, marking lines on it to make it look like hardwood boards. He'd make the superstructure the same way. Then he'd hunt along the streetcar tracks for long, skinny pieces of bamboo that flew off the brush of the sweeper that kept the tracks free of snow. They were for masts and spars. Tiny bits of canvas cut and sewed made the sails, and crochet thread made the lines with which he could raise and lower them. A complete four-master, correct in every detail, it proudly sat for a month in the window of Walker's Drugstore on Second Avenue. The only thing he wasn't good at was school work.

Chick was my best friend, but I couldn't do any of the things he did so well. I'd try of course, but my drawings and cartoons were hopeless. I even got a piece of pine and started carving it, but I never got very far. That piece of pine may still be in the basement of Chick's house at six-twelve Temperance Street. (Our house was across the street at six-o-seven.)

Chick and I spent a lot of time together. I liked to stay overnight at his house and sleep with him in the attic room. One night when his mother and dad were out of town at a church meeting, it was so hot in his attic room that, after a pillow fight that didn't cool us off any, we went down into the cellar where there was a galvanized-iron cistern, about eight feet high and eight feet in diameter. It was full to the brim with rain water, a thin scum of dust covering the surface like a blanket. We lowered ourselves into this water to cool off, and then hauled our covers down from the attic and went to sleep on the kitchen floor. Chick's older brother Waldo, who worked in Walker's Drugstore, came home late from a date and found us there. He kicked our asses up the stairs to bed.

Chick introduced me to beaten eggs and Grapenuts which I've been crazy about ever since. We'd go down in his cellar where there was a case of twenty-four dozen eggs and we'd search around for two of the biggest ones. Then we'd take them up to the kitchen, break them into a bowl and beat them with an egg beater until they were stiff. Then we'd fold in sugar and Grapenuts and, man oh man, what a treat!

Oh, we had a lot of fun together, the quick, skinny, wiry kid and the slow stout one. Just the two of us, mostly. We'd play catch endlessly and fool around with a soccer ball and pitch horseshoes, and in the winter play road-apple hockey on the corner of Temperance and Fourteenth under the street light.

In the summer holidays we'd go fishing for goldeyes in the Saskatchewan River. The only kind of fishing I've ever enjoyed because there was always something else to occupy our time. The way we did it was to get a ball of strong thin cord down at the Fifteen Cents Store and cut it up into fifty-foot lengths. To the end of each line we'd tie a railroad spike and attach about five hooks back from that. Then we'd cut a willow gad about four feet long and shove it into the clay at the water's edge. We'd attach one end of the line and a small harness bell to the top of the gad so that when it wiggled the bell would announce that we had a bite. Then we'd bait the hooks with worms and pitch the spike out into the swift-running river and go about more important pursuits.

These included filling our faces with saskatoon berries or choke-cherries or gooseberries, whichever happened to be ripe at the time; trying to persuade my dog Pal, who hated water as no other dog ever has, to chase sticks that we threw into the river; endless wrestling matches (Chick was quicker and slipperier but I was stronger and heavier, so that we always ended up about even); chasing frogs; making whistles out of willow sticks; and generally having a great time. When a bell would jingle we'd rush to the gad and pull in the line with a goldeye or chub or sucker on the end. Then we'd string the fish on a line if it were a goldeye, throw it back if it were one of the other two, and go back to playing.

Sometimes we'd sleep out in a home-made tent in our back-yard so as to get an early start. Then we'd stuff some food into our pockets and walk the two blocks to the river bank, as the sun was getting ready to come up and the air was crisp and clean.

But every now and then Chick would disappear from me and I knew not why. I'd call at his back door and his mother, who was short and plump and knew very little English, would answer it, put her finger to her lips to signal quiet, and say in a hushed voice, "Hees wreading!"

I would go away baffled. I did plenty of reading myself in those days, but never anything so important that I couldn't drop it and go out and play. It wasn't until much later that I learned that every Wednesday afternoon Chick spent a couple of hours with his father "reading" the catechism.

These times I've been describing were when Chick and I were in grades seven and eight. Before we went to high school we both moved to other houses that were almost a mile apart. Besides, as I said, he was in E School and I was in A School so that we both made new friends and saw little of each other. But we were still friends.

Then, one day when we were in grade eleven, Chick announced to me that he was quitting school.

"What will you do?" I asked. The idea of quitting high school before graduation was unheard of. The modicum of guidance we did get consisted of lectures on the importance of finishing high school and going on to university.

"Go to Seattle," Chick told me.

"Seattle! What will you do in Seattle?"

"Go to art school. My brother lives there and he said he'd pay my tuition and let me live with him."

"Art school!" Suddenly I had a tiny glimpse of a whole new

world. A world away from the flat prairies and farmers and insurance jobs and the Sunday school. A world where people studied art and maybe made a living at it. "Gosh, that's great! When will you go?"

"About a week."

Right in the middle of the school term he was leaving. Thumbing his nose at the sacred portals of formal education. What a bold, daring, reckless, altogether keen thing to do!

I saw him off at the CNR station and just before he got on the train he said, "Maybe you could call Susie once in a while and let me know how she is."

"Susie?"

"You know, Susie Summers." Chick was blushing.

Yeah, I knew Susie Summers and I was surprised. She definitely wasn't in Chick's league. Her father was rich and they lived in a big house on University Drive. Besides, she was just about the prettiest and classiest girl in Nutana Collegiate. "You've been going around with Susie Summers?"

"Only once actually, but, well you know . . . ."

I knew all right. The guy was badly smitten. I wanted to tell him to forget all about her when he got to Seattle where there were surely plenty of girls, but I refrained.

And he didn't forget her. Alone and lonely in a big strange city, he thought of her constantly and built up their one date into a big romance. This can happen to a seventeen-year-old kid.

He wrote to me often and I answered his letters. He sent me some pictures he'd drawn at art school and I still have one of them. But mostly he talked about Susie. For two years he talked about her, especially after he'd graduated from art school and got a good job with a commercial art firm and, God help him, was in a position to get married.

"Everything I've ever done," he wrote in a letter, "I've done for Susie. When I had an exam I'd say, 'I'll pass this one for Susie.' When I was looking for a job I said 'I've got to get this one for Susie.' "

And what about Susie? Well, she'd graduated and gone on to university. I'd seen her once in a while. Couldn't help it. She was into everything. And popular. When I could scrape together enough money to go to a dance I'd see her, always surrounded by guys. I danced with her once and she was very friendly. "What do you hear from Chick?" I asked.

"Who?" She really didn't remember.

"Come on. You remember Chick Thorwaldson. Used to play the Hawaiian guitar at the Lits."

"Oh, yes. He was kind of cute, but why should I be hearing from him?"

Why? Uh . . . no reason." I thought, "My God, the poor guy was too shy to write to her. Instead he's been pouring out the tender feelings of his vulnerable heart to me! Well, can't do any harm. What they both don't know can't hurt them."

Then I got a letter from Chick saying that he had some holidays and was coming back to Saskatoon for a visit. He'd be there August 19 and could I meet the train? I knew he intended to stay at our house, which was fine with me, and I also guessed that he expected to take Susie back to Seattle with him, which was terrible.

I scarcely knew Chick when he stepped off the train. He'd grown taller and filled out some, but mostly it was the "big city" look of him. He had a new brown fedora that must have cost ten bucks anyway, and a new summer suit of the type you didn't get at Tip Top Tailors for twenty-seven fifty. New two-tone shoes with fancy socks. A classy dude.

But there was something else about him that removed my old friend a million miles from me. An air. A self-assurance. An easy way of talking and moving. Chick looked and acted and smelled of success.

I didn't have a car, of course, and so after we'd shaken hands and sort of cased each other I said, "Here, I'll carry your bag and we'll catch the streetcar over on Second Avenue."

"Never mind," Chick said easily, waving his hand at a taxi that pulled up in front of us. I felt foolish for not thinking of a taxi, but to tell the truth I'd never ridden in one. It was either walk or take the streetcar. And suddenly I was nervous about taking Chick home. All my brothers and sisters were living at home then and Mother had rented the attic to a couple of working girls. Chick would have to sleep with me. He'd done it plenty of times in the past, but I wasn't sure how he'd feel about it now.

But Chick's urbanity took care of that. He greeted my mother fondly and my older brothers and sisters when they came home from work and my younger brother whose face and teeth were stained dark brown with choke-cherry juice, but it was obvious that it wasn't to see us that Chick had returned to Saskatoon.

That evening after supper he was nervous and uneasy. He shaved again, although he didn't need to. Put on an even fancier shirt and different tie and lots of aftershave lotion. "Do you think Susie will be surprised to see me?" he asked.

"Aren't you going to phone her first?" I enquired uneasily.

"No. I want to surprise her."

And here's the part I've always felt bad about. Should I have insisted that he phone? Would that have helped at all? I doubt it. But in any case, I just couldn't bring myself to tell him.

It was a beautifully warm August evening, with crickets singing in the dry grass and the leaves on the box elder thinking about turning gold. The sun went down gorgeously and a harvest moon, big and red and beautiful, showed itself above the houses in the east. Chick phoned for a taxi and set out for Susie's house and his long-awaited appointment with destiny.

I was restless myself that night and paced around the house waiting for him. That he didn't return right away was, I thought, a good sign, but when twelve came and then one and then two and then three with no sign of him I began to worry. After all, Susie's house wasn't far from that same river on whose broad bank Chick and I had fished and played not so long ago. The river was swift with undertows so that no one ever swam in it. Just a few months earlier a despondent youth had leapt to his death from the Twenty-Fifth Street bridge. And that bridge was not more than a block from Susie's house.

I thought of phoning the police, but realized that could do no good. If he'd jumped he'd be beyond help. At four o'clock I went to bed, and shortly after that I heard the front door softly open and close and somebody coming slowly up the stairs in stocking feet. Chick undressed in the dark and climbed into bed beside me. I pretended to be asleep. I heard absolutely nothing from him, neither sigh nor curse nor sob. After a while I dozed off, but I knew that Chick never did.

The next morning Chick was a different person from the one who'd set out the night before as the conquering hero. Nothing you could put your finger on. What had happened to him is what happens in one way or another at some time to all of us. Idealism had been replaced with pragmatism. Youth was gone; manhood had begun.

Chick left for Seattle the next day. Neither of us mentioned Susie. I don't think he blamed her; I know I didn't. How can a girl know, after one casual date, what happens in the mind of a shy, sensitive youth? On that one date years earlier she'd kissed him good night at the door, but how could she know that her soft, moist lips had burned their way into his heart and would remain there for all time?

A Privilege
and a Pleasure

The memory of the sixties still makes parents and many twenty-five-year-olds squirm for it was a decade of upheaval unprecedented in Canada. Teenagers, high-school students, university students . . . all youth . . . were in rebellion. Parents, preoccupied with making it big and driving impressive cars and entertaining each other, were often in shock. Their kids were into drugs, into sex, obsessed with doing their thing. Many young boys and girls just took off from good homes and either hit the streets in the big cities or went hitch-hiking across the land. And then as suddenly as it had begun, like a bad fever, it all stopped. But the feeling, the shock, and the terror lived on with many parents.

Sociologists and behaviourists and others who like to get big grants for research have been studying the phenomenon ever since, and they are just about as close to finding a cause as those who study the influenza epidemic of 1918. There doesn't seem to be any rational cause for its beginning or its end. Oh, after the fact, it's easy for preachers and others to shake accusing fingers in this or that direction, but nobody knows. Perhaps it was the Vietnam War or the atom bomb that triggered explosions that destroyed millions of dollars worth of university property and caused riots and killing on campuses. Some people, such as June Callwood, quietly went about the task of providing shelters and food and medical help to the wayward wanderers, but the rest of us parents shook our heads in bewilderment and hoped that it wouldn't happen to our kids.

And that's part of what *A Privilege and a Pleasure* is about. It is also about ecology, service clubs, and the influence of one powerful personality on an apparently well-ordered and tranquil Ontario town.

It was a quarter to eleven when
Mal finally got home from the Foursquare meeting. That bunch
of "old women" on the executive, he thought. Quibble over
everything. All they had to do was set up committees . . . Publicity, High-school Liaison, Clean-up Week, and so on.
Shouldn't take more than half an hour. But those guys. Love to
talk . . . that's their trouble. If I ran my business like that,
nothing would get done.

When he opened the door, Julia called from the kitchen,
"That you, Din?"

"Nope. Me. Din still out?"

"Yes, she is. And she's been out past midnight every night
this week."

"What about her school work?"

A shrug. "She's completely lost interest. School phoned
again today to ask where she was."

"Where was she?"

"I don't know. She's been skipping classes all week."

"And you didn't tell me?"

"What's the use? You've got enough worries. Besides, what
could you do?"

She was right, of course. What could he do? Can't drag a kid
to school by the hair. "What did she tell you?"

"Nothing. Won't even talk to me. I can't get a thing out of
her." Julia had a drink of gin and tonic in her hand. It wasn't the
first. "I can't talk to her at all. Not a bit. She hates me."

"That's crazy. Why in hell would she hate you?" He got
down the bottle of scotch from the kitchen cabinet and poured
himself a good one. "Why?"

"I don't know, Mal. I honestly don't know. She's always
been . . . you know . . . a private person. Not one to talk about
her feelings, like Bob, for instance. But now . . . Mal, what's
happening to her?"

"Nothing. Just a phase. You run into them. Business goes bad
and you can't explain it . . . but it always improves."

"Mal, this isn't exactly business. This is our daughter."

"O.K. . . . same difference." He went down the steps to the

recreation room, jangling the ice in his glass. She followed him, forehead wrinkled with worry.

"Relax. It's barely eleven. The kid's seventeen, remember. Hey, we're just in time for the news."

He switched on the television for the national news, settled back on the couch to watch. The newscaster, a smooth-haired, lean, smiling young man, said that the main items involved Kosygin's visit, the Common Market, and further protests over the underground blast on the tiny island of Amchitka.

"God-damned protesters," Mal grunted. "What the hell's wrong with people anyway? Whatever their government does they're against it. Don't trust anybody any more." There were a bunch of them on the street in front of the American Embassy, carrying placards and shouting while the cops watched.

He got off the couch to turn off the set when Julia gasped. "Wait!"

He turned to face her. "What the hell? It's a lot of crap!"

"She was there! I saw her. Just for an instant with a group of hippies. I swear!"

"Who?"

"Din. I know it was Din!"

"Where?" He wheeled around to look at the set but the news item now was the federal minister of finance explaining the new tax laws. He wanted to turn back the way you can with a home movie. But the picture was gone forever.

"You thought you saw Din . . . with that bunch?"

"I know it, Mal! She's run away . . . to Toronto. Oh my God! I've heard of kids doing that, but I never thought Din would. Where will she stay? What will she do? My God, do you realize what they might do to her?" She was close to tears.

"Take it easy, honey. You're not sure it was Din. After all, those kids with their long hair all look alike."

"Don't talk like that. We've got to get her back. We've got to go and find her! Come on!"

"Just a minute, honey. That picture was taken hours ago. There won't be anyone near that place now. Even if it was Din . . . and mind I say *if* it was . . . we couldn't find her."

"What are you going to do then? Just sit here and drink?"

"What's the drinking got to do with it?"

"Well, we've got to do something. Phone Daddy! That's it. He'll know what to do."

"No . . . we won't do that. If she was in Toronto she'll probably be back tonight. It's only fifty miles. And the T-bird will eat that up in . . . ." As soon as the words were out, he realized that he had recognized the sound of the old T-bird's engine the other night . . . the one he had sold to that hippie.

"T-bird? What T-bird? Mal, do you know who she went with? Who she's been seeing?"

"No, not exactly. One night last week when she came home late, I thought the roar of the car that drove away sounded like one I sold to a guy some time ago. A real weird guy, in some ways."

"What? And you never told me?"

"It wasn't anything to tell . . . really . . . just a flash impression. You know how I can detect the sound of an engine. But I could have been mistaken." He got up and went to her. "Now, don't get upset. We'll just wait. Chances are Din'll show up any minute now. Just cool it and have another drink. She'll come . . . you'll see."

So they had another drink and they waited.

They heard Bob come in upstairs. One thing, Mal thought, never need to worry about that kid. A good head on his shoulders. Knows what time of day it is all right. From his room came the wail of Bob Dylan. No use bothering him about his sister. The two didn't seem to have anything in common any more.

It was two in the morning when Mal and Julia finally went to bed. Mal tried to comfort her, but she turned her back on him. Her last words were, "My God . . . what will Daddy think?"

The next morning, as he grabbed a fast bite for breakfast, Bob said, "Hey, where's the brat?"

"She stayed over at Marg's last night," Julia answered hurriedly.

"Funny. I saw Marg at the Love-in Club, but no sign of Din."

"That's a stupid name for a club!" Mal exploded.

176

"You know, Dad . . . make love, not war. That's us. Of course you gotta understand it's love in the broader sense, not the more intimate sexual . . . ."

"Bob!"

"O.K., Mom, for gosh sake don't blow up. You must have heard of the sex revolution. They keep us up on all the latest stuff in school these days. Old Bernard, who teaches sex education, knows almost as much as some of the more backward kids. But to get back to Din . . . ."

"Never mind Din." Julia's lips were tight. "Do you hear? Not one word about her at school! Is that clear?"

"But what's up?"

"Nothing is up."

"Uh . . . just a minute," Mal cut in. "Something is up. Din didn't come home at all last night. We know she wasn't at Marg's . . . . Just a minute, Julia, I'll handle this. We're up against something here. We thought we saw her on TV, in a mob of protesters at the American Embassy."

"Wow! Great stuff."

"Now listen, you . . . ."

Mal stopped Julia. "We want a little family solidarity in this instance," he said to Bob. "Dig?"

"Course I dig. What the heck do you think I am? And don't worry, Mom, she'll be home."

He went out then, but Mal could see that he was worried. Julia was on her third cup of coffee. "Well, big brain, what do we do now?"

"We don't panic at all. Jesus, I feel like I'm living through that movie we saw last week. You know, *Taking Off*. We laughed ourselves silly at it."

"It's not funny! This is real!"

"Remember how the guy went out in Los Angeles or wherever it was to look for his daughter and got stoned." Mal couldn't help laughing.

"It's not funny! I'll kill that kid when I get her! One thing for sure, we aren't going to the police. Would those newspaper hacks like to get hold of this? Colonel Worthington's granddaughter disappears."

"We may have to go to the police, honey, some time."

She snapped, "She's only been gone one night."

"I know. I'm only thinking ahead. How about your father? He must know something about the city . . . ."

"Not the part of the city she's likely to be in. No, I've now decided to keep the colonel out of this."

"Oh come off that colonel crap . . ."

"Colonel! Colonel, Colonel, Colonel, Colonel, Colonel Colonel, Colonel!"

He grabbed her and held her arms tight at her sides while she squirmed to get loose, still shouting.

"O.K., O.K., we won't fight over this. We mustn't. We won't tell the police and we won't bother your father with it. I'll go into Toronto. I want to see the finance company, anyway, about that new plan we're starting. I'll go to that Rochdale place on Bloor Street. According to the papers, that's where all the runaway kids show up sooner or later. Maybe I'll get a lead there. But we won't do anything for another day . . . O.K.?"

She clung to him then. "Oh Mal, find her. Please. I want her back!"

Mal got off the subway at the Museum stop and walked west on Bloor towards Rochdale. On the west side of the museum he passed a gate that led down some steps into the university grounds. Down there he could see green lawns and immense maple and oak trees whose last red and yellow and purple leaves were drifting softly down in the autumn sunlight. Boys and girls were walking along the paths and some were lying on the grass, feeding the squirrels or reading or necking. To the right of him the street was packed with cars and the air was foul with carbon monoxide.

Two girls approached him. About thirteen, he judged . . . long, stringy hair, dirty tattered shirts, patched jeans and bare feet. He noticed their feet. They were very dirty and one had a cut on the big toe. The little blonde girl came directly towards him. "Have you any extra change, sir?"

Mal stopped, bewildered, "Extra change? Why . . . why do you ask?" It was a damned fool question. He knew that as soon as the words were out. But she'd taken him by surprise.

She smiled again, and Mal noticed that one of her front teeth was missing. "Because we are hungry."

"Hungry? But . . . where do you live . . . I mean . . . ."

The girl frowned. "Never mind. Come on, Ruth."

"Wait!" Too late. There were ten people between them now. Ten people who paid absolutely no attention to the little drama. Damn! I could have given them something. They sure as hell did look hungry. Then another thought. I bet those little broads would do anything for you if you gave them a dollar. The thought turned sour. His only daughter was here. Maybe she had to ask people for money on the street.

From St. George Street, Mal could see Rochdale College. Twenty stories high. Looks like any respectable high-rise apartment building, he thought. But he knew better. He'd read and heard plenty about this place. Newspaper and television reports had been full of it. "Waste of taxpayers' money." "A home for hippies and drug users masquerading as a new experiment in education." Reports of young people falling from seventh-storey windows onto the sidewalk below. Police raids with doors smashed in by fire axes. Elaborate warning systems. Arrests. Mal felt his anger rising. Jesus Murphy! Why do they keep a place like this right on the edge of the university grounds? The world is crazy!

As he got closer he could see brightly coloured curtains on the windows, psychedelic paintings on the front, goofy signs. On the widened sidewalk in front of the building were a dozen or so motor bikes. And a huge grotesque statue that Mal supposed was meant to be a pregnant woman or something.

Most of the bottom floor was an immense health-food restaurant. Beside that, a small door that Mal judged to be the entrance. He stopped before it. Well, this is it.

He pushed open the door and was in a dimly lit hallway. Sitting on a table, legs dangling, was a huge youth with a heavy beard and hair down to his shoulders, granny glasses, tight black T-shirt over bulging chest, patched jeans, wide black belt from which dangled an immense bundle of keys. On his breast a ticket with Rochdale Security printed on it. Mal was very aware of his own expensive fedora, clean-shaven face, well-cut suit and gaberdine topcoat.

A sign on the table read:

NOTE - YOU MUST GIVE THE FULL NAME AND ROOM NUMBER
OF THE PERSON YOU'RE GOING TO VISIT TO THE SECURITY
GUARD IN ORDER TO GET INTO THE BUILDING

The bearded one slid off the table. "Yeah?"

"I'm looking for my daughter."

"Does she live here?"

"I don't know. She left home." Mal's anger was growing. "Didn't tell us anything. Just left."

"Figures."

"What?"

"A lot of kids leave home now. And a lot of them come here. What's your daughter's name?"

"Din . . . Dinah Mawhinney."

The security officer turned and studied the page of ragged scribbler and turned back. "Sorry, nobody here by that name."

"Could she be here without you knowing?"

The guard indicated the sign and shook his head.

Mal didn't know what to say next. The whole thing was so stupid. "What kind of a place is this, anyway?" he demanded.

The guard grinned. "It's a school. We grant degrees . . . Ph.D., M.A. Want one? They're for sale."

"For sale? A university degree?"

"Aren't they everywhere?"

"No. Christ, you've got to study and learn a lot to get a degree."

"You got one?"

"No, but my wife has."

"Uh huh."

A couple of others had sauntered up and were listening. One coloured man in a black jacket was eating an ice-cream cone. "What's up?" he asked.

"This man's lost his daughter."

"Lost her. She fall out of his pocket? Or maybe somebody lifted her?"

"No, damn it!" Mal said. "She just didn't come home last

night. And we saw her on television at this crazy Amchitka protest."

"Um hm. And where might home be, eh?"

"Godston. It's a town about fifty miles from here. Up in the hills."

"And why would a chick leave a nice home in a nice little town . . . up in the hills . . . and come to this bad old city? Tell me that, Daddy-o," a skinny, stoop-shouldered youth with a pony-tail asked.

"How the hell should I know?" Mal took Din's picture from his wallet and showed it around. "Have any of you guys seen her?"

One small man with a big beard and about four strings of beads around his neck whistled. "No, I haven't seen her. But I'd sure like to. I'm not sure I'd send her back to Godston, though."

Mal bristled. "You filthy little bastard!"

The small man moved towards him. Mal was ready.

"Cool it!" the guard warned. "Mister, your daughter hasn't been here."

Mal turned to go. He had all he could take of this crowd.

The guard called after him. "If I were you, I'd try Sanctuary House. Kids with no money . . . new in the city often go there. They see a lot more of these waifs than we do. It's not far from here. North on Spadina. White front."

Mal went back into the bright light of Bloor Street. Directly across from him was an immense stone church, big and solid and familiar. Well, at least somebody here goes to church, he thought. Got some idea of decency. He crossed Bloor at the crosswalk and stood reading the church sign:

IS THE BEAT GENERATION
REALLY BEATEN?
Rev. G.O. Ackerman
Sunday 10 A.M. : 8 P.M.

As he passed the big door a harried-looking cleric came out and walked rapidly west. Maybe he could help, at least give some advice. But the cleric was swallowed up in the hurrying crowd on the sidewalk.

Mal stood for a moment looking after him. Then he turned.

Just over two blocks east was the Park Plaza Hotel, a place where he'd been a few times after salesmen's meetings. The roof-top bar, he knew, would be cool and quiet and, most important, civilized. He went towards the bar.

Back on Bloor Street three double scotches later Mal felt 100 per cent better. Even the street looked different. Businessmen leaving offices and stores and hurrying for their cars. Mal's kind of people.

He strode along past store-fronts and restaurants and the stately old York Club back to St. George Street and on to Spadina. Here he turned north, keeping a look-out for a house with a white front. On his side of the street the houses were ancient and stately. Of stone and brick, they had once housed the well-to-do, the secure. Now they sheltered – two and three families to a house – the poor and insecure. Houses waiting to be torn down and be replaced by high-rise apartments that already crowded together on the opposite side of the street.

Two blocks north Mal found the white front. A house like the others, only more battered. A girl with long hair and jeans was sweeping off the verandah that was cluttered with tattered old chairs, tables, and other bits of furniture. She stopped her broom, tossed her hair over her shoulder and smiled at Mal as he came up the walk. Probably high on pot, he thought.

"Yes, sir, can I help you?"

"Sure can, honey. I'd like to see whoever is in charge of this here establishment."

"That will be Miss Quinn." She made a dainty half curtsy like an usher at a high-school play. "Come this way. What is your name, please?"

Mal told her and followed her into a large hallway and through a door into what had once been the library and was now an office. A busy young woman at a table looked up.

"Charlie, this is Mr. Mawhinney. He wants to talk to you about his daughter."

"How did you know that?" Mal demanded.

"Just a guess. I'm right, aren't I?" She smiled and left.

The room was square and untidy with an untidiness that told of much work being done by not enough people. The walls were covered with what looked like the original wallpaper and pinned onto it were notes, magazine cartoons, signs, posters, and incredibly striking pencil drawings.

But most striking was the woman sitting in the middle of the room at an old kitchen table covered with papers and books. Charlotte Quinn was small, not more than five-two, with glowing chestnut hair that hung down the sides of her face. Luxuriant hair. It gleamed in the light from the big window, reminding Mal somehow of the tail of a horse he'd once owned. But softer, and he wanted to feel it, hold it.

Her eyes were large and dark and looked directly at him. But the feature that dominated her face was the mouth – thick-lipped and ripe and mobile. Mal stared at that mouth.

She smiled at Mal and her smile was friendly. "Please sit down. The chair is hard, but it's all we have."

He pulled up the kitchen chair and sat on it, not more than three feet from her. Her blouse was of some sheer material, open at the neck and through it Mal could see the shadow of two beautiful breasts. He stared at the breasts and tried not to. "Thank you," he said, and continued to stare.

She wasn't at all embarrassed or put out by his staring. She was a girl used to being stared at. She smiled, picked up a pencil, and asked, "Some boring details first. What is your daughter's name and have you a photo?"

Mal supplied both, still staring. He wanted to be brilliant and witty and charming, but all he could say was "That's her."

She looked at the photo. "Charming. Eighteen?"

"No. Just seventeen. Still in high school, as a matter of fact. When she goes."

Miss Quinn checked through a page of a black-covered scribbler on the table. "I'm quite sure she hasn't been here. What makes you think she might be in Toronto?"

"We saw her. On television. With a crowd of hippies at that stupid protest over the atom bomb."

The eyebrows lifted. "Stupid? Then you approve of the Amchitka test?"

He had until this moment, but now he wasn't sure. "Well . . . they say it's safe. I guess they know what they're talking about."

"Others say it isn't safe."

"I know, but . . ."

"Have you been to the police? There were some arrests after the protest."

"No. Not yet. Don't want to unless absolutely necessary. But I've been to that cockamamie dump they call Rochdale."

She looked up from the scribbler where she'd been rechecking for Din's name. "Oh? You consider Rochdale a cockamamie dump?"

"Isn't it?" He leaned towards her feeling the effect of three double scotches on an empty stomach.

"Some of my good friends live there. A professor, an Anglican minister, a writer. I teach art class there every morning."

"You do? Why?"

"Because it is a school, and because I'm an artist."

"Oh. Then why . . . ." He looked around the room.

"I work here every afternoon for two hours. A volunteer."

"Why?"

"Let me see. I don't want to sound like what our prime minister calls a 'bleeding heart,' but I just happen to think some kids are having a rotten time and I like to try and help them."

"What is this house?"

"Hmm . . . that's rather hard to explain. Call it a refuge. A really remarkable lady began it to help the kids on the street who have no place to go. The city loaned the house. It's going to be torn down to make way for the expressway. We get money where we can."

"What kind of kids?"

"Hungry kids, confused kids, kids on drugs, mentally disturbed kids. Some are so undernourished that we send them straight to a hospital."

"That's terrible. What the hell's eating kids these days?"

She leaned back, tapping her white teeth with a pencil. "I've often wondered about that. Suppose you tell me. You are a parent. And your child has left home."

"Oh, God. Here we go again."

"Pardon?"

"Always the parents." He rubbed his hand wearily over his forehead. It had been a long day. "When I was a kid I was the one to blame. Now I'm a parent and I'm still to blame. Kids to-day have it too easy. Now when I was . . . ."

"Please." She held up an incredibly small, incredibly pretty hand. "Not that old bit about the paper route and the chores and walking to school!"

He giggled. "No, not that." Those breasts again. So round, so firm, so fully packed, he thought. Aloud he said, "How about coming out with me? A few drinks. A few laughs. A good dinner. And . . . ."

"And?"

He realized that she knew what was in his mind. "O.K. I withdraw the offer. But I wasn't just making a pass. No kidding, you get to me. You really do."

The girl from the verandah stuck her head in the door and said something Mal couldn't exactly make out. Miss Quinn stood up. "I'm sorry, Mr Mawhinney. A minor crisis with one of our new arrivals. You'll have to excuse me."

"Sure. Of course."

"If your daughter comes here or if we hear of her, we'll contact you immediately. Leave your address and phone number with Jean." She held out her dainty hand and Mal clutched it. She looked at him quizzically and took it away. "Goodbye," she said. "And good luck."

She was gone. "God, what a woman," Mal thought. "There is one hell of a woman." He gave the girl, Jean, the information required and went back out onto Spadina. His mouth felt dry. "I need a drink," he muttered, and steered a direct course for the Park Plaza.

The Western
Plains

One of the most successful series of books with which I've been involved is *The Illustrated Natural History of Canada*, published by McClelland and Stewart with Peter Crabtree as editor-in-chief and Pierre Berton as editorial consultant. It was to be a Canadian Centennial Series and the work was begun in 1966. Each of the eight books in the series was to deal with one geographical region of the vast land that is Canada. And each book was to be profusely illustrated with photographs, paintings, line drawings, and maps. All of which, of course, cost a great deal of money. So much, in fact, that the company ran out of funds and had to spend a number of years trying to raise more. The books were not finally published until 1970. They are, I think, the best description to date of the land forms, geology, plant life, animal life, and ecology of Canada.

Since I had become a sort of resident expert on the Great Plains of Canada and had written a great deal about them, I was offered the job of doing the book titled *The Western Plains*. Although I had a considerable knowledge of the plains, the work required a great deal of additional research. Some people thrive on research; I find it tedious in the extreme, preferring creative writing. But I stuck with it and finally, with the help of my wife Aileen and the editors, managed to produce a creditable book.

The section that follows is about grass. From earliest times, the many members of the grass family, which include wheat, oats, barley, and the other cereals along with a host of forage grasses, have been essential to the life of animals and man. The plains have often been described as "a sea of grass," and "the bread-basket of the world" because of the millions of bushels of wheat grown there each summer. Grass in its many forms is as important to the plains as the forests are to British Columbia.

When a prairie dweller thinks of home he thinks of grass – looking with eager anticipation for the first signs of grass in bare places between the banks of melting snow; playing catch on the new grass; lolling on a grassy bank, lazily pulling out the stems and eating the tender tips; watching fields of grass undulating in the wind; playing in the long grass, finding mouse runs and rabbit paths; watching a dog jump through the grass in search of prairie chicken; inhaling the smell of new-mown hay.

His memory may go back much further, to sitting on a wagon piled with window frames and boards, urging a team of horses along a trail through the grass; of tethering his team in the grass for the night; of gathering grass to make a softer bed for his wife and children; and finally, when he got to his homestead site, of ploughing up the sod in straight rows and piling it like bricks to make four walls, and placing those window and door frames in the walls to make his first sod house. Some are still living who remember these things.

Before the settlers came the southern plains were almost completely under grass, more than one hundred and forty different species; some tall, some short; some growing in bunches, others in solid patches; shooting up green in the spring, flowering and producing seed to be scattered abroad by wind and animals; dying and rotting away to provide the basis for the humus-rich brown and black topsoils of the prairies.

The grass was doing a lot more than feeding the buffalo, antelope, and other grazers. Grass, with its great mat of fibrous roots, was keeping the prairie soil from blowing away. Many a settler learned this to his sorrow years later after he had removed the grass cover and left the land naked to the winds. Only in recent years has he come to realize its importance, and put back much of the land to grass.

Although most of us walk on grass every day – even if it's just a two-by-four plot outside the apartment building – few stop to think of what a remarkable plant grass is. It will grow literally anywhere: half-submerged in the water, on the soggy shore; on the windswept desert, and on the highest mountain top; in the Arctic and on the equator. No place is too wet or dry, high or low, hot or cold for grass. It's almost impossible to kill grass. Trample on it, bury it, cut it to the ground, break it, burn it; it will rise again.

Why is grass so durable? Pull up a grass plant and look at it. Or better still, dig it up so that the roots can be seen. Of all plants grass has the best structure for survival. In the first place, most wild grasses are perennials. Like the trees, the plant grows year after year from the same root, at the same time spreading seeds to produce new plants. Many of the domestic grasses – wheat, oats, barley, rye, corn, for instance – are annuals, but they have the tender care of man to help them survive.

Let us assume the grass dug up is creeping red fescue, a favourite grass in the aspen prairies. It's an extremely hardy plant, growing in almost every part of Canada; it also flourishes in such diverse regions as North Africa, Eurasia, and Iceland. In fact, there are over a hundred different species of the fescue group of grasses growing in many parts of the world. The creeping red variety is the best known member native to the plains.

Look at the flowers of the plant. They are arranged in a rather loose-knit group known as an "open panicle"; other grasses have spikes, columns, sickles, spears, closed panicles, and feathery panicles that wave back and forth with the slightest breeze. Each of these flowers is wonderfully constructed for producing seeds. In the first place, pollenation is a simple matter, requiring the services of neither bees, nor other insects. The tiny pollen grains from the stamens of the grass flower find their way to the pistil of the same flower or one nearby, into the ovary, by contact or by being carried on the wind.

The seeds are encased in tough coverings called glumes (the chaff on wheat) which in many varieties are formed like wings to carry the seeds off on the wind. Others have little hooks on them for catching onto the hair of animals and thus hitch-hiking a ride to a new location. Creeping red fescue seed, like all grass seeds, is oval-shaped and pointed. A tiny spear-like awn attached to the seed digs into the hides of animals or into the ground for germination. The spear, needle, and porcupine grasses have long, tough awns that twist and turn with varying moisture conditions causing a corkscrew action that actually propels the seed into the ground.

The grass stem is hollow with few exceptions. Its job is to hold the flowers and seeds up above the ground so that they can germinate and be distributed – and they do this by one of the most ingenious mechanisms in nature. The hollow stem is separated into sections by solid nodes that not only give the stem strength, but perform another specialized job when the plant has been blown or trampled down. The turgescent tissue of the nodes contains, cells capable of elongating under the influence of gravity So, when the plant is in a horizontal or oblique position, the cells on the lower side of the node stretch and thereby bend the stem upwards to the light, the sun, and the wind.

When the stems are broken or bitten off, new ones will immediately and rapidly grow from the crown at the base of the plant. This is also true of the leaf, which accounts for the fact that lawn grass has to be cut a couple of times a week during the growing season. The leaves of the grass plant are few and they are long and narrow. The limited surface area ensures that a minimum of water is lost through transpiration. At the same time, the leaves have the power of curling themselves closely around the stem in time of drought so as to cut down even more on water wastage.

But it is the incomparable grass root that plays the major role in the plant's ability to survive and spread. It is a fibrous root of unbelievable extent and flexibility, that may grow to depths of ten feet, and can spread out at least that far. The total lengths of a fully developed grass root, if it could be completely separated from the soil, would measure well over 350 miles. But such separation is impossible, because literally billions of root hairs, thinner than the thinnest thread, probe among the clay and sand particles to absorb the droplets of moisture that cling there. Thus, when there has been no rain for months, these hard-working fingers squirm their way deeper and wider into the subsoil, to take in water that may have been suspended there for many weeks.

Besides their remarkable water-gathering ability, the grass

roots help propagate new grass plants. Underground rhizomes and stolons at ground level grow out from the main stock. Each is noded, and from each node there springs a new grass plant, capable of beginning the entire process over again. Attempts to eradicate quack grass from a plot of ground give sufficient frustrating evidence of this process. No matter how many of the scaly, yellow, underground stems are dug up, there are always others left in the ground to grow more quack grass.

This same plague of the lawns is a variety of wheat grass, *Agropyron repens*, much valued by stock raisers of the aspen prairie for its durability and beast-fattening quality. Besides its ability to survive anywhere under almost any conditions, grass constitutes a complete diet for grazing animals. Its high protein (up to 25 per cent) assures growth, while the starch it contains provides plenty of energy for galloping across the plains to avoid enemies. Grasshoppers, rabbits, ground squirrels, antelopes, buffalo – all live exceptionally well on a straight grass diet.

For those mammals, including man, whose stomachs can't handle the grass stems and leaves, there is the grass seed. Long before the white man came and used the land to cultivate grasses, Indians were grinding the plump seeds of Indian rice grass to make flour for bread.

Grasses are highly specialized plants. Some grow best on the heavy clay soils, others on the light, sandy soils; some like moderately wet weather, others like it dry; some like shade, others prefer bright sunlight; some even grow in sloughs. Thus each region and condition of the plains supports those grasses best suited to it.

When the first settlers came to the eastern part of the plains, either by York boat over Lake Winnipeg, or by Red River cart from the south, they found themselves neck-deep in grass. There was plenty of pasture for their cows and oxen and horses; more than enough to store as hay for the long, cold winter. It was grass unlike anything they had seen before, stretching from horizon to horizon, covering the heavy clay soil of the Red River Valley. They called it big bluestem, or blue-joint turkey stem, or simply beardgrass. Its proper name is *Andropogon gerardi*.

The word *Andropogon* comes from two Greek words, *andros* (man) and *pogon* (beard), because the head of the grass is bearded with long hairs, branching out from the bottom to resemble a turkey's foot. In a good wet year its pith-filled stems will grow to a height of six feet, and cover the ground so thickly that it is hardly possible to walk through it. But as the land that grew it was also the best for growing wheat, most of the big bluestem was ploughed under. Today only scattered stands are found along the Souris and Assiniboine river banks.

There were other grasses too, because in all parts of the plains grasses are mixed, with one or more varieties predominating. On the lighter, sandier land, as found in the Interlake district, grow dense stands of a smaller brother of the big bluestem, known appropriately as little bluestem. As a forage crop it does not compare with its larger relative. Only in the early spring are the leaves succulent and palatable to grazing animals, and when it matures, it drops drastically in both tastiness and protein content.

As the settlers moved farther west along the southern margin of the plains, they encountered progressively shorter grass that, instead of growing in thick patches, tended to grow in bunches. These are the grasses of the shortgrass region, and the most common of them all is blue grama (*grama* comes from a Spanish word for grass). This tough, short, sickle-headed grass provided good pasturage for cattle and other grazers during the early spring, but was not so popular during midsummer. Perhaps most important, it is a favourite with all grass eaters during the late fall and early winter when many other grasses can't be eaten. Blue grama can take a lot of trampling and grazing and still survive.

On the same cattle ranges with blue grama are found june grass, *Koeleria cristata*, and spear grass, *Stipa comata*, often called needle-and-thread grass. June grass rarely grows in thick stands, but rather scattered among the other grasses, except in the mixed grass region between Kindersley and Kerrobert where it is the dominant grass. Spear grass is the kind that irritates; the sharp-speared seeds stick to clothes and prick the skin, but it's one of the best forage grasses of the West. Even so, studies have shown that it takes about five thousand plants to feed one cow for one day.

Further north in the mixed grass and aspen grove regions are three more members of the needle grass family: porcupine grass, western porcupine grass, and green needle grass. The latter is a great favourite with all wild and domesticated grazing animals. Besides that, it has a high protein content that is maintained after curing, and is satisfactorily resistant to severe changes in the weather, since its roots often penetrate to a depth of ten feet.

Another grass that likes the heavy clay soil of the aspen grove region is the indomitable wheat grass family. Four varities are native and four have been introduced from Europe or Asia. Of the native varieties, western wheat grass, *Agropyron smithii*, is the most common. It has the advantage of a triple root system, one feeding near the surface, another delving five feet into the subsoil, and a third that creeps along just under the surface and propagates new plants. Thus it has survived many droughts. Northern wheat grass is almost identical with western wheat grass and will grow equally well in clay or sandy soils. Slender wheat grass and awned wheat grass are the other two native varieties, both of which provide pasturage, natural and cultivated, in the aspen grove prairies.

In the western portions of the aspen grove prairie the *Festuca* family of grasses is prevalent. Ranchers in the foothills and Cypress Hills like the bluebunch fescue because of all the grasses in the area the cattle eat it most readily. Besides, the plant has a deep root and spreads from tufts. Even in the short-grass regions it is a good grass for irrigated areas. Its first cousin, creeping red fescue with its creeping roots, is also used to line irrigation ditches in Saskatchewan and Alberta. Many ranchers cultivate it both for summer feed and for hay.

Rough fescue requires an annual precipitation of at least eighteen inches and so is much better suited to the Cypress Hills, where there is more moisture than on the flat surrounding prairie. It grows well in association with the aspens and pines of the region, and its only drawback seems to be that in the spring the protein content is low. All the fescues are susceptible to overgrazing. If the plants are kept cropped too low, weeds, other less desirable grasses, and sedges will take their place. It's a wise rancher who adheres to the carrying capacity of the land – 1 to 3.5 acres per cow-month.

These grasses, together with many others – the Canadian Department of Agriculture lists sixty-three varieties – covered the plains for millions of years before man appeared on the scene. Some, with their close relatives the sedges, grew in the wet, low places and adapted themselves to an abundance of water. Others fought it out in the dry sandy places, establishing their roots, consolidating land against the pressing winds. Wherever there was a patch of earth or swamp, some grasses grew.

Finally the white man arrived on the scene with his bags of cultivated grasses: wheat, oats, barley, rye. He tore up the millions of acres of native grasses and planted the foreign varieties, thus upsetting the natural growth pattern of the prairies. Today, after thousands of experiments, he is still trying to better adapt himself and his crops to the stubborn land.

Saskatoon Berries

In the summer of 1954 Aileen and I took the family on a camping trip to western Canada. As usual, I had some research to do along the way but mostly it was an excuse to get out and live under canvas for a month or so.

Colin was only a year old at the time and every evening we had to wash his diapers. Sylvia was four, Chris ten, Shari twelve. Beryl, who was eighteen, didn't come because she had a job in Ontario.

We drove those long, tiresome miles through northern Ontario and then, like going out of the door of the house, we hit the prairie with its big sky and waving wheat and wild-flower filled ditches. As usual I was giving the kids their mandatory geography lesson about the plains and as usual they were ribbing me about it. We'd got almost to Winnipeg when I abruptly applied the brakes, pulled over to the shoulder and shouted, "Saskatoon berries!"

The reason is explained in the following piece.

The other day I went walking down a long, winding, seldom-used trail through the birch and hardwood trees, up and down over the humps of granite to a beautiful point on the shore of Brandy Lake. Down close to the rocky point there is a sort of meadow with some black spruce trees and beaver-chewed aspens and a lot of grass and wild flowers. On the edge of this I saw a spindly tree with many trunks, about eight feet high, with purple and red berries on it.

Saskatoon berries!

Most of them were worm-damaged or covered with hairy fungus or swelled to twice their size, but a few were edible. And as I stood there eating this lush fruit, another walker came down the path. He stopped and stared in obvious disbelief and horror.

"You eating those things?"

"Damn betcha."

"But aren't they poisonous?"

"If they are, I've been dead a long time. Been eating them since I was a kid in Saskatchewan."

"What are they called?"

"Saskatoon berries."

"Never heard of them."

He walked on towards the lake, shaking his head, and I stood there amazed and a little sad. It was hard to think that a Canadian had never heard of saskatoon berries.

They grew all over the prairies, in coulees and along the river banks. They provided vitamins and good taste for the Indians and the early settlers and everybody else, and especially for kids. As a matter of fact, I don't think I would ever have lived to maturity, at least not as strong and healthy as I've been, without the aid of saskatoon berries and choke-cherries. We picked them along the river bank in Saskatoon (named after the berry) and stuffed them into our mouths by the handful. Along with the family, we went on berry-picking expeditions and filled wash-tubs with them. Then Mother would put up dozens of quart sealers full of preserved berries, and we ate them all winter as a fruit or in pies. You could also make jams and conserves of them.

There were no fresh fruits or vegetables in our home during the long, long winter months, and the saskatoon berries, along with a few other wild berries that grew in abundance, were most important. There were no vitamin pills and only cod-liver oil to provide some extra vitamins. Like the Indians before us, we depended on wild fruits for survival.

The prairie Indians had a different system of preserving their saskatoons. Lacking preserving kettles or sealers or sugar, they dried the berries in the sun, as they dried long strips of buffalo, deer, and antelope meat. Then they pounded the dried meat and berries into a fine powder, which they mixed with melted fat. This was poured into skin moulds and allowed to harden. This pemmican could be eaten as it was, or boiled with herbs and roots and other edible wild plants to make a stew. It has been described as "the most concentrated food known," and it helped make life on the prairie possible.

I like to think of those Indian men, women, and children on their berry-picking expeditions. The hot summer sun beating down on them as they filled their skin containers with berries. The children stuffing their mouths with the lush purple fruit, and dashing into the Saskatchewan River when they got too hot. And I like to think of me and my younger brother Dennis running along the winding paths of the south side of the river in Saskatoon, stuffing ourselves with berries and now and then going into the water to cool down.

There was no television or even radio, or electronic games to distract us and waste our time. In some respects, we were like the Indian children. Our feet were bare, our clothes minimal, our skin tanned almost red, and our principal aim in life to keep our bellies full.

The Year of
the Killer Flu

As I have often told my kids, and anyone else who would listen, I have been sick only once in my life. And that was in 1918 when I was six years old and our entire family, along with hundreds of thousands of other Canadians, came down with the flu in the terrible world-wide influenza epidemic that followed the First Great War.

I think I almost died. I can still remember the days and nights of delirium I spent with an ultra high fever, and the worried look on the face of Doc Brown, Sr., who later was a victim of the same disease.

But no one in our family died. After all, if Great-grandmother Copeland and her nine kids could survive the rigours of a six-week voyage in the hold of an immigrant ship and cholera and diphtheria and pneumonia and the other ailments that plagued those gallant people, we surely could handle a little thing like the flu.

So when Ian Sclanders, then articles editor of *Maclean's*, suggested a Flashback about the flu I jumped at the chance. There was plenty of information available. The *Toronto Star* library and the Toronto Reference Library had files on the flu. At the University of Toronto medical school there were doctors and scientists available to discuss it. And in Brampton, Ontario, I found a retired doctor who had been in practice during the epidemic and had good stories about it. In addition, a retired undertaker remembered how he and others of the profession worked day and night to take care of the victims. And of course there were my own personal recollections. The following is the result.

The fall of 1918 was one of the toughest Canadians have ever known. Germany had its back to the wall in the Hindenberg Line but wouldn't quit. Each day's casualty list showed more than a hundred Canadians killed in action with many more wounded, missing, and sick. At home there wasn't enough coal for the nation's fires or sugar for its tea. There seemed no end to death and suffering and hardships.

But Canada and the rest of the world hadn't seen anything yet. A killer far more deadly than German guns or gas or bombs was stalking across the earth in the sheep's clothing of the common cold. This was the influenza pandemic (an epidemic of world-wide scope) of 1918, the worst of its kind ever recorded and, next to the plague of 542 AD and the Black Death of 1348, the most deadly scourge mankind has ever seen. It hit the country full force in October and during that one dreadful month killed an average of almost a thousand persons a day.

Everybody called it Spanish flu – possibly because first news of it came through Spain – but to this day nobody knows exactly where it began or why or, for that matter, what caused it. But we do know that it killed more than twenty million people, most of them in the prime of life – twelve million of them in India alone, more than two millions in Europe.

In North America more than a half a million U.S. citizens died, and almost as many Mexicans. It is impossible to discover exactly how many Canadians died, but estimates range between thirty thousand and forty-five thousand. The Department of Health and Welfare in Ottawa states, "one-sixth of the population was affected."

Flu broke out everywhere: in crowded cities, on farms, in lonely trading posts. Many people believed the germs were carried on the winds, and nobody has come up with a more satisfactory explanation for their almost simultaneous appearance in so many widely scattered areas.

It would be almost impossible to find a Canadian over forty who doesn't remember the flu, either because he had it himself or someone in his family did. It struck with devastating suddenness. In Nokomis, Saskatchewan, in my own family, my father

G. A. W. Braithwaite, my mother, and the seven of us children were all in bed at the same time. A visiting uncle was also sick. Mother barely managed to prepare meals. Neighbours were no help because they had it, too. Finally the town policeman came to the house to milk the cow and kill a chicken. Both of the town's doctors were so busy that the father of one of them came out of retirement to assist. I remember the old doctor promising me a bag of chocolates for taking a dose of castor oil – I was six at the time. I never received the candy because the elderly physician, like so many other medical men, worked himself into a state of exhaustion, caught flu, and died.

Similar stories are told about nearly every Canadian community. In Calgary a young mother whose husband had been killed at the front caught the flu and died suddenly, leaving two small children. In Montreal a sick mother was found in bed with her two-year-old daughter dead beside her. A Brandon, Manitoba, wife remembers desperately giving her critically ill husband cold baths at night in their apartment above a hardware store while from the street below she could hear the eerie rattling of the carts collecting the bodies of the day's victims.

Prairie homesteaders, living great distances apart without telephones, had no means of calling for assistance. A woman near Hanley, Saskatchewan, remembers how she and her family lost several of their best cows because no one was strong enough to milk and feed them. Their greatest problem, she remembers, was keeping the wood-burning stove supplied with fuel in below-zero weather. By taking turns they barely managed enough trips to the woodpile.

The Rev. T. D. Jones, a retired United Church minister now living in Streetsville, Ontario, has vivid memories of the fight against the flu in Lamont, Alberta. The four schools in the area were converted into hospitals and every able-bodied person recruited to help take care of the sick. "The thing I remember most vividly," he says, "is how the big, strong, deep-chested chaps seemed to take it the worst. One young man came to the school where I was in charge and said that although the doctor had ordered him to bed he really wasn't sick. His temperature was 104.5. We put him to bed but soon he was delirious and we had to tie him down. Poor fellow died within two days."

A Halifax doctor tells how on some ships, especially those with Asiatic crews, more than half the ship's company would be down with the disease. Many ships were held in quarantine and their crews taken ashore for treatment.

Montreal was one of the hardest hit cities. Three thousand and twenty-eight citizens died in one month, 201 of them on the worst day, October 21. In his book, *Four Centuries of Medical History in Canada*, John J. Heagerty estimates that one hundred thousand Montrealers had the flu. Persons living along streets leading to the cemeteries, he states, kept their blinds drawn to hide the "almost continuous procession of hearses and other vehicles conveying the dead to their last resting places." Coffins were piled up at the cemeteries, grocery wagons were pressed into service to supplement the hearses.

An undertaker in Toronto recalls, "At the peak we were holding funerals every hour, day and night. I once went for three days and two nights without sleep. Several times we buried whole families, mother, father, and two or three children, within one week. Another undertaker downtown had twenty-three bodies stacked in a garage for a day because there was no room in his establishment. Double and triple funerals were common.

"It was almost impossible to get help. As soon as an assistant learned that a person had died of Spanish flu he was out of there like a shot. At the cemetery they were storing bodies in vaults while the grave diggers got caught up."

Doctors who worked through the pandemic remember it as their hardest and most hopeless job. A Brampton, Ontario, physician remembers finding whole families in bed and not a nurse to be had. "It wasn't like anything we'd ever seen," he said recently. "It struck so fast that people were seriously sick before they realized it."

The first signs were usually severe pains in the back and loins. A businessman who walked to work in the morning was stricken at ten and carried home on a stretcher. A carpenter couldn't complete the sawing of a board. One woman took ill in the middle of a game of whist and couldn't finish the hand. In some cities hotel managers hired nurses to take care of guests suddenly hit by the flu.

The attacks were characterized by exceptionally high fever, severe pains in the limbs, neck, eyes, and head, prostration, and often delirium. Sometimes there were violent nosebleeds or stomach disorders. Often the lips and other parts of the body turned blue. The disease ran its course in two to three days, after which the patient either recovered rapidly or developed secondary infection – pneumonia or empyema – in which case there was little hope. Often the attacks were attended by a feeling of deep depression; suicides were common.

Doctors prescribed complete rest along with quinine or castor oil or brandy. Sometimes these remedies worked and sometimes they didn't. "If everybody could have stayed in bed and got all the rest they needed, my guess is that the death rate would have been cut in half," one doctor says.

Investigation has shown that there were three waves of flu during 1918 and 1919. The first, often called "three-day fever," broke out in June 1918. It was common in western Europe and soldiers on both sides came down with it. Many Canadians at home had it, too. It didn't amount to much, was like measles without the rash, and caused few deaths. The second wave hit in the early fall of 1918, reached its peak in October and, in many localities, hung on until December. This was the bad one that accounted for nearly all the deaths. The third wave came in February and March of the next year and was much like the first one.

As far as can be ascertained the killer flu of the second wave first appeared in Canada among troops stationed in the Hamilton-Toronto area on the last day of September. Although the pandemic had already been raging for a full month in the United States, Canadian health officials displayed a peculiar nonchalance towards it.

Two hundred RAF cadets at Toronto had come down with the disease, but air-force authorities said the situation was well in hand. Dr. C.J.O. Hastings, the city's medical officer of health, said it was "just plain grippe." Col. J.W. McCullough, provincial health officer, reported sending out a circular letter of instructions to all doctors in the province, but remarked that "the public has been unduly alarmed already." Mayor Tommy Church criticized the military for failure to move troops to warmer winter quarters in the exhibition grounds provided by the city, and demanded action from medical health officials. A number of cadets at Hamilton Air School also had the disease and the authorities were giving them "plenty of outdoor exercise, route marches, and athletic games."

The first reported death in Toronto was that of a twelve-year-old girl from an outlying suburb. Before leaving home on a Wednesday she complained of a slight cold, but nobody thought anything of it because the rest of the family had it, too. On the journey into the city she complained to her mother of chills and a severe headache. Before she reached Toronto she was delirious. Her mother put her in hospital on Thursday. Saturday morning she died.

There were three cases in the Toronto hospitals and they had been placed in the detention ward for communicable diseases.

On October 1 Hastings issued orders for children with colds to be sent home from school and advised the public to walk more and keep out of streetcars. At the same time he stated that there was "absolutely no need for anxiety."

By October 4, 540 members of the armed forces in Toronto were down with flu. Reports of the epidemic were coming in from outside points. Cadet Jeoffry H. Scott, stationed at St. Johns, Quebec, died within six days of the first symptoms. Georgetown, Ontario, reported 50 cases, Renfrew between 500 and 600 with 9 deaths. All hospitals in Renfrew were full, doctors were working night and day, and it was impossible to get enough nurses. Schools had been closed.

Sherbrooke, Quebec, reported 8 deaths; London, Ontario, had 65 cases; Brantford reported 2,500 cases and the closing of all public buildings.

By the middle of October the disease was raging all over Canada. Ten thousand of the 66,000 Toronto school children were out with it along with 124 teachers. Sixty-eight Toronto citizens died in the twenty-four hours of October 15. Police forces and fire departments were working at half strength. At one point it was almost impossible to place a long-distance call because so many operators were home sick. An Ottawa-McGill football game was called off and racing was suspended at most tracks.

Schools, theatres, pool halls, and sometimes churches were closed in most cities and towns. House parties and social gatherings were discouraged. In Winnipeg all public assemblies were discontinued. In Toronto conventions were banned, including that of the American Public Health Association. Some judges stopped kissing the Bible in their courts. But nothing had any apparent effect on the spread of the disease.

According to the *Toronto Star*, pathologists at the University of Toronto asked the Riverdale Zoo for three monkeys on which to experiment. They promised to pay thirty-five dollars each for the animals if any harm came to them. Zoo officials said nothing doing. They didn't want any monkeys that had been inoculated with flu germs and insisted on cash on delivery. Towards the end of the pandemic the Connaught Laboratories, with or without monkeys, did produce a serum consisting of dead flu germs for the prevention of the disease, but there was no evidence that it saved any lives.

In their desperation and helplessness people tried anything and everything. Streetcar conductors, store clerks, and others forced to face the public tried wearing gauze masks that covered the nose and mouth, but they proved too much nuisance and were soon abandoned. Others carried wads of cotton soaked in eucalyptus oil and sniffed them constantly. Sulphur was burned in houses. Many people hung camphor bags on strings around their necks. Others advocated eating garlic and onions. Some believed that plenty of alcohol taken internally was the best treatment and pubs and bars advertised, "Come in. Don't take a chance on the flu." Dr. J. B. Cullen scoffed at the drinking cure but advocated bathing in alcohol instead. Still another doctor claimed to be curing the disease with a combination of iodine and creosote.

The sellers of patent medicines and cure-alls had a field day. An advertisement for a remedy called Pep described it as a germ killer that was handy, convenient, pleasant to take, and causing no disorder to the stomach. Another proclaimed: "One yeast cake a day will keep the flu away." In a Brampton, Ontario, weekly paper, the *Conservator*, the only account of the widespread effect of the disease was an advertisement for a tonic called Tanlac.

It is probably the only time in history that druggists wished for less business. Customers filled their stores during the day and banged on their doors at night. They couldn't stock enough cough syrup and cold remedies. One wholesale firm that normally sold 6,000 bottles of cough syrup a week sold more than 3,000 a day during the worst days of the flu. Customers lined up for the limited supply of quinine and aspirin.

Since the disease lasted for only three or four days, unless the deadly pneumonia followed, and recovery was remarkably rapid, survivors swore by the particular remedy they had used.

Hundreds of trappers, prospectors, and other frontiersmen caught the disease from heaven knows where, fought their way through it, or died unattended. In Labrador whole villages were wiped out and nobody knew anything about it until the spring thaw restored communications months later. In some areas there was no one strong enough to bury the dead. Missionaries brought out shocking stories of sled dogs – starving when their owners died – eating corpses. At Okak, 207 died in a population of 266.

In other communities there were no hospitals and few doctors. Here the Red Cross, the Victorian Order of Nurses, the Salvation Army, and other welfare organizations visited the sick, and helped staff the emergency hospitals. Citizens' committees visited homes to discover where assistance was needed. Police and firemen delivered fuel and groceries to stricken families. Women's organizations delivered broth and jellies from central kitchens.

The disease died down as quickly as it had flared up. By the end of October it was on the wane in most communities and by Armistice Day, most people were able to be out dancing around the bonfires, where spiked helmeted effigies of Kaiser Bill burned to a crisp. By Christmas the virulent wave of the influenza pandemic had passed leaving thousands of orphans and wrecked families behind.

Today, there are still many unanswered questions about the disease. Why, for instance, was it so deadly to the young-adult group and comparatively harmless to the very young and the very old? A graph of mortality rates by age groups covering the period of the pandemic shows the greatest increase in the thirty to thirty-nine-year-old group. The twenty-to-twenty-nines suffered just a little less, the fifteen-to-nineteens less again, while those under ten and over forty showed a comparatively small increase.

Although an immense amount of research has been done in several countries since 1918, there has been no great advance in sure knowledge about influenza. Pathologists are pretty well agreed that the pandemic was caused by a filtrable virus, but the Rockefeller Institute of Medical Research warned recently:

> If and when another pandemic of influenza should occur, it is to be hoped that it may be possible to establish directly the etiology (cause) of the disease. Until such time, however, it is of great importance to recognize that the cause or causes of previous pandemics, including that of 1918-19, are not yet known.

Researchers have isolated strains of influenza viruses which they call A and B. But there appear to be many others. Of thirty-two strains of influenza virus isolated from fifty-eight throat washings taken from different parts of Canada in 1949 only two could be identified with certainty. All of Canada's post-war cases have been mild except, for some unknown reason, those on Victoria Island in the Arctic where seventeen of sixty-seven Eskimos who caught the flu died.

What are the chances of another influenza pandemic and what can science do to prevent it?

The disease has descended upon men since earliest times. Hippocrates describes an outbreak – undoubtedly the same disease – in Greece in 412 B.C. Canada has had epidemics in 1700, 1830 and 1889-90. None of them, however, was as severe as the 1918 attack.

207

There has been talk of magic vaccines that would prevent a future outbreak but so far few doctors care to guarantee that any of the vaccines yet developed would be of any practical help. Vaccines have been developed for A and B strains of the virus. The culture is grown in eggs, removed, and refined by an involved and costly process. According to Dr. Arthur F. Peart, chief epidemiologist of the Department of Health and Welfare, Ottawa, "the immunity is specific for each strain of virus and is relatively short and uncertain. The results so far have not justified the widespread use of influenza vaccine in influenza pandemics."

Other epidemiologists state flatly that no vaccine yet discovered could give any practical protection. In the first place a vaccine must be given before the disease is contracted so that the body can build up its own defenses. This would mean vaccinating everybody every two months (the effective length of the vaccine), an impossible task. In the second place, if another pandemic were to break out it would first be necessary to isolate the virus that is causing it, then develop a vaccine for that virus. By that time, since flu strikes fast and hard, it would be too late to do much good.

What, then, are our defences? Medical men believe that secondary infections which were found in the lungs of many fatal cases in 1918 were the main causes of death. These can be combatted, they point out, by sulpha drugs and antibiotics. Some doctors even speculate that some of the flu scares of recent years might have developed to pandemic proportions if it hadn't been for these drugs.

But nobody knows for sure.

What Are You Doing Now, Darling?

A humour writer, which I jokingly call myself when there is nobody about to dispute it, often writes about his family. And this can get him into trouble.

I've always tried to avoid taking cheap shots at little old ladies or mothers-in-law or wives ("Take my wife . . . please."), but I took a chance on this one because it happened just as I have recorded it. I swear.

Now I'm perfectly aware that mothers have, as my daughter Sylvia is wont to say, "a hard row," and I have the greatest admiration and affection for mothers of all sizes and ages. I hope they will forgive me for this. But I'm sure they won't.

The other day I was sitting on the back stoop with my brother, who had just arrived with his family from Saskatoon. The sun was shining on us and the birds were hopping around and we were just sitting there talking about our happy childhood . . . like the time I threw a butcher knife at him for teasing me.

Then his wife appeared at the screen door and said, "What are you doing now, darling?"

He said, "Nothing."

She said, "Will you put this jacket in the car?"

He said, quite naturally, "Why?"

She said, "Well, you're just sitting there. You might as well."

Now, I'm all for wives. I think they are here to stay – despite the divorce statistics. But what I want to know is, why does the female mind become so riled up at the sight of a resting male body?

A wife just can't be happy if she is standing and her husband is sitting. It makes no difference that up to the moment of sitting the husband has been breaking his back in the garden or shovelling ashes or driving through thirty miles of screaming traffic. He'd just better not sit while she stands.

It isn't that they don't want their husbands to read. They do. Any wife will tell you that. My wife often says to me, "Now you go right into the living room there and relax. I don't need any help with the supper at all."

So I do. I take off my shoes and get hold of a magazine and start looking at the cartoons. Then from the kitchen I begin to hear remarks like this:

"Sharon, don't sit there reading like a big lump. Set the table!"

"Beryl, see what the baby is into, can't you?"

"Christopher, come and stir the pudding. I've only got two hands, you know."

Now, none of these remarks is directed at me, but somehow they all hit me . . . hard. I get up and go into the kitchen. I don't have to help. Just so long as I'm on my feet it's okay.

What happened one afternoon a week ago is fairly typical. I had put in a tough morning thinking. I hadn't done any actual writing but, as I have often complained to my wife, thinking is as tiring as any amount of physical labour.

After lunch my wife said, "Now you just go right up to your room and lie down. You look done in." I agreed to this because I recognize how important it is for the bread-winner to be in good condition at all times and not let himself get overworked.

So I go up to the bedroom and I pull down the shade and I close the door and I hunch up my shoulders and pull the comforter over my right ear and close my eyes.

All is quiet for about two minutes. Then I am aware of a puffing and grunting on the stairs, followed by a pitter-patter of little feet along the hall and a small voice says, "Daddy-dad, are you in there? I want in."

Naturally I ignore this and after fifteen minutes or so she goes away and there is silence . . . a bad silence. Then my wife calls up from downstairs, "Is the baby up there?"

I grunt that yes she is.

"What is she doing?"

"I don't know."

"Well . . . that's all right, but don't let her in Beryl's room because she gets into everything on the dressing-table and makes a terrible mess. Don't get up, though."

So I get up and get the baby from the mess in Beryl's room and put her in bed with me and tell her to lie down and go to sleep. This is like telling the wind to stop blowing. She sticks her fingers into my eyes and giggles. I turn over and present her with my broad back. She climbs over top of me and sticks her little face a quarter of an inch from mine and whispers, "Daddy seeping?" I realize I'm licked and get up and go down to the office where, for some reason, my wife never lets anyone bother me.

Or take the evening when the dishes are all done and I sink into an easy chair for a well-earned rest. My wife sits down to the sewing-machine to mend three or four pairs of pajamas. That's the trouble with women. They don't know how to relax.

I'm just nicely into my Pogo book when she sighs and says, "Oh dear." After eighteen years of married life I still can't ignore those two words. I look up from my book but she isn't speaking to me at all . . . just to herself.

She says, "I left those scissors up in Christopher's room where I was fixing the curtains this afternoon."

I keep quiet.

She says, "I don't suppose you'd be going upstairs for anything."

I say, "Yes, as a matter of fact I am going up . . . for the scissors."

She says, "No, no, you stay there. I'll get them."

But she doesn't make a move.

Now, I don't mind getting the scissors, you understand, or a sweater or a magazine. It's just that . . . why can't a wife make a direct, straightforward request just once, for goodness sake? What husband hasn't been sitting quietly in his chair or reclining on the sofa and hear his wife say, "On your way through the kitchen would you mind shutting off the oven?" The poor guy had no notion of going anywhere . . . least of all through the kitchen. That is, up to that moment he hadn't.

I guess this is just another of those things about wives husbands will never understand. It probably goes back to caveman days when a recumbent male was easy prey to a leaping sabre-toothed tiger. But in these days of stress and strain when husbands are dropping off with heart attacks like flies from a sticker, it behooves us to come up with some sort of a solution. Our survival depends upon it. And – I am happy to report – I have hit upon just such a solution.

Since it is the sight of the reclining male that infuriates the woman, I have learned to rest standing up. It isn't hard; horses do it all the time. Just so long as I'm in a vertical position my wife ignores me. I can stand in the middle of the kitchen and read or sleep or listen to the radio while she goes about her little duties happy as a lark. I pass this bit of information along to other males with the request that it go no further. Wives are very adaptable.

The Night
We Stole
the Mountie's Car

This book, which won the Leacock Memorial Medal for
Humour in 1972, is, like the other two books in the prairie
trilogy, mostly autobiographical.

It is set in Saskatchewan during the 1935 to 1937 period
when the Depression, drought, dust, and misery had reached
their highest point. And yet it is a happy story, for it was then
that I married the dearest girl in the world, started my family,
which has been an unmitigated joy to us, and began my
writing career.

I have often been asked how we managed, in the face of
disappointments and rejection slips from just about everybody to whom I submitted my stuff. The answer is simple.
Desperation. A drowning man doesn't stop struggling. It was
either resign myself to teaching school, which I hated, in a
part of the country I found incompatible, or pull ourselves out
of it and do something I did like doing.

Other people have escaped from the prairies by becoming
professional hockey players or opera singers or famous actors
or politicians or outstanding businessmen or scientists. I had
no talent for any of these professions. But I did have some
talent for writing. This would be our means of escape.

This excerpt gives some idea of those early times when we
were poor and desperate and frustrated and mad, but at the
same time happy, for we had each other. After all, I'd told
Aileen when I was courting her that if she married me I'd take
her "away from all this." I had to put up.

The post office in Wannego was at once my hope and my despair. Through the post office I could reach out to any place in the world. Just write the name and address on the envelope, stick on the required stamps, drop it through that slot in the front of the counter at the post office, and a host of eager, busy hands would see to it that the missive reached its destination.

Mr. Harold Ross,
Editor, *New Yorker*,
25 West 43rd Street,
New York, N.Y.

Within the week my story would be on the desk of Mr. Ross or one of his assistants. There it was. Something to be reckoned with. Somebody had to do something with it, even if just take it out of one envelope and put it in the return envelope I'd provided. It was a fascinating thought.

It was almost as though I were on speaking terms with the editors.

"Hello, Harold."

"Hello, Max."

"How are things?"

"Pretty good. Read your last piece. Good work . . . just the sort of thing for the *New Yorker*. I'd like you to have lunch with me at the Algonquin soon."

The first short story I attempted was one thousand words for *Liberty*. And with every word I set to paper I thought of that One Thousand Dollars that I would get for it. In fact, I thought more about the money than I did about the story. Actually I should have been writing a story about a man who suddenly found himself in possession of One Thousand Dollars.

I remember the plot of that story in detail. There were these two crooks who had robbed a Saskatoon bank of a bundle and were heading north in their speedy V-8 automobile to the relative safety of the hinterland.

It was the perfect crime. In fact I probably titled it "The

Perfect Crime." Every loophole had been plugged, every contingency thought of. They'd covered their trail completely. Nothing could possibly go wrong. And as they sped north, jubilant at their cleverness, I tried out all the thug and gangster dialogue that was kicking around in my mind from seeing dozens of gangster movies. There's no doubt that my two thugs bore a strong resemblance to George Raft and Edward G. Robinson.

All went well until they came to the new bridge that crosses the Saskatchewan River south of Radisson. They'd no sooner driven onto the bridge than they saw a group of people at the other end and among those people were three Mounties, red coats gleaming in the sun. One of the Mounties stepped out and held up a gloved hand for them to stop. What to do? Too late to turn back. Make a run for it. Shoot it out. So with guns blazing they roared through.

Well, of course the Mounties gave chase in their own V-8, and the chase ended with the thugs' car hitting the ditch and both the villains dead. Then the Mountie, shaking his head, remarked, "And all we wanted was to get their names as the one thousandth car to cross the bridge."

Sound familiar? Of course it does. Variations of that plot have been used hundreds of times and will be used hundreds of times more. I thought it was new and original because it was new and original to me. I had actually thought it up, not borrowed it. And this is the greatest pitfall for the beginning writer. Naturally the first ideas and plots that come to his mind are the same ones that have come to the minds of writers since printing was invented. Young writers are still doing it, except that now that many more of the plots have already been used. There is nothing new under the sun.

I wrote this story with great care. Rewrote and polished it. Typed and retyped it. Finally I had it perfect. Not one single typing error. Spacing – exactly one-and-one-quarter inch margin on both sides. Name and address in upper right-hand corner of the title page. Not a blemish or a blot on any of the five pages.

Then the self-addressed envelope. I'd contacted Puss Ellingson, with whom I'd gone to high school and who was then in Seattle working as a commercial artist, and he sent me American stamps for the return envelope. Then the whole thing went into a bigger envelope. My wife and I each put our good-luck sign on it and I trundled off down to the post office.

The post office, when we first went to Wannego, was in the general store of Nathan R. Smith, a short, dapper, greying man who had come from Ontario as a young man and was trying to make enough money to get back. There were three main factions represented in Wannego and the surrounding farm community – the Old Ontario, United Church group of which Smith was the leader; the French Canadians led by old Orland Beltier, a small nervous man who ran the principal hardware store; and the Ukrainians whose most influential member was Peter Nikoluk who ran the other general store halfway down the block. Of the three groups, the Anglo-Saxons were in the minority.

For this reason, Smith and his group looked upon themselves rather like Pukka Sahibs in India. It was their duty to uphold the principles and mores of the white man in this savage land. They mustn't ever allow themselves to become contaminated by association with the "lesser breeds."

So it happened that Smith never spoke to the French Canadians or Ukrainians who were his fellow townspeople and indeed his neighbours. It was something to see him meet with Orland Beltier on the main street at noon, for instance. Neither looked at each other. There was always something on the road to engage their attention, or somebody across the street to whom they could shout a greeting. To each, the other was a non-person.

This lack of communication presented special problems as Orland's son, Danny, had the contract for carrying mail between the railway depot and the post office. This contract was awarded separately, I suppose, so that the government could spread the cash and paying jobs around as much as possible. The government, then as now, was scrupulously careful to let no hint of political patronage enter into the awarding of jobs.

So great was Smith's dislike for Danny Beltier that not only would he not speak to him but he wouldn't even mention his name. So when the townspeople were in his store waiting for the mail, Smith would mutter darkly, "*He* hasn't shown up with it yet!" as though "he" was part of a diabolical plot to keep the mail from its rightful owners. Or he'd mumble, "Don't know what's happened to *him* now," suggesting clearly that *he* was either drunk somewhere or off in the livery barn with Ruby.

When Danny did arrive with the mail and plodded through the store speaking pleasantly – in French – to all his friends and pointedly ignoring the rest, he'd plunk the heavy bags down as far from the door of Smith's cubby-hole as was allowed by his contract and clump out of the store again. Smith would go very red in the face, kick the mail bags into the "post office" and start sorting. The ritual never varied.

The situation was compounded by the religious and political factors. The French Canadians were Roman Catholic which, in the eyes of an Orangeman like Smith, made them first cousins to the devil. Also they voted Liberal to a man and, since there was a Liberal government in both Saskatchewan and Ottawa, Smith was convinced they received more than their fair share of political goodies. The Ukrainians, who had their own Orthodox Church, also supported the Liberal Party, Smith believed, and shared in a lesser extent in the political patronage. This left Smith and his small group fighting the good fight alone.

Smith's house on the edge of town stood out among the other shabby houses of the street like a flower in an ash pile. Large and white and always freshly painted, with glassed-in verandahs, it was surrounded by about two acres of green lawns enclosed by a picket fence. The lilac, rose, forsythia, and other shrubs were always neatly trimmed, the grass neatly mowed. His well, the deepest in the district, provided ample water for watering lawns even through the worst years of the drought. As nearly as possible, Smith had created on the bleak and dust-ridden prairie a bit of the green and grace of southern Ontario.

When I took my envelope into Smith's store after school on Monday the place was empty. The groceries were at the front of the store, then the dry goods, and at the very back the tiny wicket of the post office. "You'd think the old bugger would at least put it at the front of the store," Danny Beltier complained. "But not him. He thinks he might make a sale if you have to walk past all those shirts and piles of underwear to get to the post office."

Smith was busy somewhere in the back warehouse when I opened the door of his store, but the tinkle of the little bell at the top of it warned him of a customer. He came out, peered at me over his glasses, grimaced a greeting. I had my envelope under my arm and I didn't quite know how to present it. After all, nobody else in town sent manuscripts to *Liberty Magazine*. I sort of eased it up onto the counter in front of his wicket and, half-turning, became very interested in the pile of trousers on a table. Smith took the envelope, read it, looked at me and growled, "What's this?"

Somehow his cold eyes, wrinkled forehead, and forbidding mien reminded me of every teacher, preacher, Sunday school superintendent, parent who had ever stared at me for doing something wrong. I couldn't help myself, I felt guilty. Instead of saying, "None of your damned business, you hack civil servant," I fumbled and mumbled and finally blurted out, "Uh . . . a story."

"A story? What kind of story?"

"Uh . . . just a fiction story."

"Aha. About the people around here?"

At last I came to my senses. "Look . . . it's just a story that I'm sending to an editor. Will you please weigh it and tell me how much it is."

Well, he had to do that. So he did. But after that each time I mailed out a story he looked at me as though I were sending secret documents to the Kremlin. Peered at the envelope, weighed it in his hand as though testing for explosives, and let me know clearly by his scowls and grunts that there in Wannego they didn't take kindly to people who carried on in such a crazy way.

Getting the story back was much easier. The train arrived at Wannego at four-fifteen in the afternoon. By the time Danny Beltier delivered the mail and Smith got it sorted into its little boxes, it was five o'clock. The school kids who lived in the country usually waited to take the mail home with them, hanging around the poolroom or the drugstore. At mail time they, along with whatever adults were downtown, converged on Smith's store and waited in groups, talking in hushed tones as befitted the establishment of so eminent a man.

I gave the editor of *Liberty* two weeks in which to receive my manuscript, read it, approve it, and mail me the cheque.

After that I waited in the store with a feeling in my mid-section as though my guts were gone. I watched those mail bags being brought in and listened while the mail was sorted behind the closed wicket. When the wicket opened I approached it tentatively, almost afraid to get my mail. When I did get it I'd forgotten about the self-addressed envelope bit and didn't recognize my own typing. Who, I pondered, could be sending me a brown envelope from New York? Then I remembered.

My story had come back, all right, looking as fresh and clean as when I'd posted it. And there attached to it was a small white slip with the big word "SORRY" printed on it, followed by, "We did not find this story suitable for our magazine. This does not imply that it hasn't merit. Please try us again. The editors."

That is a rejection slip. Some magazine publishers tried to dress them up a bit more; others were even more curt. Either way they informed me that I hadn't made it. My brain child had been rejected, scorned, refused, declined, ejected. They didn't want it. My first reaction was despair, my second anger, and the third determination – or stubbornness, whichever you prefer. I was to collect enough of those slips to paper a room before I ever sold a story.

After trying a few more stories for *Liberty* and having them rejected, I got the idea that perhaps I should try to learn something about the craft of writing. So off I went to the Saskatoon library for books. "The Art of the Short Story" – as a rough guess I'd say that one million four hundred and eighty-four books have been written on this subject. And none of them will write a story for you.

I bought a copy of *Roget's Thesaurus* to help me with words. Fowler's *Modern English Usage* was a must for all writers, they said. So I got that. Then I subscribed to a magazine called *Writers' Digest*, which was full of tips and advertisements for more books and the names of "agents" who would read your manuscripts for a fee and help you become a writer fast. I didn't have money for a fee so I never discovered if it really worked.

Then I learned two things about myself: first, I was a writer, and second, I couldn't write. That sounds contradictory, I know, but it really isn't. A writer, I'm convinced, is a certain type of person. He's been described as "a watcher and a listener." Bernard Shaw said something about a writer seeing the world through different eyes. A writer is a person who pays attention, who ponders, who considers, who assesses. Nothing really escapes his notice. He wonders why. Why is that woman doing that? How did she get that way anyway? What would happen if she were to do this instead of that? A person is born with this faculty. It is part of his nature.

But this doesn't mean he will be a successful writer. There are people who have a natural aptitude for doctoring, for instance, or judging. But unless they put in years of training to learn how to do it they'll never become doctors or judges.

So it is with writing. The techniques of the craft must be learned. The use of words, sentences, paragraphs. Selection – what to put in and what to leave out. Form, style, suspense, and all those things that make a reader want to keep on turning pages to find out what comes next. These must be learned.

I had little natural skill at this. I hadn't written stories for the kiddies' section of newspapers when I was a boy. I'd been too busy playing hockey and delivering the papers. I was no great whiz on the Nutana Collegiate paper, *The Saltshaker*. Although I was on the staff, the editor complained he could never get anything out of me. I wrote one excruciatingly funny story about tennis but the printer couldn't read my handwriting and so it never got into the paper.

So I had to learn. And I learned writing the way I'd learned practically everything else in my life. By doing it. Trial and error. Outside of school, I've had no formal instruction in anything.

I learned to swim by getting in the water and swimming, by figuring out the best way to do it – for me. And that was the side-stroke. Now you'll never win an Olympic gold medal doing the good old side-stroke. But I knew I was never going to win an Olympic medal or any kind of a race with the Australian crawl, either, even suppose I practised it twenty-four hours a day. So the side-stroke is adequate. It gets me there and permits me to have a lot of fun in the water. But I sure had to work at learning the side-stroke.

The same thing happened with learning to skate. I didn't come by it easily. I had to learn it. My ankles were like rubber and I developed callouses on them from ankle-walking. And callouses on my rump, too, from sitting down on the hard ice. But I kept at it, doggedly and patiently, and finally I could skate – not well enough to win a gold medal but good enough to have a lot of fun.

It was the same with learning to dive and ski and drive a car. I actually learned to drive by stealing Dad's old Overland which was parked in the backyard on MacPherson Avenue in Saskatoon when I was in grade ten. It was parked there because all the seat cushions had been stolen from it when Dad left it by the side of the road out near Warman. While they were waiting for an insurance adjustment, the car just sat in the backyard.

So one Saturday I got fooling around, rigged up a box for a seat and then started experimenting with old keys in the ignition lock. They must have made them less tamper-proof than they do now because I soon found one that would fit. Like every kid, I'd watched Dad and my older brothers shift gears enough so I knew how to do that. I backed the car out of the yard and drove out onto Tenth Street and I was away. I did this until I learned how to drive. No teacher, no book of instructions, just trial and error.

And trial and error is how I learned to write. People ask me today if university courses in creative writing or journalism schools are a help in learning to write and I have to tell them I don't know. I never took any. But then I never took courses in anything.

I just wrote – and wrote – and wrote. Up every morning at five, banging on an old rickety typewriter until school time. Nobody to bother me but our cat, Jonesy, who developed a bad habit of springing onto my back as I sat hunched in front of the typewriter and holding on with all claws. I'd pitch him over onto the couch where he'd sit glowering at me, tail twitching, and go on writing.

After dinner at night I'd try again if I weren't out coaching a baseball game, refereeing a game of basketball, directing a play, or speaking to a church Young People's group. But after a day's teaching I had little mental energy left for writing and had to drive myself. I had one rule that I didn't break: finish the story, get it in the mail. Sooner or later something would have to break.

Two things happened during these first months. The post office changed hands and Aileen became pregnant.

Next to Smith's store and between it and the restaurant was a vacant lot. It was full of weeds and old tin cans and looked as though it would remain vacant forever. Nobody was building anything in the mid-thirties. But one day, much to the surprise of the Main Street regulars, a four-horse team pulled into the lot from the lane behind, dragging on skids an old wooden shack. It was battered and broken with tar-covered sides and a flat, slanting roof. The windows were smashed, the door gone.

Two of the local carpenters went to work on it, however, and repaired most of the damage. A coat of paint made it look almost presentable. I discovered why it had been brought there on one of my trips to the post office. Nathan Smith was alone in his store and he was furious.

"There is nothing, absolutely nothing, these people won't do!" he fumed as soon as I entered.

By "these people" I knew he meant his arch enemies, the French Canadians.

"But this . . . this . . . is the lowest yet. It's the ultimate in . . . in . . . ." He was lost for words.

It turned out he'd had a visitor from the federal post office that very morning who'd informed him that it was a new policy not to have the post office in his store.

"Why?" he had demanded.

"Well there have been complaints. The French Canadians – and the Ukrainians, too – claim that they are treated badly in here."

"They're treated like anybody else."

"Well . . . there have been complaints."

"What are you going to do about it?"

"Well, we plan to move the post office out of here into a building of its own."

"You want to erect a building?"

"No. There isn't space for one on the main street now . . . and the post office has to be on the main street. But there's this building next door . . . ."

Smith could scarcely continue his recital of the crime. "You see what he did . . . you see . . . ? Got a lot of his pea-soup friends to write to the Department complaining about how I treated them. Then he moves that ramshackle shack onto the only vacant lot on the street. It's as plain as the nose on your face. They're getting it because they're political heelers!"

I couldn't believe this, of course. Danny Beltier was simply the better man for the job. But he had terrible luck. Shortly after the post office was moved into the little building, the place caught fire and burned to the ground. Fortunately there was no loss of mail or vital documents as the fire happened at night when there was little mail in the building and, besides, Danny had been working late that night in the hardware store across the street and had, at great personal risk, rescued everything of value from the building.

Then, as a temporary measure, he established the post office in the hardware store. He built in a separate door where one of the big front windows had been, so that customers wouldn't have to go into his store to get their mail. And he built a nice counter and put in shiny new boxes. It was very handy for Danny, too.

It was more interesting going for the mail now, too, because although he was a highly intelligent man in every respect Danny Beltier was almost blind.

Watching him sort mail for you was as good as a show. He would hold each letter within an inch of his thick glasses and slide it across like a man eating a cob of corn, moving his lips as he did so. He accomplished this with such speed and dexterity that he could sort the mail at least as fast as Smith had ever done.

More important, from my point of view, Danny was tremendously interested in my progress as a writer. Whereas Smith had shown nothing but sullen suspicion as to why so many manila envelopes were going back and forth to New York, Chicago, Philadelphia, Danny was fascinated.

"Don't you worry," he'd say. "Some of these days the story won't come back. You'll see." And each time that one did he was so disappointed that he could scarcely hand it to me. I swore him to secrecy, of course, because I didn't want the people of Wannego to think I was a nut altogether.

"Why?" he asked. "I should think you'd be proud of the fact that you're a writer."

A writer! That was the first time anyone had ever called me that. I didn't go about telling other people that I was a writer. I couldn't. But the realization that at least one man in town called me a writer was a great boost to my spirits.

For I had learned one important thing about the trade of writing. It is the loneliest occupation in the world. You work alone – always alone. Talking to others about what you are doing won't help much because talking is easier than writing and given half a chance any writer will talk his story rather than write it. It's a lonely occupation even for an established writer in a city. For a beginner, in a small Saskatchewan town, it is like being in solitary confinement.

At least it would have been without my wife. Everybody, I guess, must have somebody who believes he can accomplish the impossible. Somebody he can complain to, enthuse with, and even swear at, if necessary. Aileen was then, as she is now, the perfect wife for a writer. Her understanding and patience were complete. With that sure, confident way that women have she knew that some day we would make it. She had no nasty, mean, niggling doubts like the ones that plagued me. She was sure.

By this time Aileen had become considerably pregnant and we were glad. We were so poor that if at the end of the month we had sixty cents left over from our $60.00 cheque it was a cause for jubilation. There was no doctor in the town to provide all that pre-natal care that women need. We had absolutely no idea where we'd get the money for baby carriage, crib, clothes, or even diapers. Our water supply was so wretched that washing diapers daily or even bathing a kid would mean back-breaking chores. But just the same we were glad.

Why?

Several reasons. We'd both come from large families where brothers and sisters had been reasonably compatible. Aileen had a great love for babies – anybody's babies, and let's face it, we still had that ridiculous pre-population-explosion idea that raising a family was a worthy thing to do. We actually felt proud that we were going to produce a human being.

In due course of time our first child was born. Aileen went to Saskatoon for the last week so as to be close to the doctor and when she went to the hospital Harry King gave me the day off to go in and be with her. The baby was a girl, healthy and whole. And when I saw her I felt good. No rejection slip here. But I had to take the train back to Wannego that afternoon. Harry didn't believe in pampering his staff.

And it was then that it finally happened. I sold my first short story. What's more, the acceptance letter was accompanied by a cheque and that nearly ended me in Wannego.

I have to go back a bit here. After months of writing stories for *Esquire, Liberty*, the *Saturday Evening Post, Scribners Magazine*, and various other class magazines and getting back nice, clean, crisp rejection slips, I decided on a new tack. I would begin with the lesser markets, something in the manner of a neophyte hunter starting on gophers and working up to lions. Now to find some gophers.

In a copy of the *Writers' Digest* – which was full of helpful hints for beginners – I learned of the newspaper syndicates. "These markets may pay less than the top markets," the item said, "but they are considerably easier to break into." The magazine was always talking of "breaking into" markets and it gave the beginner a nice feeling of putting a broad shoulder against the door of adversity and crashing through.

The syndicate they liked best was the McClure Newspaper Syndicate. The address was given along with the information that they would send a writer copies of recent stories they'd bought so that he could study their length, format, style, and so on. So I sent for, and they sent to, and much to my surprise I discovered the names of some well-known writers attached to these stories. They were very much in the style of the *Liberty* Short-shorts, a format which I already had studied assiduously.

Hitler was much in the news then, of course, and so was the Nazi Bund in America. They were wearing swastikas on their shoulders and harassing Jews and I got the idea for a story about a Bund member who'd been badly wounded during a demonstration and needed a blood transfusion immediately. The only donor with his type of blood available was Jewish. The denouement – all of these stories had great denouements – came when the recovering Nazi learned that he now had Jewish blood.

I got a letter back from McClure's almost immediately saying they liked my story fine but that somebody else had already used this idea. How about another story? Another story! I had a million of them! But such are the cantankerous caprices of memory that I can't remember what this next one was about.

When I got back to town and went to the post office wicket for my mail Danny Beltier was grinning all over. I was just about to tell him about the baby when he handed me a letter with a celluloid window in the front.

"How about this?" he said.

"Another rejection slip?"

"Nothing doing. This is the kind of letter they send cheques in!"

A cheque! The first I'd ever received as a writer. I stood there holding the thin envelope in my hand afraid to open it. The article about the syndicates had said they paid less than the top markets. Well, less than One Thousand Dollars was Nine Hundred Dollars. Or even Five Hundred Dollars. Hell, I'd settle for One Hundred Dollars, I told myself, but I knew I was just hedging. It couldn't be as little as *One* Hundred Dollars.

"Aren't you going to open it?" Danny said, grinning. He was as excited as I.

But it isn't so easy to open a letter that might change your life. That might contain news that will rescue you from poverty and frustration. Fame and fortune came suddenly for writers. I knew this from biographies of Edgar Rice Burroughs and Jack

London – oh, almost any writer you want to mention. Fame and fortune! It's no wonder I hesitated to open that envelope.

And then I did. And it contained a cheque, just as I had hoped, crisp and brownish and official, attached to a letter of acceptance. And the amount stamped into that cheque so that it could never be tampered with was $5.00.

"Well?" Danny enquired, and I tossed the cheque on the counter in front of him. He picked it up and ran it in front of his eyes. I knew what he was thinking. Five dollars for all this work! For spending every minute of your spare time hunched over a typewriter, for study and planning and rewriting and more rewriting. For hope and faith and confidence. Five lousy dollars and a story published in the weekend supplement of the *Milwaukee Journal*. This is fame and fortune?

I guess this is the moment that really separates the reasonable from the unreasonable, the sensible from the insane, the rational from the blindly stubborn. Rejection slips you can take. You say – well, that editor doesn't know a good story when he sees it, or the story was never read, or they had another story like it, and you know that some day somebody will recognize your worth and your story will sell.

But to sell a story, have it read and appreciated, finally to break through the great wall of indifference, to enter into the world of payment for them, and then get five lousy stinking bucks. It just plain wasn't worth it. Any sensible person could see that. Now was the time to quit and try something more practical – like taking a course in show-card printing, or learning to play the piano in ten easy lessons, or raising chinchillas in your basement, or studying for a lucrative civil service position, or becoming proficient in the growing field of electronics. Hell, the publications were full of pleasant ways of bettering your station in life with half the work of learning to write.

I must admit that, standing there with that five-dollar cheque in my hand, I felt like quitting all right.

"By the way," I said. "Our baby was born this morning. A girl. Eight pounds, two ounces."

Danny reached through the wicket and grabbed my hand. "Now," he said, "you can buy new shoes for the baby."

Then I knew what I must do with this money. The only thing that could possibly restore my perspective. "To hell with shoes," I said, beginning to feel better already. "I'm going to get a good bottle of scotch and I'm going to celebrate my success. Are you with me?"

"I sure as hell am," Danny said. "We'll have it at my house. I'll get Vincent and Maurice and Jean and a few others and we'll have a big one. We'll celebrate the new baby and the new cheque."

The people he mentioned were all his friends and all French Canadian. Vincent Denis was the municipal secretary, Maurice DeSante was the accountant in the bank, Jean Bouchard was an insurance broker. There were more. A couple of farmers, assorted nieces and nephews – including a buxom, bosomy brunette I'd never seen before but who was very friendly.

This was my first real association with French Canadians. Like most other good Canadian WASPS, I'd had no direct contact with them and therefore harboured an attitude of suspicion and dislike. For one thing they talked French and, after my dismal experiences with that language, I had a strong suspicion that anybody who spoke it must be pretty devious. Since my father had once been an active Orangeman, I'd heard some of the stories of how the Catholics were taking over the country, and God knows I'd heard enough from Smith about what liars, cheats, and generally dirty bastards all Frenchmen were.

I didn't care. At this point I felt reckless.

There is certainly one thing to be said for getting drunk with people; you get to know them. The party started up at Danny Beltier's house and his tall, graceful, dark-eyed wife welcomed me and my bottle of scotch with a big hug. That was a good beginning.

As each of the others arrived with their wives, I realized that when they said party they meant party. Each brought a bottle of booze and some had taken a few nips before they arrived. They greeted me like a friend of long standing, enfolded me in warm embraces, and insisted that I have a drink from their bottle. Everybody was glad about the baby.

I'd never seen anything like this before. I'd been on parties with my Anglo-Saxon friends, but they tended to be rather stiff and furtive affairs, degenerating gradually into drunken brawls. Like most other Canadians of that time, we didn't know how to drink. Having been instructed from infancy that alcoholic beverages were tools of the devil – not something to enhance enjoyment and make life good, but rather something to degrade and destroy – we went about drinking guiltily, secretly, defensively, and stupidly. And since we'd already taken the first step towards perdition we figured we might as well go all the way, and so we did crazy things like breaking furniture and fighting.

But this was drinking for fun. For enjoyment. For ecstasy. For gaiety and frolic. We danced and laughed and patted each other and, for the first time in public, I emerged from my school-teacher shell. I lost my stiffness, my reserve, my foolish notions. It was fun to hug and kiss the beautiful brunette without being expected to take her into the bedroom. I also learned that I was a very funny fellow when properly lubricated, and that when people finally got through to me they tended to like me. I developed a lot that night, as a person and also as a writer.

I also nearly got fired from my job. I was not then, nor ever have been, what is described as a good drinker. In fact I am a bad drinker. I tend to get very very happy and very very reckless. So it was that when the party had reached the stage that we were marching from house to house and singing, I decided to pay a visit to Mr. McElvey, the bank manager who, you will remember, was also a member of the school board.

Now Mr. McElvey didn't actually disapprove of French Canadians. He knew that the bank had to deal with them and that it was necessary to have an accountant who could speak French – God knows he'd never learn the crazy language himself – but apart from that it just happened that he had no French Canadian friends.

Well, as I rollicked up the street with these wonderful people we passed his house and I somehow got the idea that it was incumbent upon me to climb up on McElvey's front porch roof and sing "Alouette" through his bedroom window.

"You can't do that," Maurice DeSante protested halfheartedly. "It's two o'clock in the morning!"

"And everybody know," said his petite wife who was the only member of the group with any accent, "that these Anglais are never awake after ten."

"But what if they are making love?" somebody asked.

This brought a considerable laugh from the group and it was obvious they considered that WASPS don't make love, at least not in the sense that they thought of it.

I don't think I ever would have gone any further in this – and I soon wished I hadn't – if somebody hadn't spotted a ladder lying beside the house, put it up the verandah and said, "Voilà!" So up I went, unsteadily, and got onto the verandah roof which was steeper than I'd thought. Gingerly on hands and knees I crawled up to the big double window and began to sing, loudly, drunkenly, and off-key.

Then I was aware of a strange thing. There was no noise behind me. The laughter and banter that had been there had all gone. I looked down on the dark street and it was empty. My friends too were all gone.

Instead of them I made out a dark figure coming down the street. It turned in at the gate. It was Banker McElvey who had obviously been out at a party himself and who was just returning. And there I was, the drunken teacher perched on the porch of the member of the school board.

My mind raced over possible courses of action. I might jump down on top of him and knock him over so that he'd be so stunned he wouldn't see who it was running down the street. No. I might really hurt him. I might jump off the side of the verandah and run around the side of the house. No, I'd probably break a leg or at least sprain an ankle. I even considered diving off the verandah head first and ending it all right there, but the thought of my wife and new baby deterred me.

So I just sat there and looked down foolishly at the figure below. And he looked up at me.

"Braithwaite!" McElvey roared in a big voice.

"Yeah."

"What in hell are you doing sitting on my porch roof singing French Canadian songs, off-key?"

"Well . . . it, uh . . . seemed like a good idea. Now I'm not so sure."

"Come down."

So I came down the ladder, which he held for me, and when I reached the bottom McElvey looked at me and said, "That's a hell of a way to sing!"

I had no answer for that. It wasn't the first time my singing had been criticized. But it did seem a little strange that he should be concerned with the quality of my voice at a time like this.

Because I couldn't think of anything else to say, I blurted, "My wife had a baby today. A girl."

"She did? Congratulations! Come on in, I'll buy you a drink. I'll also show you how those songs should be sung. My wife's away, too."

So we went in and it turned out that he was as high as I was and that under the influence, instead of climbing porches, he sang French-Canadian songs. And sang them, and sang them, and sang them. For hours I sat there and drank his whisky and listened to these songs. He also liked to teach other people how to sing.

Then he became serious and told me how it was being a banker. "These farmers around here think I'm some kind of Shylock because I won't lend them any money. Hell, it's not my money. The bank inspectors come around and rake me over the coals for not collecting what is out. If I lend money on land – what good is land? Who wants it? The bank owns more land than it knows what to do with now. They don't realize what I'm up against."

It was a sad story. I wished he'd go back to singing.

When I finally got out of there it was four in the morning. I walked down the dusty road and then along the cracked sidewalk to the hotel. "Gosh," I said to myself, "bankers sure do have a miserable time of it."

McGruber's Folly

This is one of two novels I wrote about men who had been forced to retire. In the case of Ranse McGruber, chief of detectives in a large city, he retired at the age of sixty when his mental and physical faculties were still strong. He found himself with the time to do what he'd always wanted to do – write crime plays for television.

But he couldn't do it.

That left him with a loving wife and a loving family, including grandchildren, a cottage on a lovely lake in Muskoka, and the worst case of boredom imaginable. After he'd caught fish in the lake and built all the additions to his house that he could think of, he found himself with nothing challenging to do. It might be said that the Devil finds work for active minds and bodies that have nothing worthwhile to do.

So Ranse devised the perfect crime. He worked out a scheme for robbing the local bank that was absolutely foolproof. And he pulled it off. Then he discovered that this one act had changed his character and his personality. One lie led to another and soon he was lying to his wife and his grandchildren and his neighbours and friends. After chasing crooks all his life, he had now become one.

It's an old story, of course. Lust and greed have done for many a man and woman. But it was all new to Ranse. He got what he wanted. Or did he?

As soon as the boat touched shore on Rattlesnake Island, the twins leaped off the bow and, clutching their equipment, ran into the woods. They'd been sitting on the bow peering out, like a couple of figure-heads, as the island got bigger and bigger in front of them. Theirs was a singleness of purpose rarely seen except in ten-year-olds. Before the adults could move, they were gone.

"Well, that's a switch," Zeke said. "They didn't even want to eat first."

"Is it safe, Dad?"

"Yeah, mostly," Ranse assured her. "But we'll go and find them."

He and Zeke pulled the boat up on the shore and helped the women unload the food. Ranse was uneasy. He knew from experience the uncanny ability of kids to find things. No matter where he hid his fishing pole or his walking-stick or his electric drill, it was no time before they located it. He could hear the boys off in the bush, shouting excitedly. He called to them, but they didn't answer.

"Come on," he said to Zeke. "There's a bit of a path through here." He led the way along an overgrown path through thick hemlock and white pine. The path ran parallel to the shore for about two hundred feet and then ended against the sheer cliff that faced the clear, deep water of the lake.

There they found the boys, peering upwards.

"How can we get up on that rock?" Timothy asked. "Our teacher says that this time of year snakes like to sun themselves on ledges."

"I bet we could climb it," Patrick said.

"Not a chance," their father warned. "Straight granite for forty feet, with no footholds."

The two boys stood holding their complicated snake-catching equipment, foreheads creased with thought.

"How about around the other side of the island?" Timothy asked.

"Sheer rock. That's why nobody has ever built on this island, why they left it for picnickers. It's really just a great big rock, with this narrow crescent along this shore."

"Hasn't anyone ever been up top?"

"Probably. But not that I know of."

"With a helicopter we could do it, easy."

"Or with ladders. Maybe we could cut trees and make a ladder!"

"That would take all day and more tools than we've got. You'll just have to do your snake hunting along this shore," Zeke told them. "I'm going back and get something to eat."

"Me, too," Ranse said. The two men went back along the path, but the boys didn't follow.

"Bet they find a way to get up there," Zeke said with a certain amount of pride. "Won't give up until they do."

Ranse was afraid he was right.

They built a fire in the old stone fireplace and Ranse laid his metal grill over it.

"There you are," he said. "When that burns down a bit, it will be perfect for hamburgers and hot dogs."

The women had set up an old folding table, covered it with a cloth, and were laying out the food. Josie was happy. Ever since she was a little girl she'd loved picnics. She could remember how her father would shine up the old six-cylinder McLaughlin, which had what he called "the grub-stake box" bolted onto the right-side running-board. They'd load it with food and set out for a picnic somewhere along the Ottawa River. Since then, every time she went on a picnic, she'd think of him and of her mother in her neat driving costume.

Soon the hamburgers and wieners were sizzling on the grill.

"Get the boys," she told Ranse. "It's just about time to eat."

Ranse shouted for the kids, but there was no answer. Then Zeke shouted even louder, and then, from somewhere far above them, came an answering call. "Hey, we're up here!"

"Up on the top?" Ranse could hardly believe it.

"There's a secret path," Patrick shouted. "About halfway along the rock wall. It's hidden behind an old hemlock, but we found it. Come on up!"

"No!" Zeke commanded. "You come down. And right now! All the food is ready."

"Aw, nuts!"

"Can we come up again after we eat?"

"It's sure neat up here. Pine trees and moss all over the rock, and, boy, is it ever warm!"

"O.K.," Zeke said. "We'll go up with you after we eat."

Ranse sat on an immense fallen log and poked at his food. So it had come down to this. Beside him the boys were wolfing down their food and jabbering like jays.

"Jeez, Ranse, wait till you see it!" Patrick said. "The moss is all dry, brown, and brittle."

"But there's some green stuff growing, too. Hey, I bet we're the first people ever been up there!"

"Except the Indians. They'd know about that secret path. Maybe they went up there for, you know, ceremonies and things."

"Oh, sure. And the place is probably loaded with buried treasure," Zeke scoffed. "Places like that always are – on television."

"Maybe it was a burial ground and we can find some bones!"

"How thrilling," their mother commented. "There are more hamburgers here. Don't you boys want any more?"

"No, thanks," Patrick assured her. "Come on, let's get going!"

"I thought maybe I'd do a little fishing off that rock there." Ranse knew there wasn't much hope, but he had to try. "Great place for bass."

Usually the mere mention of bass would arouse unbounded enthusiasm in the twins, but now they couldn't care less.

"Jeez, Ranse, we can fish any time. This might be the last chance we'll get to explore that cliff!"

The last chance indeed.

"Are you coming, Dad?" Patrick shouted, as they disappeared into the woods.

"Wouldn't miss it for the world."

"Me neither," Susie said. "After all, how often do you get to see an authentic Indian burial ground?"

"Complete with buried treasure," Josie laughed. "I'm coming, too."

"You?" Ranse objected. "It might be quite a climb."

"Well, I'm quite a climber. Come on, Ranse." She took him by the hand and there was the old comradeship and affection there. How many times had they explored new places together? How often had they shared, enjoyed, loved together? That simple act of taking his hand took Ranse's mind back to it all. And how often at times like this, when they'd been alone together in the outdoors, had they just naturally and enthusiastically come together and enjoyed each other, while butterflies flitted by and birds sang? But he had no urge to do that now.

Instead, he followed the others.

With the excited shouts of the twins leading, they found their way through the woods to the hidden path.

"See?" Patrick shouted, like an archaeologist who has unearthed a new find. "Nobody would ever know it was here!"

"I still can't see it," Susie said.

"Well, just look." Timothy pushed aside the long, low branches of a hemlock whose crown had been chewed off by porcupines, and there, sure enough, was a narrow split in the cliff. It slanted up among the roots of pines that clung precariously to the rock.

Patrick was already halfway up. "Come on!" he shouted. "It's easy. Even for you, Grandma."

They all followed, with Ranse bringing up the rear. Halfway up was a ledge, covered with dried blueberry bushes and fallen debris. More roots helped them get up over this ledge to another, and finally, with a certain amount of pulling and boosting, they all reached the top.

"Oh, look at that view!" Josie exclaimed. She was flushed with excitement and exertion, and looked younger than Ranse had noticed her looking in the past two years.

It was a view indeed. Below them was the beautiful clear surface of Wigwam Lake dotted with other wooded islands.

"I can see our bay," Susie said. "Doesn't it look grand! There's more red in the maples than I thought."

Their reverie was broken by a shout. "Hey, we found one!"

"Be careful!" Josie called. There was little growth up here, and the boys were visible, standing beside a rock and looking down.

"Keep back!" Ranse shouted, running towards them. They were standing still, leaning over something on the ground.

Patrick looked up in wonderment and said, "It's dead!"

Ranse looked at where he was pointing and sure enough

there, lying on its back, was a short, fat snake.

"Gosh!" Timothy exclaimed. "Just a minute ago it was coiled up spitting at us, and shaking its tail. It's not a rattler," he said. "Is it, Ranse?"

"Nope. See, there are no buttons on its tail," Ranse explained. "Apart from that, it looks a lot like a massasauga and, believe it or not, it tries to act like one, too."

"How?"

"By shaking its tail and rearing up. This is a hognose snake. Quite common and absolutely harmless."

"Why did it die?" Patrick asked.

"Watch." Ranse took the stick Patrick was carrying and gently turned the "dead" snake over on its belly. Immediately it flipped over onto its back and lay motionless again.

"Holy cow!"

"Just pretending to be dead. This rascal is full of tricks. First, he mimics a rattler to scare you off, and then if that doesn't work he plays dead. Watch what happens when we leave him."

The group withdrew about twenty feet from the snake. Sure enough, after a few minutes the hognose came to life, rolled over on its belly, and wriggled away among the stones.

"Hurry up and let's catch him!" Patrick shouted, springing forward with his crotched stick. But the snake was gone.

"Heck! Well, maybe we'll find another." They began looking among the big rocks, getting closer and closer to the juniper bushes under which Ranse had hidden the money.

Ranse tried to think of a diversion, but, before he could turn them back, Patrick shouted, "Hey, here's one!"

"Does he have rattles on his tail?" Timothy yelled.

"Keep away from it!" Zeke shouted, and ran towards the boys with a heavy stick he'd picked up.

"He went in there!" Patrick exclaimed, pointing to the mass of juniper. "How can we get him out?"

"Was it really a rattler?" Josie asked.

Carefully, Zeke parted the juniper with his stick. There was the rock, and, sticking out from under it, the end of a tail.

"Gosh, it might be," Zeke said. "Looks like something on its tail. What about it, Ranse?"

Ranse bent over and took a close look at the tail that protruded out of a small crack beside the big rock he'd placed there.

"Can't be absolutely sure," he said, "but it looks like one."

"Oh, boy, let's get him!" Timothy yelled. "All we have to do is move that big rock."

"Gosh, a real live one!" Patrick was jumping with excitement. "Maybe if I grab him by the tail – "

"No! Don't even think of it!" Josie said. "And stand back!"

"Leave the poor thing alone," Susie added. "It's not hurting anyone."

"Normally I'd agree," Zeke said. "But this may be one of very few rattlers in Muskoka. It's up to us to kill it before there are more."

"Kill it? No!" Timothy yelled. "I want to catch it and take it to school. We can do it easily!"

"Nothing doing," his father said. "We kill it!"

Ranse stood back, observing the little tableau as he might have watched a scene on television. If they move the rock, he thought, they'll find the box. Zeke will have an idea what's in it. But there is no way anyone can tie it to me. He'll turn the box over to the police, being careful, of course, not to get fingerprints on it. The police will return it to the bank. The kids might even collect the reward.

And the whole thing would be over. He'd be back where he was before this crazy idea took hold of him.

All he had to do was urge them to go in there after the snake, which undoubtedly had crawled into the crevice where the neat pine box was hidden.

He stood there, knowing that this was the moment of decision. He looked at his family about him, and he knew how precious they were to him. He started forward towards the group.

But Josie had taken command. "I don't think we should kill it," she said. "I most certainly don't. Even if it is the first rattler around these lakes – which I doubt – it's living up here where nobody ever comes, in this beautiful, lonely place, one of the few where man hasn't laid his greedy hand. Why should we dig it out and bash it to pieces?"

"I just want to catch it," Timothy said.

"That's worse. Take it away from here to Toronto for a bunch of people to stare at, and keep it in a cage until it dies?"

The boys were looking very uncomfortable.

"Grandma's right," Timothy said seriously. He'd had many lectures on ecology from his teacher, and had read about conservation, and seen innumerable shows on the subject on television. "Anyway, we saw it," he said. "We can tell the class that."

"To heck with that!" Patrick said. "Gosh, we came here to get a snake and there it is!"

"I say leave it alone," Susie said.

"What do you say, Ranse?" Patrick pleaded. "We could move that rock."

Ranse looked down to where the snake's tail was disappearing under the huge slab of stone. He paused, and looked out over the lake.

"I say, leave it alone."

The sun was almost straight overhead, making it so hot that Ranse could scarcely stand to be out of the shade for more than a few minutes. He thought of the sun in Muskoka, low in the sky, shining through the bare branches, throwing long black shadows on the white snow. Muskoka was one of the few places he knew where the snow remained white all winter.

It was just past the shortest day of the year, what the radio announcers and weathermen called the beginning of winter. Beginning of winter! Hell, they'd have had winter for at least a month up there. The Grey Cup had been played. He'd listened to it on the short-wave radio, and Edmonton had won again. The Argos hadn't even made the play-offs. Well, there was always next year.

The round table at which Ranse was sitting was sheltered from the sun by an immense coconut palm. On the table beside him was a rum punch, cold and strong. The sand was as white and as clean as sand can be, and the ocean was clear and blue. Maybe this afternoon he'd go snorkeling. He'd finished his tossed salad, which he'd mixed himself at the salad bar under another tree. But he hadn't grilled a hamburger. He had to watch his weight.

But Madelaine, he knew, would want to go sailing on the barquentine riding at anchor about two hundred yards off shore, red sails shining in the sun. She had become quite the sailing enthusiast, Madelaine had, ever since their first cruise.

It hadn't been much of a cruise, really: just around to some of the islands, with the tourists play-acting as crewmen, pulling on ropes and swabbing decks and doing jobs that they'd never hire out to do. But it was all a game, with Turbo shouting the orders, and telling them to "Step lively" and "Heave to." And then they'd put ashore in Pirate's Cove, always the same cove, and have the two rum punches that were part of the deal. They didn't do much heaving-to on the return trip, being content to doze in the shade of the big red sails.

Red sails in the sunlight. What fun!

Ranse had enjoyed it somewhat the first time, although he didn't take kindly to being ordered about by that bronzed, flat-stomached, massive-chested Turbo. And he didn't care much, either, for the way Turbo put his arm around Madelaine to il-lustrate the proper way to grasp a rope when she was heaving-to. Anybody could see what he was up to. But women never catch on to the tricks of jokers like Turbo.

Then his mind went thousands of miles away to the shore of Wigwam Lake. Christmas holidays. They'd all be there, he knew. Josie and Zeke and the twins and Susie, and maybe even Helen and family from Regina. And Allenby. Oh, yes, he'd more than likely be there too. Ranse had no way of knowing for sure, but he had a pretty good idea. Josie was not a woman to be long without a man, and Allenby had certainly shown great in-terest in her. Any man would show great interest in Josie.

He could figure Allenby's thinking. The ex-British In-telligence man, of whom there were none in the world more pragmatic and devious. Undoubtedly he suspected that Ranse had robbed the bank; then, when Ranse left like that, he would be sure of it. But he had no proof. Proof would take long and careful work and planning, and there was a good chance he would never get it, supposing always that he could discover where Ranse had disappeared to.

Far better, Ranse interpreted Allenby's thinking, to let him go. It was only money, and insurance companies have lots of that. They expected to pay off. So, Ranse gets the money, and Allenby gets Josie. Allenby, he knew, would be satisfied with the bargain.

But he didn't really want to think of Allenby now. He'd always known this would be a bad day for him. But it was, after all, only one day, and like other days it would pass away and he would be all right again.

Christmas – a day for extremes of feelings. The happy it made happier; the miserable and lonely it made more miserable and lonely. Those with families enjoyed them; those without families missed them more on this day than any other. Maybe it was the only day they felt the lack.

He took a big gulp of the rum punch and let his mind wander where it would.

There was that Christmas day when the twins were about six, and Zeke had bought each a pair of skates and hockey sticks. Ranse and Zeke had worked hard all Christmas morning, shovelling snow off a square of ice near the beach, had set up sticks in the snow for goals and, with an adult and a boy making up each team, had played a game of hockey.

"I'm Guy LaFleur!" Timothy had kept shouting, as he stumbled along the glassy surface on his ankles after the tuna can full of ice they were using as a puck. Then he'd trip and slide on his belly across the ice, get up again and chase the puck, with the kind of determination that makes Canadians the greatest hockey players in the world.

"I'm defence!" was Patrick's cry. Not knowing the name of any great defenceman he could emulate, he included them all in his cry, "I'm defence!"

Zeke and Ranse were on skates, too. Ranse had been skating since he was the age of the twins, and once had been a star forward for the police team. But Zeke was far better, having played semi-professional before he joined the force. Ranse envied his skill and energy. Ranse envied a lot of things about Zeke.

He wondered what Allenby would be like on skates. Probably not worth a damn.

Josie, in her youth, had been a wonder. The first place Ranse had taken her was to the old Mutual Street arena, where they had glided around the ice to the strains of "The Skater's Waltz." At the corners he would lift her clear off the ice and swing her around. He could kiss her without missing a stride.

Ranse glanced down at the new wrist-watch he'd bought from a pedlar on the beach, for two hundred Canadian dollars. The pedlar, whom Ranse figured as a fence for stolen goods, said that it was worth a thousand new. But Ranse had no way of knowing. It told the day, the month, and the year, and had several other gadgets on it that he had never tried. The watch said twelve forty-five, which would be eleven forty-five at Wigwam. The place would be a mess, he knew. The kids, up early, would have ransacked the tree that stood in front of the glass doors that led to the patio. In winter these double-glazed doors were never opened, for the patio would have at least a couple of feet of snow on it already. Wrappings and ribbons and boxes and bows would completely cover the floor, wrappings that Josie had spent hours perfecting. Josie loved Christmas.

And, by now, the kids would be outside with their new sleds or skis. Zeke would have cleared a coasting path down to the lake. Allenby (Ranse was sure he'd be there) would have helped. Ranse could see them in their down-filled jackets and tuques and mitts, shovelling away, panting breaths coming from their mouths like smoke.

But mostly he could see Josie inside, cleaning up the mess and now and then testing the immense turkey. No matter how many people were coming, Josie always insisted on an immense turkey. She would be wearing all the new things she'd received – she always did that – probably a new dressing-gown and a sweater and a scarf and beads. She would wear them all. When it came to Christmas presents, she was a child.

And later the men would come in and make rum toddies with dark rum and boiling water and maple syrup, always maple syrup, and nutmeg. And they'd sit with their feet up while the kids used the new slide. Or maybe Allenby would introduce them to some new English drink. What was it the Cratchits had? A bowl of steaming porter.

And from outside would come the shouts and arguments of the boys, who already would have figured out some contest with the new slide, probably to see who could go the farthest out on the lake.

Ranse shut the picture off then. He didn't want to see any more.

A motor boat had set out from the barque, skimming along over the calm, clean water. It pulled up on the white, smooth sand. Turbo and Madelaine jumped out and came running and laughing up the beach towards him.

"We're going to paint the deck black this afternoon. Turbo says black is the only colour."

She looked marvellous. All worry lines were gone from her face, her large brown eyes squinted against the brightness. Madelaine was made for this life. And he was a lucky dog to be here with her.

The bronzed giant leaped into the empty chair beside Ranse and took a sip of his punch.

"Sure thing. Want to help us, Pops?"

Christ, I wish he wouldn't call me Pops, Ranse thought.

The Commodore's Barge Is Alongside

The Commodore's Barge Is Alongside comes from my stint in the RCNVR, which I tried to join as an executive officer, but was enlisted as schoolmaster when the navy, in its infinite wisdom, decided I'd make a better teacher than fighter. How right they were. I joined at HMCS *Unicorn* in Saskatoon, which was an old, abandoned downtown garage, far from any water. Some very good men (boys, mostly) came there to learn the first rudiments of sailoring and went on to distinguish themselves in corvettes and other small fighting ships in the North Atlantic.

Like many another writer, I've always been struck by the absurdity of military training (war itself being the ultimate absurdity). I know it's essential in time of war for some men to be given the task of shouting at and bossing and bullying other men, and for others to be the recipients of all that shouting, bossing, and bullying. But just the same, many of the aspects of service life are, along with being tragic and grim, downright comical.

Most prairie boys, used to rugged individualism and independence, didn't take kindly to the regimentation. But they suffered it with their usual stoicism and good nature. Besides, it was the first job and pay cheque that many of them had ever had. And the glamorous uniform, the travel, the opportunities for drinking and wenching had their own attractions.

The title of the book comes from an incident that took place at HMCS *York* (the Automotive Building in the CNE grounds), where I finished my service as head schoolmaster. On this occasion, the commodore who was in charge of all

naval divisions was coming to inspect the ship. All was, as
they say, shipshape. Everything that could be painted was
painted and every speck of dust removed from behind filing
cabinets or wherever, for the Commodore had a habit of feeling with his white-gloved hand into the most inaccessible
crannies searching for dirt.

The ship's company had been equally prepared. All
shined up, lint removed from our best dress uniforms, we
lined up for inspection. The officers, in order of rank, were
lined up beside the captain at the front door (poop deck)
waiting for the commodore to come aboard. It was a long
wait, with the bosun's mate nervously peering down the
driveway and the rest of us sweating in our starched white
collars. Finally, when the limousine pulled up to the door, the
bosun's mate stepped smartly through the door, tooted his
whistle, saluted the captain, and announced, "Sir, the commodore's barge is alongside."

It struck me then, and still does, as typical of the slightly
Gilbert-and-Sullivan flavour of navy life ashore.

The Monday after our show, in-
stead of being dismissed after opening exercises we were left
standing at attention while Lightson reported to the Old Man. A
little shudder of apprehension ran through the ranks, for we
knew that when the commanding officer spoke to us it could
only mean trouble.

We were right.

He stood there looking very natty in his freshly pressed
blues and his new cap, and informed us that on our behalf he
had issued a challenge to the commanding officer of Number
Ten Air Training School of the RCAF to a boxing card.

He explained that not only would it be good for us, but since
it would be held in the hockey arena it would provide entertainment for the civilian population. He said that match-ups would
be made in all weight categories, and gave us a little pep talk on
the importance of boxing in the armed services.

"Boxing," he said, "is an education. You learn self-control, to
give and to take, to punish and be punished, smiling all the
time."

To say that the Old Man liked boxing is like saying squirrels are mildly interested in nuts. He was crazy about boxing. He loved boxing. To him it was the manly art, the true test, the ultimate contest, the measure of a man. The idea of punishing and being punished gave him a real high – just so long as somebody else was doing the punishing and getting punished. He would take care of the smiling.

I don't know where he got the quote. Probably from some book. He was a great one for second-hand quotes about manliness and true tests. Anyway, now that the softball season was over and we had won the inter-service championship, boxing was the thing that would absorb the interests of the athletically inclined ratings of HMCS *Porpoise.*

Group Captain Gorson, a craggy-faced First World War flier who was commanding officer of Number Ten Initial Training School of the RCAF, was also a raving, slavering boxing nut. So, a good healthy rivalry developed between the two men. I always thought that the best way for them to have settled it would have been to put on the gloves themselves and, like Sohrab and Rustum, have at each other to the death. But then I had nothing to do with the arrangements, and I suspect the idea of such a one-on-one contest never entered the minds of these two raw-meat tigers.

It so happened that at the time *Porpoise* had a real boxer. His name was Howard Wilbur Transvil, but he was always called Turk. About my size, but considerably better built, Turk was a mild-mannered, pleasant fellow of about twenty-five. A brick-layer by trade, he'd had a number of professional fights and had gained for himself the title of Middleweight Champion of Western Canada. This last fact we were instructed to keep from the air force.

I liked Turk and he liked me. The first time I boxed with him I learned the difference between a professional and an amateur. His punches were solid, even when he was holding back, as he did with me, and they were so quick that I never saw them coming. He taught me how to put my body behind my own punches so as to make them more solid. He also taught me how to handle the small bag and hit the heavy bag without injury to my wrists, and how to skip rope.

When the Old Man saw Turk boxing, his enthusiasm for the sport increased tremendously. He even put on the gloves with Turk himself. Watching this encounter, I remember how I wished it were me in there against the Old Man and that I were as solid a hitter as Turk.

The best man the air force had at the Initial Training Base was also a middleweight. His name was Rostough and he'd been a plunging back for a professional football team. In the off-season he did quite a lot of boxing, and the word was that he'd knocked out all his opponents. Gorson was sure he could do the same to Transvil, and Featherby was just as sure that he couldn't.

Thus it came about that all our recreation time was taken up with training for the big boxing card. First came the weigh-ins, where every man who looked as though he could lift a boxing glove was weighed in the nude, to determine in just what weight class he fitted.

I weighed in at 162 pounds and was immediately instructed by the Old Man to get that weight down to less than 160 so that I could qualify as a middleweight. I didn't quite understand how I was to do this since, at that stage. I had little extra fat anywhere.

Then training for the final show-down between navy and air force began.

"Don't ever forget," the Old Man admonished us, "that the navy is not only the senior service, but also the superior service. You aren't just fighting for yourselves, you are fighting to uphold the reputation and honour of His Majesty's Navy." He failed to mention that we were also fighting so that he could win a one-hundred-dollar bet from Gorson.

The ten of us upon whose frail shoulders the reputation of His Majesty's Navy rested were, except for Turk, a motley group. We had no flyweight, but we did have a bantam, a skinny little guy named Rowels who was a Métis from Duck Lake. He had got into the navy as a cook, I suppose on the supposition that if he was strong enough to lift a soup ladle he could cook. Among the host of other flaky ideas that inhabited the Old Man's handsome dome was the one that any man with a drop of

Indian blood in his veins was a natural killer. Actually, Rowels was a peaceful little guy who, at the tender age of seventeen, had already acquired his senior matric and determined to become a doctor after the war. He didn't say much, but his words when they did come were carefully weighed and tended to be rather ponderous.

Like the rest of us, Rowels was over the 113-pound limit for bantams, but the Old Man was confident he could pare that down.

We also had a featherweight, a farm boy named Dornoski, who was very short and very wide. So far as I could ever gauge, he had no neck at all, just a big head sitting on a pair of Charles Atlas-like shoulders. He was immensely strong and could climb a rope with ease without using his feet at all. He'd just grab it and hand over hand himself to the top. I rather pitied anyone that the air force might match against him.

We had two lightweights, and in this class there was some controversy. The weight limit for the class, according to American rules, is 135 pounds, but by British rules it is an even ten stone, or 140 pounds. Naturally, the Old Man, who was British to the toenails, insisted on the 140-pound limit. Both of the tigers we had for the class, a stoker named Gluck and a writer named Barstow, might possibly get down to 140 pounds but could never be sufficiently pared to meet the lower weight.

There was of course, a plethora of welterweights from which to choose. They had one thing in common, none of them knew the first thing about boxing. There was a sick bay tiffy named Arsenol, whose name, like mine, would make a fighter out of anyone; Ordinary Seaman Corbett, who at least had a good name for a boxer, but who moved like the famous Gentleman Jim as a plough horse moves like a racehorse. And then there was Ronce who, when picked for the slaughter, remarked, "Well, I might as well get killed in the ring as on some gawddamned ship."

We had two lightheavies. A big blond Swede from down south named Warse, who was surely one of the best hockey players ever to come out of the prairies, but whether he could box or not was another question. But whereas Warse was a natural athlete, the other lightheavy, a shy grain buyer of about thirty years of age, was anything but. I suspect he was picked because Lightson hated him almost as much as he hated me and, in his sadistic way, was looking forward to both of us getting our brains knocked out.

So there, as they say, is the boxing team. Let's hear it for them. Our training began at once. Diddle, who from his Boy Scout days believed in being prepared, somehow got boxing mixed up with marathon running. His idea of preparing us to meet the air-force tigers was to get us out in our navy blue shorts and run the chuffs off us. We ran to the edge of town and then along dry, dusty roads straight out over the prairie, with the harvested wheat fields on either side, the bemused country folk staring at us as though we'd gone mad. Which we had.

Actually I became very fond of the road work. Because out there on the outskirts of the city on Queen Victoria Road there was a farm implement dealer named Brick – famous for Brick tractors – in whose office Patricia worked as a stenographer. And so I took to doing extra road work, which was readily agreed to since I knew all my bends and hitches, knots and splices and the rest of the stuff backwards. This extra road work consisted of running as far as Patricia and spending a half hour or so in her delightful company.

The only flaw in this arrangement was Patricia's eagerness to talk about Lieutenant Commander Featherby. "Don't you think he's the most distinguished-looking man?"

"Yeah. Distinguished. They tell me the wolf who met Red Riding Hood had the same air of distinction."

"What do you mean?"

"Well, I'm not giving away any secrets, since everybody knows it, when I say the Old Man will try to make anything in skirts."

"That's just gossip. His manners are perfect."

"Didn't your father ever warn you against guys like him?"

"Don't be silly. I think he's charming."

"Think what you like, but don't let him get you alone. Especially if he's got a snootful of those pink gins."

"Silly. He's asked me to go to a supper dance with him at the Colonial Hotel."

"Jees. You didn't accept?"

"Not exactly. But I may. I've never been to one of those dances. They say they're marvie. You're just jealous."

She was right, of course. Jealous as hell. But I think I was really concerned for her, too. Another time we talked about the boxing match for which I was supposed to be training.

"Why box anyway?" she pouted. "It's just silly, punching somebody in the head and getting punched back."

"And smiling," I added. "Don't forget the smiling."

"But why do it?"

"It's my duty. The Old Man says box, I box. We're in a war, you know. What do you want me to do, be a shirker?"

"Oh that's just silly."

She was right again, but a surprising number of things that are obviously silly and crazy and insane in peace-time seem absolutely logical in time of war. Like Patricia, I had a sneaking suspicion then of the absurdity of the whole operation, and in the light of what's happened since then, how right we were.

It became perfectly obvious that not one of the tigers we'd selected was making any progress whatsoever along the lines of becoming a boxer. Diddle had taught them how to stand with left foot and left hand extended towards the opponent, and had emphasized that they were to keep their feet in that position and not take a step forward or back, but rather to shuffle forwards and backwards. "Maintain balance at all times," he commanded, "ever ready to move without losing that balance and ready to strike the opponent with either hand."

Turk's instructions tended to be more direct. "For chrissake hit him! This isn't a game of pattycake, you know. You've got to put some weight behind those punches or you'll get killed!"

Diddle and the Old Man discouraged such talk. They wanted our tigers to think of it as a game of pattycake, otherwise they knew damned well we'd all quit. I never in my life saw a group of men so gullible concerning something that was going to happen to them. The only thing I can compare it to, in the light of my vast experience, is an operation for piles. Everybody tells you, especially your doctor, that there is nothing to it. And you think there will be nothing to it and so you blissfully go to sleep on the operating table counting backwards, and then

251

you wake up with a pain in your anus so excrutiating, so absolutely mind-boggling that if you'd known about it you'd never have consented to the operation in a million years.

So it was with our tigers. I can see them now, blissfully trying to skip rope and stumbling over their own feet, pecking away at the punching-bag, dancing about in the ring and making tentative little jabs at each other, with Diddle yelling, "That's it, chaps, you're getting it. That's right, counterpunch, counterpunch!" There wasn't one of them could punch his way through a piece of toilet paper.

At least that's what I thought.

And then events took a turn towards disaster. I first got wind of it two days before the fight card was to be staged, at one of our training sessions when the boxers were prancing around the deck making ineffectual jabs at nothing. Diddle, I noticed, had a look on his thin face that was decidedly grim. I'd never seen him looking like that before, and I was puzzled until he called me over and told me the reason, and then I was devastated.

"Oh, Diespecker," he began, "I've got something to tell you."

"My opponent has dropped dead from fear?"

"No. Nothing like that. I don't know how to tell you this, and I want you to know I had nothing to do with it."

"I've been scratched. Well, that's okay, sir."

"No. Stoker Transvil has been scratched."

"What? Why?"

"It's that wretched air force C.O. He heard about Transvil being middleweight champion of western Canada and he says he's a professional."

"So?"

"Well, he won't go through with the tournament unless we find another middleweight to fight Rostough."

"But we haven't got another middleweight, except . . . ." I had a horrible empty feeling in the region of my bowels. "No, you can't mean me!"

"That's what has been suggested."

"Me? Box with that guy? That's ridiculous, sir, crazy! Who ever got an idea like that?"

"Well, the scuttle-but around the ship here is that you

knocked out a sub-lieutenant who was practically a professional boxer."

"No, no, we were just fooling around. It was a lucky punch and I didn't knock him out. Just knocked him down. He probably slipped."

"Whatever happened, it gave you a reputation."

"But, sir, this is awful. I can't. Besides, half the guys on the ship have bet on Transvil."

"They've bet on the main bout. I'm afraid the air-force men they've bet with will insist on their honouring the bets."

"This gets crazier and crazier. Sir, you've got to . . . ."

"I told you, it's not my idea. I'm sick about the whole thing. With Transvil in there we'd have had a good card."

"Then we'll have to call the whole thing off."

"We can't do that. Over five thousand tickets have been sold. All the publicity the newspaper and radio station have given us." He smiled weakly. "After all, it's only three rounds."

"A man can get killed in three rounds! Listen. Can the navy make me do this?"

"No, technically they can't. But the captain and Lightson can put a lot of pressure on you."

"Don't I know it!"

"I can't promise you anything, of course, but if you do this it might make a difference. Besides, it would show Chief Petty Officer Lightson . . . ."

"Show him what? What's he got to do with this?"

"Nothing. Except he said . . . ."

"What?"

"Well, I guess he didn't really mean it."

"What did he say?"

"Oh, I forget his exact words. Something about your being too yellow to do it."

"He said that, eh?"

"I'm sure he didn't mean it."

"He meant it. I'll show that sonofabitch." It came out before I realized it. And that's how I became the navy representative in the main bout in the infamous boxing card at Wabagoon Arena in front of thousands.

Wabagoon's biggest and, for all I know, only boxing card was held in the downtown arena where the senior and junior hockey games were played. It wasn't a big arena but not small either, with banks of seats along each side and a few at each end. A ring had been erected in the centre of what was normally the ice surface, and the space between it and the boards filled with folding chairs. These were the dollar seats. The regular arena seats, or rather benches, cost fifty cents.

The first shock to our boxers – other shocks would come later – was the number of people who came. Long before the first fight was commenced the place was jammed to the rafters.

"Holy Palooka!" was the comment of our lightweight Barstow. "We got to get up in front of all these people?"

The Old Man, resplendent in his best dress uniform, and his officers filled the seats along the west side of the ring, while the seats on the east side were occupied by Gorson and his bevy of brass. At the north end sat Diddle and the air-force sports officer who, along with a neutral representative from the local YMCA, were to judge the bouts. A couple of sports writers from the local paper sat next to them, along with a cameraman to record the event for posterity.

The mayor of Wabagoon and sundry other VIPs were on the south side. All wore evening clothes and all the ladies wore long gowns. Most of these had been guests at a cocktail party in the *Porpoise* wardroom since about five in the afternoon and were, to say the least, in a festive mood. So, for that matter, were the rest of the members of this eager fight crowd. The ordinary seamen and the air-force chaps had had their own little gatherings in the beer parlours and had placed their bets.

I can still see those fine ladies with their fancy hair-dos and well-made-up countenances, flushed with booze, peering expectantly and happily up into that ring. None of the females had ever seen a boxing match except perhaps a short shot in a newsreel, and they had no idea what a fight was like. They would find out.

The fight announcer was some yahoot from the air force

who stood in the middle of the ring and bleated, "Ladeees and Gentulmen," in a poor imitation of Clem McCarthy, whom we used to hear on radio. "Tonight, in this ring, thirrreee rounds of boxing between the best of the navy and the best of the air force."

Wild cheering from the assembled throng, like unto that which I imagine greeted the lions and the Christians in the Roman Colosseum.

The bouts began with the smallest men, appetizers before the main feast, and that meant that Rowels was the first man in the ring for us. His opponent looked about twice as heavy as he but I may have been prejudiced; besides, I was watching the fight from the passageway that led to our dressing-rooms under the west side seats.

As Rowels passed me in the passageway, wearing an old gaberdine over his shoulders, I whispered, "Good luck!" but he didn't answer. His eyes were glazed and unseeing, like those of a calf going up the ramp behind the judas goat into the slaughterhouse. He reached the ring and climbed in and sat down on a stool in the corner where Steward Smiley and Sick Bay Tiffy Reagan were waiting for him. They pinched his shoulders and flabbed his muscles as they thought they were supposed to do. The referee announced the first bout, three rounds of three minutes each, and the fighters advanced to the centre of the ring.

At the bell Rowels went in there, as he'd been taught, with his left hand extended, shuffling along in a daze. He made a tentative little flick of a glove towards his opponent, whereupon his opponent hit him hard on the nose and sent him back on the seat of his pants on the floor. Blood spurted from his nose and splashed on some of the ladies at ringside. Two of them screamed and one fainted dead away after shrieking, "It's blood!" Their idea of the evening's festivities hadn't included great gobs of very red, very sticky blood.

As for Rowels, he'd no sooner hit the floor than he let out a roar like a wounded Cree, which he half was, leaped to his feet and, forgetting all about keeping one foot in front of the other, waded into his enemy with both fists going like windmills.

There was a lot of power in those skinny arms, and his opponent, trying to back up to escape them, fell over backwards. With another blood-curdling scream, Rowels leaped on top of him and continued to pound him with all his might. It was quite a sight, I can tell you, with everybody on their feet and the air force screaming "Foul!" and the sailors cheering their heads off. In no time several secondary bouts had broken out between matelots and flyboys, and there was considerable consternation about.

Well, the referee finally managed to pull Rowels off his bloody opponent and the city police managed to break up the fights in the crowd. The timekeeper wisely bonged on his gong and the first round was over. The second round was splendid. Rowels, realizing that a fight was a fight and to hell with all this fancy stuff, waded into his opponent and tried to kill him. He just slugged for all he was worth. Most of the blows, to be sure, landed harmlessly on arms and shoulders and even buttocks, but enough found their way to the air-force lad's head to make things uncomfortable for him. But he kept flailing away, too, and by the end of the round both fighters were so tired they could hardly stand.

The third round was anticlimactic. The short rest had done nothing for either of them, and they were barely able to stagger around the ring, hugging each other and being pulled apart by the referee. The fight was finally judged a draw.

Our featherweight, Dornoski, was next up. Like Rowels, he was nervous, frightened, and determined to do his best for the honour of the navy. His best consisted of advancing to the centre of the ring with his hands held in front of him, taking a wild swing from the air-force fighter and being knocked out cold.

As a matter of fact, we saw four knock-outs altogether during the evening, two for us and two for them. Which may seem an inordinate number for inexperienced punchers, except that inexperience goes two ways, and none of our so-called fighters knew much about self-defence. They could duck the odd punch and pull back from a few and guard themselves to some degree, but too often they were so eager to swing at the opponent's jaw that they left themselves wide open for lucky punches. And these boys were all strong and in good condition, so that when they landed one on an unprotected jaw the result was disastrous.

But the crowd loved it, as crowds have always loved the spectacle of two individuals – be they dogs, cocks, bull and man, bear and dogs, gladiators, jousters, wrestlers, or boxers – fighting to the death, or at least a reasonable facsimile. They cheered and booed and roared and, as often happens, the women became the most bloodthirsty. The sight of an otherwise demure, timid, tender, kind, loving female standing up with fire shooting out of her eyes and screaming, "Kill him! Kill him!" must surely indicate something about the human condition, but I've never been able to figure out what.

When my own fight was just about due, I stood in the dressing-room with Turk Transvil. To say I was apprehensive would be a gross understatement. I was sweating like a racehorse, shaking like a nuptial bed, and fearful I would soil my baggy shorts.

"Now just remember what I told you," Turk said.

"What was that?"

"I've been telling you all week that you've got to box a fighter and fight a boxer."

"I don't even know what that means!"

"It means that this joker Rostough is a fighter, a slugger; he'll try to get in close and pound you with those short arms of his. So stay away from him. Keep him at long range."

"How am I going to do that?"

"Box him. Use your left jab. Keep jabbing him and moving to the left. Back up. Don't let him corner you."

"To quote the immortal words of Joe Louis: 'I can run, but I can't hide.' "

"You don't need to hide. Just keep the jab working. They'll give you points for those just the same as for harder punches. You're in much better shape than he is. All that road work will pay off."

I didn't tell him that most of the road work consisted of sitting in a corner ice-cream parlour eating banana splits with Patricia. I wished now I'd run more. I got a bright idea.

"Why don't you go in and fight this guy? They can't call the bout off now."

"No deal. The Old Man would kill me."

"Better than Rostough killing me." But I knew it wouldn't work.

Then it was time to go. I took that long, lonely walk down the aisle through the crowd and climbed in.

As the announcer went through his silly stuff about this being the feature event of the evening, I stared across the ring at my opponent. He was big. And athletic. Joe Louis had nothing on this guy. God, but he looked strong.

Beside him I looked rather ridiculous. I'm not really built like a boxer. My arms are too long, my hands too small and my head too big. But I was nimble and fast on my feet. If I could just stay away from this brute, as Turk suggested, for three rounds and use my extra reach so that he couldn't get in close with those short, muscular arms, I might have a chance.

Thinking of this I began to think of Charlie Chaplin in *City Lights*, when he became a prize-fighter to earn some money for his blind girl, and of how he managed to keep the referee between him and the other fighter all the time, dancing about as only Chaplin could. The thought of this made me laugh out loud which brought a very funny look to the face of my opponent.

"What the hell's the matter, Dink?" Smiley muttered as he dumped a sponge full of water on my head. "You feeling okay?"

"Yeah, yeah," I said. "Fine." But I couldn't help giggling. I knew a fighter was supposed to look stern and put the evil eye on his opponent, but I couldn't help it.

Somebody hit a gong and I got up to do my stuff. The other fighter advanced towards me in a crouch and so I said to myself, All right, I'll fight straight up. This guy Rostough sure looked like a slugger.

I stuck my left hand out as far as it would go and tried jabbing him with it, at the same time moving to the left. He brought up a round-house right that I could see coming a mile away and so I stepped back and, after it whistled by, moved in with another jab. This one caught him flush on the end of the nose and I knew it hurt him. He swung another round-house right and I managed to get out of the way of it, too. Well, so far so good. I'd hit him once and he hadn't hit me at all . . . so far.

Then a left came from nowhere as I was moving to the left and caught me flush on the kidney. And that hurt. So much that my arms suddenly seemed made of lead and I could hardly hold them up. So I wrapped them around my opponent, pinning his arms to his sides, and held on for dear life. The referee broke us apart and I began to back peddle for all I was worth. I had practised, as Gene Tunney said he'd done in getting ready for his second bout with Dempsey, running backwards.

The round went pretty much that way.

"Jees, Dink, you're never going to win a fight running away like that!" Smiley admonished. (He'd bet on me, too.) "You got to get in there and punch!"

I don't know what real boxers think of in the ring, but I know what I thought of. Survival. Staying alive. The essential ingredient of a boxer's make-up – the killer instinct – was entirely lacking in me. I didn't want to kill anybody. I just wanted to get out of there alive.

During the second round I got lucky. I hit him a pretty good belt in a solar plexus and to my surprise my glove sank in further than I'd expected it would. He looked a little sick for a second or two and brought his hands down and I caught him a pretty good shot to the button. This staggered him a bit and I got in a couple more before he put his short arms around me and held on. That lucky shot did me until the end of the round, when he began to come on strong again.

In the corner Smiley was ecstatic. "You've got him, Dink, you've got him! He's finished. All you have to do now is stay away from him."

To tell the truth, I felt pretty good, too. So good that I allowed myself a glance at the Old Man. And there sitting beside him in a beautiful long dress cut on the bias was none other than my true love, Patricia. That sonofabitch and Patricia! What was she thinking of? Hadn't she paid any attention to my warnings about him? Poor, sweet, innocent Patricia!

As I look back on it now I realize that even considering the sexual mores of the times and my Sunday school upbringing I was unbelievably, absurdly, disgustingly naïve.

I was still sitting there in a daze, my poor broken heart sunk down somewhere around my gym shoes, when the bell went for the third round. I still sat there.

"Get up, Dink! What the hell's wrong with you?" Smiley yelled, and pushed me off my stool into the ring.

And then I got mad. Mad at the Old Man, at Patricia, at the navy. All the frustration of the past weeks came boiling up in me and I completely lost my temper and tore into my opponent as though I'd kill him.

Here I'd dearly like to say that all this adrenalin pouring through my veins changed me into a tiger and that I knocked the stuffing out of the big air-force champion. But no, truth is sadder than fiction. Everybody knows that a mad fighter is a helpless fighter if his opponent keeps his cool. I rushed at Rostough and for a while did all right, throwing rights and lefts at random. I should have been throwing them at his head. It would have worked if Rostough, like Rowels' opponent, had been a novice. But he wasn't. He simply waited for his chance and then socked me on the side of my head, hard enough to knock me down on the seat of my pants.

I got up all right, but all the fight was gone out of me. I hung on and ran backwards for the rest of the round, and the decision was unanimous for Rostough.

Epilogue

So this brings to an end the story of my first thirty-eight years as a professional free-lance writer. During that time I supported myself and my family entirely from writing, without benefit of grants or teaching fees. We never got rich, but it's been a hell of a lot of fun. Looking back on it, there is nothing we would change.

And it ain't over yet. I continue to write novels and will do so until my fingers or brain stiffen up and I can no longer function. I have a finished novel and one that's half-finished yet to be published and ideas for a few more. At age seventy-two I find that I can't, nor need to, work as hard as I did at age forty-five, but one of the great things about being a writer is that there is no need for retirement. Nobody hands you a pink slip and a gold watch and says, "We don't need you any more."

We live six months on Brandy Lake and six months in Florida (with a total hip replacement I can't risk icy roads or sidewalks), and I still walk two miles a day, either on the Atlantic beach or the Falkenburg Road. Each has its charms.

Most of the good people I have worked with over the years are dead. Ralph Allen, Andrew Allan, Alan Savage, Don Fairbairn, John Drainie, Howard Milsom, Tommy Tweed, Johnny Cantelon, to name a few. But others who sustained and helped me are still around: Jim Harris, Jack Mosher, Scott Young, Trent and June Frayne, Farley Mowat, Jack McClelland, Bob Ferguson, Pierre Berton, and others.

Visiting and being visited by our five kids and twelve grandchildren is great fun for us. We still consider Canada to be the greatest country in the world. A bit absurd, but great.